Jonathan Coe was born in 1961 in Lickey, a suburb of south-west Birmingham. His first novel, *The Accidental Woman*, was published in 1987. His best-selling novels include *What a Carve Up!* and *The Rotters' Club*. He is the recipient of many prizes and awards, including both Costa Novel of the Year and Prix du Livre Européen. He won France's Prix Médicis for *The House of Sleep* and Italy's Premio Flaiano and Premio Bauer-Ca' Foscari. His most recent novel is *Bournville*.

MR. WILDER AND ME

Jonathan Coe

MR. WILDER AND ME

Europa
editions

Europa Editions
27 Union Square West, Suite 302
New York, NY 10003
www.europaeditions.com
info@europaeditions.com

Library of Congress Cataloging in Publication Data is available
ISBN 979-8-88966-001-9

Coe, Jonathan
Mr. Wilder and Me

Art direction by Emanuele Ragnisco
instagram.com/emanueleragnisco

Cover design and illustration by Ginevra Rapisardi

Prepress by Grafica Punto Print – Rome

Printed in the USA

CONTENTS

For Neil Sinyard

MR. WILDER AND ME

O ne winter's morning, seven years ago, I found myself on an escalator. It was one of the escalators that takes you up to street level from the Piccadilly Line platforms at Green Park station. If you've ever used those escalators, you will remember how long they are. It takes about a minute to ride from the bottom to the top and, for a naturally impatient woman like me, a minute standing still is too long. Even though I was not in any particular hurry that morning, I soon began walking up the escalator, easing my way past the line of stationary passengers on the right-hand side—thinking to myself, all the while, "I may be almost sixty, but I've still got it, I'm still fit"—until, about three quarters of the way up, I found myself stuck. A young mother was standing on the right-hand side and on the left, holding her hand, was her daughter, a girl of maybe seven or eight. She had blonde hair and was wearing a red plastic mac with a hood that made her look a bit like the little girl who drowns at the beginning of *Don't Look Now*. (Everything makes me think of a film, I can't help it.) There wasn't room to push past her, and in any case I didn't want to rupture this lovely moment of connection between a mother and her child. So I waited until they reached the top of the escalator and then I watched as the little girl prepared herself to jump off. Even from behind, I could sense her anticipation, the way her eyes must have been fixing themselves on the moving track ahead of her with concentrated energy, the coiled readiness in her tiny limbs and muscles and then, when the moment arrived, the sudden fierce movement as she leaped forward and landed safely on *terra firma*, following which, no doubt relieved and elated by the manoeuvre, she performed two little skips, still clasping her mother's hand and pulling her slightly forward in the process. And I think it must have been these skips, more than anything else, that made my heart flip, that made me catch my breath, that made me watch in wonder and longing as the mother and her daughter headed off towards the ticket barrier together. It made me think at once of my own daughters, Francesca and Ariane, children no longer, and how for them, when they were seven or eight years old, the mere act of walking was sometimes not enough, it must have felt simply too ordinary, too boring to express the intensity of their delight in motion, in the joyous novelty of their relation to the physical world, which meant that sometimes they, too, would randomly break into a skip, or a hop, and in the process they would carry me forwards with them, each of them clasping one of my hands, and sometimes I would skip too, to keep up with them and to show them that I was also capable of sharing their joy in the world, that middle age had not yet drained it out of me.

All of these thoughts flashed through my mind as I watched the mother and her daughter proceed to the ticket barrier, and they all swelled and distilled themselves into a sudden, transitory but overwhelming sense of loss and longing, which flattened me and took my breath away and obliged me to rest for a moment, stepping aside from the relentless flow of passengers, catching my breath and resting my hand upon my breastbone until I too was ready to rejoin that flow, to press on with life, to put my card on the card reader and pass through the barrier and then head upwards towards Piccadilly and the thin late-morning light.

I walked along Piccadilly very slowly, reflecting on what I had just seen and the way it had made me feel. Tomorrow Ariane, the elder of my twins (by forty-five minutes), would be leaving home at last, flying to the other side of the world. It would be my job to drive her to Heathrow, to wave goodbye at the entrance to Departures while pretending to feel nothing more ambiguous than pleasure at the wonderful opportunities waiting for her in Sydney. And then my husband and I would be left only with Fran, with the problem of Fran, with Fran who in the last few weeks, suddenly and dramatically, had gone from being a child to being a problem, a problem which had floored us both, and would no doubt continue to do so for the foreseeable future, until we could find a path which led through the mess she had created and out the other side. But there was no sign of that path appearing yet.

The task I'd set myself in coming to Piccadilly was soon accomplished. I went into Fortnum's to buy Ariane a going-away present and it didn't take long to find what I wanted: tea. She loved tea—for her it was the taste of home—and I had always loved making it for her. I bought her a pack of six different blends, which came complete with its own silver teapot and strainer, and I tried to picture her in some featureless student room in Sydney, pouring tea from this pot into her Union Jack mug and sipping it and being transported back to our kitchen at home, her elbows resting on the old pine table and her hair sheened with low sunlight cutting through the branches of the apple tree in the winter garden outside.

Maybe it would comfort her. Or maybe (perhaps more likely, and even better) she would not need comforting.

The year was 2013, and it was the first week of January, that disorientating time when the Christmas festivities are over but the world has not yet quite returned to normal. Feeling the need to do something that would seem routine, quotidian, I decided to go for a coffee in the bar at BAFTA. Perhaps there would be somebody there that I knew. It would do me no harm to have a chat, an exchange of gossip and pleasantries.

The bar was almost empty. It still had that air of post-Christmas desolation. There was only one person that I recognized, sitting by himself at a table for two by the picture windows, overlooking the street. Mark Arrowsmith. Not the first man I would have picked for a friendly catch-up. But beggars, as they say, cannot be choosers. Mark it was. I went over to his table and waited for him to look up from his MacBook.

"Calista," he said. "Darling! What a nice surprise."

"May I?"

"Of course."

He closed the lid of the computer and moved some papers out of the way to make room for the cappuccino I had already bought myself at the bar.

"Sorry about all this junk," he said. "I've finally got a meeting with Film4 next week. They've asked to see a budget which I assume means they might be serious at last." He arranged the last bundle of papers into a stack and put them away in a plastic folder.

Mark must have been in his late sixties by then. Although nothing like as athletic, he had something of the look of Burt Lancaster in *Local Hero*. (As I said, everything and everyone reminds me of a film.) He had the eyes of a dreamer—or used to, about ten years before—but these days they were clouded with defeat. Mark had been trying to get the same film made for the last twenty-five years or more. Some time in the late 1980s he had taken out an option on a novel by Kingsley Amis—a name which, back in those days, still carried a certain *cachet*. It had seemed quite a realistic proposition and he had secured the services of a well-known director and three or four bankable actors. But for some reason the final tranche of money had fallen through at the last minute and then the director had become unavailable and then two of the actors had become unavailable and one of the others had begun not to look so bankable any more and before he knew what was happening the project had a bad smell hanging around it which everyone started to notice except for Mark himself. As a producer he already had a couple of reasonably successful credits to his name—a feature film and a one-off drama for BBC Two—but since then he had made nothing and the quest to get this stupid Kingsley Amis adaptation off the ground had come to obsess him. He had become one of the fixtures at BAFTA, always sitting by himself at a table for two with his MacBook, waiting to have a meeting with someone who might or might not have read the fifteenth draft of the script and who might know someone who knew someone who worked for a hedge fund which might have some money lying around at the end of the tax year and who might have nothing better to do with it than invest it in the screen version of a minor novel by someone nobody ever talked about any more and who was now so out of fashion that you might as well try to get an adaptation of the Yellow Pages onto the screen. But still Mark refused to give up, and in the meantime his moustache had turned white and a film of rheumy disappointment had begun to cloud his eyes.

The odd thing was that he also kept a house in the South of France and had two children by his second marriage in private schools and nobody knew where his money came from. But I'd often observed this state of affairs among the British and assumed that he came from a family who had plenty of money going back generations and were skilled at keeping it to themselves. It stopped me from feeling too sorry for him, anyway. And the other thing that stopped me from feeling too sorry for him was the awareness that I hadn't done a serious piece of work for about ten years either so I wasn't exactly one to talk.

"Have you been working much?" Mark asked now, speaking with a directness I could have done without.

"Not really," I admitted. "Did you see—?"

I mentioned a British film which had enjoyed modest theatrical success a few months earlier.

"I did," said Mark. "Was that you? I thought it was—"

He named a young British composer of film and library music, with a growing reputation.

"Some of it was him. I was just the orchestrator, in theory. You remember the little figure on marimba, which played whenever you saw them driving in the car?"

I sang the simple melody for him.

"Of course," said Mark. "That's what made it. That's what everybody remembers."

"That was me."

"And yet he got the Oscar nomination." Mark shook his head, dismayed as always by the way of the world. "You're so talented, Cal. Will you do the music for my film? Say you will. It has to be you."

Of course I said yes, but I did not take the offer seriously. It was as if Mark was offering to pay off my mortgage for me when he won the lottery. Never mind. It was a nice gesture, and he meant it, and it wasn't his fault that he was sure to spend what little remained of his working life in pursuit of this doomed project.

"I've got Dame Judi interested, you know," he said, as if he could read my thoughts and wanted to reassure me that he was not some deluded madman.

"I thought she was already attached," I said, casting my mind back to a conversation we seemed to have had on this very subject decades ago.

"She was attached, and then she wasn't attached, and now she's attached again," he explained. "Only now she's going to play the grandmother, not the mother."

That figures, I thought. The cast for this film remained pretty much the same in Mark's head, they just kept moving up a generation. If it ever got made, the one-time hot young leading man would end up playing Grandpa as he pushed himself around the set in a wheelchair.

"Also," I said, a tad too defensively, not wanting him to think that I was sitting at home twiddling my thumbs and waiting for the phone to ring (even though I was), "I'm writing some music of my own."

"Concert music?" he asked.

"Kind of. It's film-related, but not actually for a film. It's a little suite, for chamber orchestra. I'm calling it *Billy*." And then I added, in response to his interrogative look: "As in Wilder."

"What a nice idea. I didn't know you were a fan."

"I adore his films. Doesn't everybody?"

"Of course. It's incredible, really, when you look back. Just one masterpiece after another. I mean, how do you manage to *do* that, in this industry? *Double Indemnity*—masterpiece. *Sunset Boulevard*—masterpiece. He just kept turning them out. *Some Like It Hot, The Apartment* . . ."

"What about after that?" I asked.

Mark frowned. "I don't know . . . Did he make many films after that?"

"Of course he did. About ten of them."

Struggling to recall, he said, "Was there one about Sherlock Holmes . . . ?"

"Did you ever see *Fedora*?" I asked.

Mark shook his head. "I don't think so. If I have, I've forgotten it."

"Well, I haven't," I said, "because I was there when he shot it."

His eyes widened. "Really?" Frowning again, he mumbled, "*Fedora, Fedora* . . . What was it about?"

And I'm afraid I couldn't resist saying: "It was about lots of things. But I suppose you could say that mainly . . . mainly it was about an ageing film producer, trying to make a film which was completely out of step with the times."

That seemed to close the conversation. Shortly afterwards, Mark gathered up his things and left. From the window, I could see him crossing Piccadilly and heading north towards Regent Street. The sky was darkening, and it was starting to rain.

*

I am a contrary person, I would be the first to admit that. Our last dinner together as a family of four was perfectly cheerful and pleasant, but that was exactly what depressed me about it. There will be no more of those for a long time, I thought to myself afterwards, as I loaded the dishwasher. The girls had gone upstairs to their bedrooms, to do whatever it was they did up there. I decided to watch a film, for distraction. We were at the start of the awards season and as BAFTA voters, Geoffrey and I had about thirty DVD screeners to get through. We started watching an American action movie with a cacophonous soundtrack in which the noise of explosions, gunfire and car crashes competed with a thunderous orchestral score. After about ten minutes he was fast asleep on the sofa, his snores loud enough to drown out even the noise of the movie. I watched it to the end without the least sense of interest or involvement. Everything about it was formulaic to the last degree, and I marvelled at the time, energy and expense that must have gone into something that would be forgotten in a few months' time (and forgotten by the audience the minute they left the cinema). I followed it up with a British comedy about two feisty old dears who went on a road trip to the South of France and got involved in all sorts of scrapes. It was meant to be quirky and life-enhancing but it filled me with a deep sense of existential despair. Every time something amusing was about to happen the composer nudged us in the ribs by having the strings play *pizzicato*. (Back in the 1950s and '60s it would have been a bassoon that did the nudging.) After thirty minutes of these two lovable pensioners larking about in Provence I wanted to kill them both. I turned off the TV and went back into the kitchen, gloomier than ever.

In circumstances this desperate there is only one thing that can console me. I always keep at least three different kinds of Brie in the kitchen for emergency situations. Other people drink to forget; I eat Brie. At the moment my fridge contained a good *Coulommiers*—not strictly a Brie, but close enough—as well as a superior but mass-produced supermarket brand, but this was no time for compromise: only a top-notch *Brie de Meaux fermier* would do tonight.

Of course, it should have been standing at room tempera-
ture for a couple of hours, but there was no time for that now.
I spooned a good dollop out of the box and plastered it onto
a water biscuit. The release of those delicate nutty, mushroomy
flavours onto my tongue was exquisite. The texture was firm
but creamy. Bliss. I scraped out some more and then some
more and before I knew what I was doing I'd eaten about half
of it in ten minutes flat.

"Oh dear," said Geoffrey. He had woken up and was standing watching me from the kitchen doorway. "Bad as that, is it?"

"You will never understand," I said, with my mouth half-
full, "the consolations of a good Brie. You're a cheese philis-
tine."

Geoffrey liked Cheddar and Red Leicester, at a pinch. He
really didn't have a clue when it came to cheese.

He sat down opposite me and poured himself a half-tumbler
of Laphroaig.

"Everything will be all right," he said.

I spread cheese onto a new cracker and devoured it in two
mouthfuls.

"How will it be all right?" I asked.

"It just will. Life goes on."

I thought about this answer and found it wanting.

"So our daughters have grown up," he continued. "That's
wonderful, isn't it? They've turned into beautiful young
women."

"It's not just that," I countered, petulant.

"Why, what else is it?"

"Did you notice the music in those two films?"

"Not really."

"No—you did the sensible thing and fell asleep."

"Well, what about it?"

"That wasn't music, it was just . . . noise. Written by numbers. Not a single melody, not a single new idea . . . And that's
what people want these days. They don't want what I write.

For God's sake, no one's commissioned a score off me for fifteen years."

"The industry's not what it was, everybody knows that. Anyway, now you have time to do other things."

"Other things? Such as?"

"I thought you were going to write some new music—your Billy Wilder thing."

This was true, of course, but it wasn't enough.

"What's to become of me, Geoff?" I said, clutching both of his hands. "I have two talents. Two things that give me a reason to go on living. I'm a good composer, and I'm a good mother. Writing music, and bringing up children. That's what I do. And now I'm basically being told that neither of these skills is required any more. On both fronts, I'm finished. Kaput. And I'm only fifty-seven! Fifty-seven, that's all." I reached out for his whisky glass and took a swig. Big mistake. Whisky and Brie don't go together, not at all. "What's to become of me?" I repeated.

*

The next morning was the one I had really been dreading. The post came freakishly early, while Geoffrey and I were having breakfast. Ariane was upstairs finishing off her packing. Fran was in the shower. When she came down to the kitchen, she was in a hurry. She had a temporary job at Caffè Nero and her shift started in half an hour. There was a letter for her, with the NHS logo in the corner of the envelope. She opened it and said:

"January the fourteenth. A week on Monday."

She meant that this was the day the procedure had been scheduled, to terminate her pregnancy.

She handed me the letter and I read it, but couldn't think of anything to say.

Geoffrey said: "Well, that's good, I suppose. The sooner it's over with, the better."

I stood up and walked towards Fran, meaning to give her a hug, but she saw me coming and managed to duck out of the way.

"I'm late," she said, taking a bite out of a piece of toast, and downing her espresso in one. "I'll see you later."

"Did you say goodbye to your sister?"

"Oh—I forgot," she said, and ran back upstairs.

"She's not going to see her again for months," I said to Geoffrey. "How could she forget?"

"Teenagers are weird," he answered.

She was upstairs for a minute or two, and then she came down and put on her coat and made for the front door, apparently quite unperturbed by the prospect of prolonged separation from her twin.

"So you're O.K. with this, are you?" I said, as she stood in the half-open doorway. "The appointment, I mean."

"Sure."

"And you definitely want to go through with—?"

"Not now, Mum, O.K.? I'm late. This isn't the time to talk about it."

"It never seems to be the—"

But Fran was already on her way down the path to the main road. I looked after her, helplessly, and then went back inside.

Geoffrey was munching on a piece of toast and reading the *Guardian*.

"Am I the only person in this family who feels anything?" I asked. "One of our daughters is pregnant and the other one's flying to Australia. Why am I the only one who can't take any of this in their stride?"

"It's your Mediterranean background," said Geoffrey—an answer which infuriated me.

"Athens is not on the Mediterranean!" I shouted. "And my mother was from London and my father was half-Slovenian and I'm just as emotionally repressed as any of you."

All he had to offer in response to that was, "Everybody deals with things in different ways," another of his maddening and meaningless generalizations.

"You can't even be bothered to come to the airport with us," I said, unfairly.

"It's a teaching day," he said. "It's been in the diary for months. I'll go and say goodbye to her now."

He went upstairs. Like me, Geoffrey was finding it hard to get real work in the film business these days, and instead spent more and more of his time teaching at the National Film and Television School in Beaconsfield. Of course he would have come to the airport with us if he wasn't teaching today. I knew that. I was just lashing out, in my anger and grief. I think you're allowed to do that kind of thing, every so often, when you've been married twenty-five years.

I walked over to the French windows which connected the kitchen to the garden.

We lived (still do) in a four-bedroom terrace in Hammersmith. Cheap when we bought it, absurdly overpriced now. That's one thing, incidentally, that I've never quite been able to understand about the British: how eager they are to regard their houses as financial assets, rather than family homes. Geoffrey was constantly monitoring the rising value of our house via various property websites but to me, first and foremost, it was home, and I hoped that our daughters felt the same way. When I looked through the French windows this morning, for instance, what I saw was a map of Ariane's childhood. An atlas of memories. The apple tree that she used to climb. The long, thick branch to which Geoffrey had attached a swing, a swing which was still there, still visible behind the out-of-control foliage of the laurel bush, if you looked hard enough. The grassy corner where the girls had loved to picnic in the summer, and where, during one rare snowy winter, they had once tried to build a snowman. The wrought-iron table where Ariane used to sit and draw, her brow furrowed with concentration, her tongue sticking out between her lips. I still had those pictures, folded up in a cardboard box beneath our bed, even though she was desperate for me to throw them out.

Did she remember any of these things herself, or did she no longer care?

She would be happy in Sydney, I was pretty sure of that. The Conservatorium had offered her a scholarship and it was a fantastic opportunity, as they say. And Fran going to Oxford in the autumn was another fantastic opportunity, if only she hadn't screwed it up for herself by getting pregnant. Ending the pregnancy was the right thing to do, probably. She didn't look happy about it, but why would you look happy about something like that? The father (father! He was just a boy) wanted nothing to do with it, and nothing to do with her, so there was no point looking for support on that front. It made no sense for her to have the baby. And she had been brought up, I hoped, to see sense.

"Right, that's done," Geoffrey said, coming back into the kitchen. He grabbed the house keys from the hook on the wall, kissed me on the cheek and then he was gone, too. Which left just me and Ariane, alone for the last time.

*

Heathrow Terminal 3. A loathsome place, if you've come there to say goodbye to someone. Ariane had kept up a happy vein of chatter in the car, gossiping about friends, talking about a new book she was reading, and I couldn't decide if she was genuinely light-hearted or was just doing it to mask her distress. Personally, I'm not good at hiding my feelings. I'd nodded along, and thrown in the occasional comment, but inside I felt hollow with misery and I was sure that she knew it.

Just before joining the queue for Departures she said:

"You're not going to start crying or anything, are you?"

"Of course not," I said. "I'm happy for you. It's going to be such a huge adventure."

"I hope Fran sorts herself out."

"I hope so too. It's a nightmare, but Daddy and I will give her . . . all the help we can."

Ariane hesitated. It was as if she was going to say something momentous. I assumed it would be "goodbye."

"By the way," she said, "I'm going to call you Mum and Dad from now on. Otherwise it just sounds . . . I don't know. It sounds like we're still little kids."

"Good idea," I said, swallowing hard. After which there was a difficult silence.

Ariane moved in and put her arms around me.

"Well, I'll see you in a few months, I suppose."

"That's right," I said, returning her hug. "Not long at all."

But my body shook with a sob. She held me close and rubbed my back and said: "Come on, Mum. Don't make this hard for yourself."

I shook wordlessly.

"Did your mother do this?"

"What's my mother got to do with it?" I managed to say.

"She must have been through the same thing," Ariane said. "She saw you off at the airport, didn't she? The time you went to America?"

"That was different," I said.

"How was it different?"

"That was just a trip."

"Then think of this as just a trip."

She kissed me, gave me one last hug, and then released herself from my too-tight, over-protective clasp. I watched her shuffle down the long queue to the security area, and finally she turned and waved and smiled and then the glass gates opened and she went through, rounding a corner and disappearing from view.

I wiped the tears from my eyes with the sleeve of my coat,

then turned and began the long lonely walk back to the car park. I thought about what Ariane had said and wondered if she was right.

Had it been just as hard for my own mother, back in 1976? Since her death, rarely a day passed without me thinking of her. But strangely, this particular question had never occurred to me before.

Los Angeles

To answer Ariane's question: No, my mother did not cry when she waved me off at the airport in Athens in the first week of July 1976. At least, I don't think she did. Would I have noticed? My daughter was right: young people do not notice the feelings of their parents, are not even aware that they have feelings, most of the time. They live in a blissful state of sociopathy, as far as their parents' emotions are concerned.

I was too nervous to notice, in any case. I'd just turned twenty-one but I had still never done much travelling alone, and backpacking around America for three weeks during the long vacation was a big step for me. During the flight to New York, rather than watching the in-flight movie (which I think was a detective spoof called *Murder by Death*, but I wouldn't swear to it, because I had no interest in films back then) I pored over my guidebooks and my Greyhound itinerary. It was a long and uncomfortable flight. For a while I listened to the classical music programme the airline had provided. There were no personal stereos in the seventies, of course, so you were at the mercy of other people's choices, and someone had put together a pretty dull selection of Beethoven and Mozart and the like, all in terrible sound quality. Music was already my passion, but the composers I loved—Satie, Debussy, Ravel, Poulenc, all French for some reason—didn't get a look-in on this occasion. The hours passed slowly, and my nervousness mounted. I had wound up in the smoking section, somehow, and the middle-aged guy sitting next to me was smoking very pungent *cigarillos*. By the time we landed at JFK I was feeling thoroughly sick, and I didn't go out that first evening, just lay in my hostel feeling tired and queasy and wondering what I'd let myself in for.

After New York I spent more than a week taking buses to the West Coast. Chicago—Springfield—St. Louis—Oklahoma City, then on through New Mexico to Vegas and LA. I was pretty lonely at first but after a few days I had a stroke of good luck.

I turned up at the Greyhound station in Springfield to find that the bus ride I'd made a booking for didn't exist. And it wasn't my fault, because several other passengers had the same problem, including a British girl of about my own age, with ash-blonde hair and pale, freckled features, whose name was Gill. We had four hours to wait for the next bus, and that was enough time not just to get talking, but to become friends. It seemed like we had plenty in common: neither of us was especially confident, in fact both of us were rather shy. This trip was the most adventurous thing Gill had ever done, as it was for me. Unlike me, she hadn't started university yet, but said she would be going to Oxford in the autumn. She lived on the outskirts of Birmingham, a place I knew nothing about except that it was a big industrial city somewhere in the middle of England. I lost touch with Gill a long time ago but despite what happened when we got to LA I have the fondest memories of her. I even have a photo of us both on the desk in front of me as I type this, taken late one afternoon on Santa Monica beach. Looking at it I would have to say, without being immodest, that I was the prettier of the two—Gill had a long, angular face, and an unfortunate set of teeth—but for some reason your attractiveness to the opposite sex is not always dependent on how attractive you are, and as it happened she was the one whose trip across America led to a holiday romance.

His name was Stephen. Gill and I had made our way to the West Coast by then, taking in the Grand Canyon and Vegas among other places, but the travelling and the sightseeing exhausted us both and by the time we got to LA neither of us had much energy left. So our first two days there were uneventful. We were staying in a hostel downtown and it was pretty grim, I remember. There were no meals provided and we lived off food bought at the drugstore two blocks away: sliced bread, processed cheese, slices of turkey and ham. After a day or two of this I was starting to feel ill. Once or twice we tried visiting the tourist sites but it was too hot and getting around this huge city by public transport was too difficult. And then things got complicated on the second night when Stephen turned up at the hostel, having hitched his way down to LA from San Francisco. He was British, too, and maybe that was how Gill first got talking to him, I don't recall the details, but I do know that for the next few days our companionable twosome became a complicated threesome. He clung to us like a limpet, and gradually I could feel myself being edged out of the picture. First I noticed they were nearly always walking together, ahead of me, side by side, while I followed behind. Then they were holding hands, then they were kissing every time a suitable opportunity presented itself (or not). After a couple of days it was obvious that I had become the reluctant witness to a full-blown love affair.

I didn't realize how serious it was, however, until a few days later. Stephen was booked on a night bus from LA to Phoenix, Arizona, where he was meant to be meeting up with another traveller, a schoolfriend of his. By coincidence, this was the same night that Gill was meant to be having dinner with some-one—a friend of her father's—in Beverly Hills. She didn't seem to be looking forward to it much—was quite annoyed with her father, in fact, for arranging it, even though I'm sure he had done it with the best of intentions—and she had already invited me along for "moral support." But now that it coincided with Stephen's departure, she was absolutely furious about it. I couldn't see what the fuss was about, personally:

they had already agreed to meet up in London, a day or two after she flew home. They would only be apart for about ten days: was that really so hard to bear? (I had never been in love myself at this point, you understand.)

On the afternoon of Stephen's departure, the three of us went to Santa Monica beach. I spent most of the afternoon drifting alone among the tourist shops on the pier, or sitting on the beach looking out to sea, while Gill and Stephen walked up and down the promenade holding hands and French kissing until their lips were sore. Eventually the moment came when he had to get a bus back to the hostel to pick up his things and then make his way to the bus station. I was expecting Gill to be in floods of tears but to my surprise, and relief, she seemed very stoical about it. After she'd waved him off on the bus and watched it disappear into the distance, she came back and joined me on the beach.

"You O.K.?" I said, as she sat down beside me.

"Yes, of course."

Not knowing, at the time, about the Brits and their compulsion to disguise their feelings, I took her at her word, and decided to change the subject by asking a question which had been on my mind for a day or two, ever since I'd been told that we were going to dinner that evening with an old friend of her father's. There was something about this invitation that seemed puzzling, given that her father, from what I'd heard, was a fairly ordinary white-collar worker who had nothing to do with the film business.

"So how does your father," I said, picking my words carefully, not wanting to be rude, "know a film director from Hollywood?"

"I don't know," she answered. "My dad's quite a mysterious person. He knows lots of people. He's always going on foreign trips and not really telling us where he's been when he comes back. But they must be quite good friends, because a few years ago he made a film in England and there was a premiere in

London and my mum and dad got invited. I remember the tickets coming in the post. They were these great big pieces of card with gold all around the edges."

"What was the film?"

Gill shrugged. "I think it was about Sherlock Holmes. Dad's *crazy* about Sherlock Holmes."

"Is he famous?" I asked. "This director."

"I don't think so. He's about seventy, for one thing."

And that was all she told me. We spent the next couple of hours sunbathing, and it was at some point during those hours that the photograph was taken. I have no memory of who took it. We must have asked some random passer-by, I suppose. It captures us sitting side by side on the beach, about half a mile from the pier, watching the shadows grow long and the sun burnishing the ocean with its fading golden light, two young girls thousands of miles away from home, Gill's long skinny legs stretched out on the sand next to my own, sturdier, chunkier, tawny and smooth beside her veiny English pallor. I admit that I was selfishly pleased to have Gill back again, to have her to myself for the rest of this trip, not to have to share her with Stephen any more. As for tonight's dinner, how bad could it be, an evening spent with strangers and a nice big steak in front of me to make up for the last few days of junk food? Of course, if I'd known that this meal was going to mark a huge change of direction in my life, I might have felt differently, but I had no inkling of that, and in the meantime all I had to do was lie here on the beach with my new friend by my side, the sunlight on the water, the distant sounds of happy screaming from the roller coaster on the pier, the feel of hot sand beneath our bodies, the sense of a future that seemed to consist of pure, uncontaminated potential.

*

Gill had been given the address of a restaurant called the Bistro on North Canon Drive in Beverly Hills. This was a part of LA we had not visited so far, and it bore no resemblance to the district where we were staying. The evening sun blazed down on smart-looking bars and coffee shops and designer boutiques, and money oozed out of every building and every crack in the pavement. Miscalculating the journey time, we arrived at 7.50—twenty minutes late—and found ourselves standing, breathless and flustered, outside a faceless three-storey building onto the front of which had been tacked an incongruous porch in dark wood, with lace curtains hanging down over its old-fashioned windows. The words "The Bistro—Restaurant" were inscribed over the doorway in lettering which evoked the style of *fin de siècle* Paris.

At first, predictably enough, we were refused entry. The doorman took one look at us and blocked our way, more or less laughing in our faces. We were both wearing the same sort of things: dirt-cheap T-shirts with something or other printed on the chest, denim shorts cut off at the thigh, sunglasses, flip-flops. I didn't know much about restaurants, but I understood that we were in an exclusive neighbourhood, and even I could see that we were under-dressed.

"We're here to have dinner with Mr. Wilder," Gill said, when the doorman told her to go away.

"Yeah, right," he answered, and looked to one side, ignoring us, glancing up and down the street. He was wearing a dark suit and tie and his face was sheened with sweat from the summer heat.

"He did invite us," Gill said. Then spelled out the name syllable by syllable. "*Miss-ter-While-Der.*"

The doorman took one more look at her and, letting out a contemptuous sigh, turned on his heel and disappeared inside. About a minute later he came back out, and his expression had changed, although it was no friendlier.

"Name?" he said.

"Foley. Gill Foley."

"Gill," he repeated, clearly reluctant to believe that he was actually going to have to let us in. "O.K. Come on."

He jerked his head and we followed him inside. I can still remember his stocky, swaying bulk as we hurried along behind him, and the roll of fat at the back of his neck, straining against his starched collar.

The inside of the restaurant felt no less incongruous than its facade. Outside, you had the blue skies and unrelenting sun of California in mid-July. Inside, after passing through a small entrance lobby (where a pale girl sitting behind a desk was on the point of asking whether we had any clothes to check in, then took one look at us and decided not to bother), you found yourself emerging into a large space which seemed to belong to another world entirely. Bevelled panelling in dark wood, crystal chandeliers, mirrors everywhere, a bar running the length of one wall. All very rococo. It really did feel as if we had somehow stepped through some kind of barrier in space and time and emerged in Paris: except of course that the muted conversations all around us (the place was packed) were being conducted in English. There was even accordion music playing over the PA system: a musette band waltzing its way through *"Sous le ciel de Paris"* (one of the first tunes I had learned to play on the piano) which for some reason they had transposed a whole tone up to A minor from its more usual G.

Our doorman handed us over to a moustachioed *maître d'* in a tightly fitting tuxedo, who was too experienced and polite to look askance at our foolishly inappropriate clothing and merely turned on his heel and led us through the tables, cutting a swathe between them with lithe, expert movements. The other customers stopped talking and glanced at us as we walked by. I could feel my cheeks burning. Soon we were being shown towards a table in a corner of the room but for some reason there were already four people sitting around it, not two. Two men, two women. They seemed very elderly. That was the first thing that struck me. The second thing was that they seemed very gloomy. A kind of pall of depression hung over the table. It hung over the two men in particular. It was very noticeable. There was one couple sitting opposite each other at one end of the table, and another couple sitting at the other end, and there were two spaces in the middle for me and Gill to sit opposite each other as well.

One couple was dressed more elegantly than the other. My eye was drawn, particularly, towards a lady in her early fifties, with thick, luxuriant black hair and generous lips and good cheekbones and blue eyes sparkling behind a pair of large, slightly tinted glasses. She was wearing a chiffon blouse in autumnal brown with a pattern of small yellow leaves. Even though I knew even less about clothes than I did about restaurants, and never really thought about them, I could tell that this was an expensive blouse. Sitting opposite her was a rather older man I took to be her husband. He was almost bald but made the most of his remaining silver hair which was nicely combed back to emphasize his distinguished forehead. He was wearing a simple fawn sports shirt buttoned up to the collar, which I also assumed to be expensive, and when I thought about him afterwards (as I did, a lot) I wondered how he had managed to look so smart, so stylishly at ease with himself, wearing just that sports shirt and slacks, whilst my father, for instance, could rent the most expensive dinner suit in Athens (as he had, for his fiftieth birthday dinner that year) and still look a mess, with his collar too tight and his tie never quite straight and his shirt stretched taut over his belly. I suppose it's a question of what you've been used to all your life. And money, obviously. The money thing is always important.

This was my first glimpse, and my first impression, of Mr. Wilder. He was also wearing glasses, thick-lensed glasses, and, despite his air of dejection, behind these glasses his eyes could not help lighting up and sparkling with amusement when he saw Gill and me approaching the table in our manky T-shirts and cut-off shorts. The amusement was frank and undisguised and somewhat mortifying, but I couldn't see any malice in it. He saw this as a comic situation and he relished it as such. Who wouldn't, for that matter?

When he rose to his feet to greet us, his three dining companions stood up as well.

"So one of you," he said, holding out his hand in our general direction, "must be Gill."

"That would be me," said Gill, shaking the proffered hand.

"Ah, yes, of course. Good to meet you. Very nice to meet you. Please sit down, here in the centre of the table."

To my surprise, he had what sounded to me like a strong—very thick—German accent. Nobody had told me that he was German. I had assumed that he was American.

"My name's Calista," I said, when it became clear that Gill had forgotten to introduce me.

"Good, good, good," he said. "This is my wife Audrey, and my friend Mr. Diamond, and his wife Barbara."

"Calista," said Audrey. "What a lovely name. Is it an English name?"

"I'm Greek," I explained. "From Athens."

We took our seats. I was between the two men, Gill was between the two women. "Mr. Diamond" had a balding head, wire-framed glasses, and a reserved and scholarly air. I guessed that he wasn't going to talk much this evening, and I was right. His wife Barbara seemed friendly and perhaps the least scary of the four of them. I felt completely out of my depth. It would have helped if I'd known anything about Mr. Wilder or his films. My idea of a film director was a young man in a tracksuit and baseball cap shouting "Cut" and "Action" while crouched behind the camera in some athletic position. Mr. Wilder looked more like a retired university professor, or a Beverly Hills surgeon with a thriving business in expensive facelifts.

All four of them were drinking Martinis. They asked us if we wanted one: Gill said yes, and I said no. Meanwhile Mr. Wilder had an earnest conversation with the sommelier, which ended with him ordering two bottles of wine, one white and one red. He checked very specifically to see if the red wine had been decanted earlier, and was promised that it had been.

There were leather-bound menus on the placemats in front of us. I opened mine up. The dishes were listed in English as well as French, but the font used on the menu was so ornate that I found them difficult to understand in either language. Glancing at the list of wines at the back, I caught a glimpse of the price of the red wine and my jaw dropped.

Turning to Gill, Mr. Wilder said: "And how is your father, if I may ask?"

"He's fine," she answered.

"That's good. I'm glad to hear it." Addressing the table more generally, he said: "I met this young lady's father in London during the war. He was working at the Ministry of Information and we spent a lot of time in each other's company, working together. I liked him very much."

"You kept in touch?" Mr. Diamond asked.

Mr. Wilder shrugged. "Now and again. I'm not a great correspondent. I last saw him in London a few years ago—when we were making the Holmes picture. We met for a drink at the Connaught."

Gill said nothing, and there seemed to be no more mileage left in this particular topic of conversation. I felt rather sorry for her: it must be difficult, I thought, to know what to say to an elderly friend of your father's, especially one you'd never met before. And of course, she was sad about saying goodbye to Stephen: that much was written on her face.

"Do you like oysters?" Mr. Wilder asked us now, out of the blue.

"Oysters?" I said, picking up the menu and pretending to read it.

"The oysters here are very good. They bring them in from Humboldt Bay. Of course, real French oysters are better. But this is California."

"I might try the oysters then," I said.

"Do you like oysters?"

"Not really."

"Then I wouldn't try them. Don't be scared. You can choose anything. Choose something that you like."

He was being kind, although of course I was furious with him for noticing that I was scared.

"What are you going to have?"

"My wife and I," said Mr. Wilder, "will share a dozen oysters. And then we will share the *chateaubriand*."

"We always have the same when we come here," said Audrey.

"Have you been coming here a long time?"

"Ever since it opened. Billy owns it, you see."

I turned to stare at him.

"Really?"

"I'm one of the stockholders," he said, in a dismissive way.

"We wanted," she said (I noted the first-person plural), "to bring a little bit of Paris to Beverly Hills. Everything in this town is very . . . plastic, very new. Billy wanted a reminder of old Europe."

"I imagined something simpler," Billy said. "Check tablecloths and carafes of wine, that sort of thing. But then she took over."

"All the fittings," Audrey said, "are from one of Billy's pictures. Everything—the bar, the lights, the panelling . . ."

"*Irma La Douce*," he murmured, but I did not understand what he meant by that.

A waiter arrived to take our order. "The usual for you, Mr. Wilder?"

He gave a single nod.

"And Mrs. Diamond? What will you be having this evening?"

Mrs. Diamond ordered something light—a salad, I think—while her husband prevaricated.

"*Pâté* to start," he said, looking across at her to see if she approved, which apparently she did. "And then I know I should have a salad too, or something not too heavy, but . . ."

He looked at her again, a more beseeching look this time, and she put him out of his misery.

"Oh, go on, Iz. Have the steak. You know you want to."

"With *frites*?"

"Just this once. They're so good here."

The waiter looked down at him for confirmation:

"*Steak frites*, sir?"

He closed the menu and gave a smile of assent. It was one of the few smiles I saw him give that evening—or any time, for that matter. "Why not?" he said, and the others around the table exchanged amused, conspiratorial glances.

I ordered exactly the same as Mr. Diamond. I liked him already, and already thought he might be the most reliable, trustworthy guide through the social labyrinth I had found myself entering. Gill ordered onion soup and an omelette. The waiter departed, and the sommelier arrived, bearing our wines. An elaborate ritual of uncorking, smelling, tasting and approving ensued. Six glasses were filled.

"So," Barbara said, when this procedure was over, "you girls are travelling round America together, is that right?"

"That's right," I said, having taken a large swig of wine and already feeling better for it.

"Have you been to the East Coast yet?"

We nodded.

"And what did you think of New York?"

Looking back on that conversation, I can only cringe. Shy at the best of times, we were both completely tongue-tied that night. The whole situation was just so bewilderingly unlike anything we'd encountered in our lives up until then. Luckily, before it became too obvious that neither of us had anything interesting to say about New York, we were rescued by the arrival at our table of a man, a man in his early thirties, wearing a loud checked business suit which had those absurdly wide 1970s lapels, with a shock of curly hair and a tentative, deferential expression on his face.

"Mr. Wilder?" he said.

Mr. Wilder turned in his seat, with a look neither hostile nor welcoming.

"I don't mean to disturb you . . ."

"That's O.K. Go ahead."

"I just wanted to say—I am your *biggest* fan."

"Really? My biggest?"

"It's such an honour to meet you."

"That's very kind, thank you."

"You can't imagine the impact . . . I mean, you're really the reason I entered this business."

"You're in the business?"

"I'm in the front office at Warner's. Can I give you my card?"

"The front office at Warner's? I should be making advances toward you, not the other way around."

The man giggled nervously at the compliment and handed Mr. Wilder a business card. He raised his glasses to read it.

"*Some Like It Hot*," the man continued, "is . . . well, the greatest."

"Very kind," Mr. Wilder repeated.

"A masterpiece of American comedy," the man added. "Truly."

Mr. Wilder nodded his agreement. It was an eloquent nod, giving out a clear signal that the man's time was up and the dialogue was over.

"Well . . . I'm sorry to intrude upon your evening," the man concluded. "But I saw you across the room, and I couldn't resist . . ."

"That's quite all right," said Mr. Wilder. "It was nice meeting you."

"I don't know if you have a project you're working on at the moment, or whether you're attached to a studio, but . . . Well. You have my card."

"I do."

Before leaving, the man said, "May I?" and held out his hand. They shook hands and he left.

Mr. Wilder turned back towards the table and took a sip of his wine. Then he glanced across at Mr. Diamond and said: "Did you hear that? 'A masterpiece of American comedy.'"

"I heard."

With a short laugh, Mr. Wilder added: "Adapted from a German film which was adapted from a French film. Written by an Austrian and a Romanian!"

The ghost of a smile flickered across Iz's face, and was gone.

Meanwhile, I was stockpiling information. Mr. Wilder was the Austrian one, going by his accent. That meant that his friend was Romanian. And I was pretty sure, after listening to that exchange, that *Some Like It Hot* must be the name of a film he had directed. I confess that I had never heard of it. If someone had mentioned the name of Marilyn Monroe, perhaps, I might have been impressed, because even I had heard of *her.* But nobody did. Maybe Gill could have confirmed some of this for me, but I could see she wasn't really listening. All she could do was stare into space with a mournful look in her eyes.

"Then again," said Mr. Wilder, "maybe he never even saw it. How would we know?"

"Oh, come on, Billy," his wife reproved. "Don't be so cynical."

"I think the guy was sincere," said Mr. Diamond.

"Well, I shall keep this," said Mr. Wilder, putting the business card in the breast pocket of his shirt. "God knows, it looks like we might be needing it soon."

This remark didn't seem to be intended as a joke, and wasn't received that way. Mr. Diamond immediately looked more depressed than ever. Barbara swirled her wine around in its glass and gazed stolidly down into its depths. Audrey seemed exasperated, more than anything else.

"Snap out of it, Billy. So Marlene doesn't want to do the picture. So what?"

This, I realized later, was an incendiary thing to say. Billy did not like to discuss work on social occasions, let alone when the subject was as sensitive or as confidential as this. But he didn't get angry. (He never did, with Audrey.) He just said:

"Let's not talk about that now, O.K.?"

"Sure. So like I said, snap out of it."

Luckily I had no idea who "Marlene" was. Nor, not knowing who she was, did I know that he had been hoping she would play the lead in his new film. Nor did I know that he had received a letter from her in today's post telling him in no uncertain terms that she wasn't going to do it. Nor that this letter had plunged him and Mr. Diamond into a state of gloom which had prevented them from making any progress on the script all day. None of this was known to me. And if I had known, in any case, none of it would have mattered as much as the delicious slab of coarse Ardennes *pâté* which was now placed in front of me and which I immediately began to attack with the eagerness of someone who hadn't eaten a proper meal since leaving home almost two weeks ago. And my enthusiasm had one good effect at least, which was that it seemed to cheer Mr. Wilder up, to the point where that gleam of amusement reappeared behind his glasses and he said, after taking a long sip of wine:

"Something tells me you haven't been eating too well on this trip."

I nodded, embarrassed to think that I was making myself so obvious.

"*Bon appétit*," he added.

He began to concentrate on swallowing his oysters, which looked loathsome to me and smelled even worse, but he had only managed to get three of them down when another man approached the table. This one was in his mid-forties, probably, and had shoulder-length black hair, a droopy moustache, a cheesecloth shirt, stonewashed denim jeans and a heavy medallion dangling from his neck. He seemed altogether more sure of himself than the previous visitor.

"Mr. Wilder?" he began.

Billy, in the act of picking up the fourth oyster, turned and regarded the man with a look of resigned enquiry.

"How can I help you?"

"I know you're eating, and . . . having a nice time with your friends and all that, but can I tell you something, just in a few words?"

"Go ahead, please."

"I just wanted to say that your films . . . They changed my life." Having made this declaration, the man rushed on:

"You see, the thing is, back in the early sixties, I dropped out and moved out here to the West Coast. I mean, the drug culture and the hippie culture and the counter-revolution hadn't really got started then, but it was on its way, you know? So first of all I came to San Francisco and there was a real poetry scene, and a real jazz scene going on there at the time and I kind of immersed myself in that and started to write a bit and—well— " (a laugh)—"my poetry really wasn't so good, I have to be honest with you, but it at least made me reassess myself, you know?, it made me realize that my life up until that point had been so . . . *narrowly focused*, I mean, I was such a *square*, but I didn't really start to . . . *find myself* until the music thing got going, you know, flower power, psychedelia, the whole trippy, druggy thing, that was when I knew what I really wanted to do, so I moved to LA and began to make myself known, you know, on the music scene, I had a record store for a while, a little store on Melrose, it's not there any more, I think it's a dental office now or something weird like that, but then I got into management, I was the manager for Mother's Finest for a while, do you remember them?, they were quite big at the time, they were

playing to audiences of three or four thousand, sometimes, anyway, that doesn't matter, then I got more into the promotion
side of things, and—long story short, sorry, I know you want to
finish your meal—I opened a club in Fairfax, and now I've got
another one in East Hollywood, two venues, both doing very
well, and, basically, I feel like I'm the luckiest guy alive, I mean,
I know it's not like being a world-famous film director or anything but being a club manager does give you a certain . . .
cachet on the scene, do you know what I'm saying? I mean, I can
have a different chick every night if I want to, and sometimes I
do, not that I—" (noticing the way that Audrey was staring at
him)—"well, no offence, ma'am, none intended, and none
taken, I hope. I just wanted to share my story with you, Mr.
Wilder, and say thanks. Thanks for everything."

Billy looked at him for a moment or two and said:

"I don't understand. What the hell has this got to do with
any of my pictures?"

The man realized that he had, indeed, left out the most
important part of his story, and he gave an apologetic laugh.

"Sorry, I'm such a jerk, that's the first thing I should have
told you, it was all because of your movie, your movie *The
Apartment*. You know the one I mean?"

"I remember it, yeah."

"Well, the Jack Lemmon character, that was me in the early
sixties, you see? I was just a dumb schmuck working for a big
corporation in NYC, and I saw your movie, and realized that
I had to do what he does, I had to give it all up, I had to get
the hell out of there, you know what I'm saying?"

There was a pause. Billy nodded.

"I know what you're saying. So it's all because of me?"

"It's all because of you."

He stood there a bit longer, as if waiting to be congratu-
lated.

"Well—" Billy held out his hand—"that's good to know.
Thank you."

They shook hands.

"Thank *you*, Mr. Wilder. And no offence, ma'am."

"None taken," said Audrey, smiling at him graciously.

The man left. Billy took another sip of wine, and slid the fourth, much-delayed oyster into his mouth. I had long since finished my *pâté* and was gnawing on a piece of bread.

"Well," he said, looking across at Mr. Diamond. "There you have it."

"There you have it," Iz agreed.

"This guy is getting laid every night and we're the ones who made it happen for him."

"Kind of gives you a warm glow, doesn't it?"

Mr. Wilder shook his head, as if lost in wonder at life's small, unexpected vagaries. He was smiling. He ate his two final oysters without further comment.

I decided to venture a remark. The large glass of wine I'd just emptied had given me courage, and I said:

"It must be wonderful to hear people say things like that. That your films have changed their lives."

Mr. Wilder shrugged. "Yeah, it's a good feeling. Not everything you've done has been forgotten, you know?"

"He sounds blasé," Audrey explained, "because it happens so often. In the streets, in the shops. I promise you there will be five or six more people like that tonight."

"And I promise *you*," Billy answered, "that they will all talk about those same two pictures. Which are fifteen years old. More than fifteen. Or they will talk about even older pictures. Pictures from twenty years ago, thirty years ago. Mr. Diamond and I have written seven pictures since *The Apartment*. Seven. Let's see if anyone comes over tonight and says that one of *those* has changed their lives."

To break the solemn silence that followed, I said: "Yes, but it's great that—"

He turned towards me.

"You said that you were from Greece, right?"

"Yes."

"But your English is perfect. You even have an English accent."

"My mother's English."

"So you spoke both languages, even when you were a small child?"

"Yes."

"Say something in Greek."

"Νομίζω ότι ήπια πολύ γρήγορα το κρασί μου," I improvised.

"What does that mean?"

"It means: 'I think I drank that glass of wine too quickly.'"

He laughed. "You're very lucky, to speak two languages. You need to learn them both as a child. I was almost thirty when I came here, and when I came, I had no English. Practically none. I learned by listening to the radio, listening to baseball games. But you know, I never lost my accent, and even now, sometimes, the words, they don't come so fluently. My French is better, actually. My French is good. Do you speak French?"

"Yes, I do," I said. "And German. I studied French and German at university."

"Mr. Diamond and I visited Greece earlier this year," he now told me. "We were making a visit to some of the islands. Scouting locations. Do you know them?"

"The Greek islands? Yes, I know some. We've been for holidays to Santorini, Ikaria . . . Why do you ask?"

"We didn't find what we wanted," he said. "But if we ever get a studio to pay for this new picture—and I say *if*, because nothing is certain any more in this business—we'll have to find a Greek island."

Intrigued, I asked what seemed to me to be an innocent question—"What's your new film about?"—and I was shocked by the looks of alarm which appeared on the faces of Audrey and Mr. and Mrs. Diamond. Since then, of course, over the years I've learned that you must never, ever ask creative people to tell you about their works in progress, but in those days I was a perfect *naïf* and it seemed the most natural question in the world.

In any case, Mr. Wilder himself did not appear to take too much offence. There must already have been something about me (I don't know what) that made him talk freely.

"It's about an old movie star," he said. "A woman. Her name is Fedora. Nobody has seen her for years and all that anyone knows is that she lives somewhere on a Greek island. A recluse. A Garbo figure. So a producer comes looking for her but when he finds the island where she lives, he can't get anywhere near her. He can't get past the people who are looking after her."

"She's a sort of prisoner?"

"Sort of, yeah."

I didn't know what a "Garbo figure" was, but I was not just being polite when I said: "That sounds great. I'd definitely go and see that."

"You would?"

"Yes. I love mystery films."

Mr. Wilder looked across at Mr. Diamond with an expression of triumph. "There you are. We've reached the youth market at last."

Mr. Diamond shook his head sadly and said: "You need a bigger sample size, Billy." He turned to Gill: "What about you, do you go to the movies much?"

"Now and then," said Gill.

"What kinds of picture do you like?"

Gill shrugged. "All sorts."

"Anything in particular?"

She wrinkled her nose. "*Jaws* was good."

"Oh yes, *Jaws* was incredible," I agreed, nodding vigorously. My mother and father and I had been to see it the day it opened in Greece—Boxing Day, 1975—and I had seen it a couple more times since then.

The mention of this film, though, made Mr. Wilder sigh (in a resigned, rather than angry way).

"My God, this picture with the shark. When will people stop talking about this picture with the shark? You know this damn shark has made more money in the States than anything else in the history of Hollywood. Even Monroe, even Scarlett O'Hara, didn't make as much money as this shark. And now every stupid executive in town wants more movies with sharks. This is how they think, these people. We made one hundred million dollars with this shark, we need another shark. We need more sharks, we need bigger sharks, we need more dangerous sharks. My idea was for a picture called *Jaws in Venice*. You know, you have all the gondolas going up and down the Grand Canal, all the Japanese tourists, and then you have about one hundred sharks coming up the canal and attacking them. I pitched it to a guy at Universal, as a joke. He thought I was being serious. He loved it. Any picture you can describe to them in three words, you know, they love that, they love these simple stories, and he thought *Jaws in Venice* was perfect. So I said, O.K., fine, you can have that idea for free, but I'm not the person to direct it for you. I'm not really comfortable around fish, you know? You look back at all my pictures and you'll see that not one of them has anything to do with a big fish. I'm more of a human-being kind of director.

"This Mr. Spielberg, you know, he's really talented. He's part of this new generation, with Mr. Coppola and Mr. Scorsese. Mr. Diamond calls them 'the kids with beards'." He laughed at the expression, showing genuine admiration (I was to see it again and again) for his friend's turn of phrase. "Really I think he is the best of them all, which makes him the most talented person in Hollywood at the moment. I saw his picture *The Sugarland Express*. Did you see it?" (Gill and I both shook our heads.) "There you are, that's because it's a picture about people, and nobody wants to see those any more. Sure, there are car chases, and guns firing all over the place and so on and so on—maybe at the end there's a bit too much of this kind of a thing—but really it's a story about these characters, you know, these people that you have some interest in. But now, with the shark, he's gone the other way, he's gone for this whole make-the-audience-drop-their-popcorn kind of a thing, with the big moments and the big shocks. More like a fairground ride than a drama, a story. That's how it seems to me, anyway."

He tailed off as a pair of waiters delivered our main courses, and we were distracted, for a while, by the business of setting everything up, dividing the *chateaubriand*, sampling our food and, in my case, closing my eyes in near-ecstasy as my teeth closed on the first tender mouthful of steak, feeling the sweet release of blood and juice onto my tongue. I looked across at Mr. Diamond and saw that he was having the same reaction. It was so good. We exchanged a nice moment of complicity.

"We could have Fedora attacked by sharks," he said to Billy now, in a ruminative way.

Mr. Wilder nodded as he carved up some *sauté* potatoes on his plate.

"You mean while she's taking the boat over to her island? Sure, that could work. *Jaws in Greece*. Not bad. Maybe it would solve our problem with the second act. Sure." He speared some potato and paused before eating it. "Let's talk about it in the morning." Then he leaned back in his chair and looked over to the other side of the restaurant. In a different tone entirely—altogether more confidential—he said to his friend: "Now, you see who just arrived?"

Mr. Diamond didn't look around. I had the feeling that he had no interest in who the other diners were, however famous they might be. Barbara followed Mr. Wilder's gaze, however.

"That's Al Pacino, isn't it?"

"I believe it is Mr. Pacino, yes. And I believe that the very beautiful woman sitting opposite him, with the dark hair, is his girlfriend, who is also an actress. The other people at the table I don't know."

"Will you go and speak to him?" Audrey asked.

"I will not go and speak to him," he said. "Not while we are all eating."

Mr. Diamond, defiantly unimpressed by any of this, turned towards Gill and me again. "So what about comedy?" he said. "What makes young people laugh these days? Any movies you've seen?"

I tried to think, but nothing came to mind. As I said, I didn't go to the cinema very often in those days. As for Gill, I'm not even sure that she heard the question. In fact I was a little bit worried about her. She was looking more and more woebegone, as if she was about to burst into tears.

"I mean, do you like Monty Python?" Mr. Diamond prompted.

Hunched over his plate, Mr. Wilder said: "I don't really get Monty Python."

"Or what about *Blazing Saddles*?" Mr. Diamond asked. "Now that was pretty funny."

Once again, it was Mr. Wilder who reacted, since Gill and I had nothing to say.

"Yeah, it was pretty funny," he admitted. "I like Mr. Brooks. He's a clever guy. Very clever, very funny. But even then, you know . . ." He turned to Gill and me, as if addressing a class. "You know, you have the scene where the cowboys are all sitting around the fire, and they start breaking wind one after the other. It's not what I call sophisticated humour, right? Mr. Diamond and I have never wanted to write a scene like this. We're more from the Lubitsch school." (Another name that meant nothing to either of us.) "You don't make things obvious. You imply things. You use a bit of subtlety, you make the audience do the work. Before I met Mr. Diamond, my previous partner, Mr. Brackett, and I—we wrote a picture for Lubitsch called *Ninotchka*. A huge success, a very big success. Because it was the first time Garbo had done comedy, you know? And the publicists at MGM, they came up with a very good line, a tag line for the picture, for the campaign and the posters: '*GARBO LAUGHS*'. That's what it said, and that was enough to make the audience show up. That was what intrigued them: '*GARBO LAUGHS*'. But you notice, it did not say '*GARBO FARTS*'. Because the audiences back then, they were used to a kind of humour which was more delicate, a bit more intelligent. Now it's different, and maybe Mr. Diamond and I, we are getting out of step with the times but, as I said, we are writing a story about an old film star, very elegant, very beautiful, very mysterious, so there is not going to be a scene where she sits up in her chair and lifts her leg in the air and breaks wind in the middle of a conversation."

"Oh, Billy!" his wife said, reproving but laughing.

"No, I mean, it's not going to happen. We can't do it." He poured himself some more red wine from the decanter. "Anyway, this new picture, it's not even a comedy. It's going to be a very serious picture. A melodrama, almost a tragedy. This is why Mr. Diamond feels so uncomfortable writing it."

I glanced at Mr. Diamond to see if he did indeed look uncomfortable, but it was hard to say. It was always hard to say, with him. He looked thoughtful, and melancholy, and rather inscrutable except that he was definitely enjoying his steak.

Just then, Gill rose to her feet.

"I need the toilet," she said.

The statement was so abrupt and unceremonious that it took Audrey a moment or two to say: "The ladies' room? Sure, it's through there."

Mr. Wilder also rose to his feet and dabbed at his lips with a napkin. He said: "I think I will use the men's room, as well. Come on, I'll show you the way."

They disappeared together, but Mr. Wilder did not go to the men's room. Instead, he seemed more interested in stopping by Al Pacino's table, where he was soon engaged in a lengthy conversation with the star. He leaned over him in his chair and they were talking and laughing and appeared to be getting on very well.

After a minute or two, a waiter approached our table. He brought with him a scrap of paper upon which Gill had scribbled a message for me.

"This is from your friend," he said.

I unfolded the note, which read:

It's no good, I can't stand this. I'm going to Phoenix with Stephen tonight. I'm so sorry xx

Audrey and Barbara were watching my face closely as I read it. How could she do this to me? Leave me in a restaurant with four complete strangers? What was I going to tell them?

The truth seemed the easiest option.

"She's had to leave," I said.

They were too well-mannered to look as incredulous about this as they probably felt.

"Oh dear," said Audrey. "I hope it's nothing serious."

"Did she tell you what's happened?" Barbara asked.

"She met this guy a couple of days ago," I said. "They've been having this big romance. He was leaving town tonight. She's gone chasing after him."

"How *utterly* thrilling and romantic," said Audrey.

"Tough on you, though," said Barbara—for which I was grateful.

Mr. Wilder returned to our table and received the news that Gill had vanished with perfect equanimity (having hardly spoken to her all evening). He was much more interested in reporting back on his encounter with Al Pacino.

"So how did that go?" Iz asked him, dry as ever.

"We had a pleasant conversation," Billy replied, noncommittal at first.

"I hope he was suitably flattered that you dropped by to talk to him," Audrey said.

"I'm not sure that he was flattered, but he's familiar with myself and Mr. Diamond. He's acquainted with our work." Turning to me, he said: "You know Mr. Pacino, of course. You saw him in *The Godfather*?"

"I didn't see it," I admitted.

"Very good picture. The second part, I mean. The more recent one. Brilliant picture, one of the best I ever saw." He resumed talking to the table in general, although his eyes were mainly on his friend throughout, watching for a reaction. "It was hard to know exactly what he was saying because he was eating a hamburger and mumbling and talking with his mouth full. He talks the way that he acts, you know? You could give him Hamlet's speech, 'To be or not to be', and still you wouldn't be able to understand a word of it. And incidentally, this is not a hamburger restaurant. Monsieur Chaumeil—our head chef—does not cook them normally. They are not on the menu. So he would have had to make a special order. Look at all the things you can ask for here—*bouillabaisse, cassoulet, pot-au-feu*—and he asks for a hamburger! His girlfriend apologized for that. She told me he has no manners."

"What's her name?"

"Her name is Marthe. Marthe Keller. A Swiss lady." He looked around, quizzically. "That's odd, isn't it? There are not many Swiss here in Hollywood. There are not many Swiss actresses full stop. I can't think of any others. This is a country that produces more cuckoo clocks than it produces actors." Then, to me, he abruptly said: "So what happened with the Foley girl? Did somebody tell her that the desserts here are no good?"

"No."

"I'm glad to hear it. Because they are very good. Let's get those menus back."

He looked around and clicked his fingers and a waiter came scurrying. I thought about my father again, this sweet ineffectual man in his fifties who could never catch a waiter's eye to save his life. I thought it must be nice to command that kind of attention. And, once you had got used to commanding it, not so nice to lose it again.

"She's gone chasing after a man," Audrey informed her husband, "for *love*."

"Really?" This news seemed to amuse him. "I don't think her father would approve. He always seemed far too sensible for that. She must be her mother's daughter."

Without Gill there, I was starting to feel awkward.

"You've all been so nice," I said, "letting me have dinner with you. But now she's left, I'm not sure that I should stay. I'm only here because she invited me along . . ."

There was a loud and unanimous chorus of protest.

"Nonsense, dear," said Audrey.

"We wouldn't hear of it," said Barbara.

"Here," said Billy, filling up my wine glass, "finish this off, because we're going to order another bottle."

"But you don't even—"

Audrey laid her hand on mine and silenced me with a look. "Please, just relax and enjoy yourself. We're very happy that you're here. And order any dessert that you want, because you've already earned it."

"I have? How, what have I done?"

"I don't think you quite realize," Audrey said, "what an unusual occasion this is. Billy and Iz never eat together in the evenings. Never. Why should they? They spend every day in each other's company. They're together from nine in the morning till six at night. They see more of each other than Barbara and I see of them. And they're far more devoted to each other than they are to their wives." (Billy and Iz were looking on while she said this, nodding occasionally and neither of them disputing a word.) "But they both *wanted* to meet you tonight. You know why?"

I hadn't the faintest idea.

"It's quite simple, dear. It's because you're *young*. Didn't you notice how they've been trying to pick your brains about the movies all evening? Billy's desperate to know what the young people want from the pictures these days. And he never gets the chance to talk to any. Now come on—I heartily recommend the chocolate mousse, it's to die for."

"I would hardly say that I was desperate," said Billy, pouring yet more wine into my glass, which was practically full anyway. "But I'm always curious to know what people want from a picture. You know, I can't just make pictures for six people in Bel Air. Or to win the, the . . . Golden Chipmunk at the Liechtenstein Film Festival. This is a business. You win or lose at the box office. Everything else is just . . . *pfft!*" He glanced across at Audrey. "Do you mind if I have a little smoke?"

"Go ahead. I might join you."

"If you don't mind me saying so," Iz said to me now, "your friend was kind of putting a dampener on the evening anyway. Now, Billy and I have had a rough day, after this letter from Marlene this morning, and I for one intend to forget all about it."

"Good idea," said Barbara, filling his glass, and everyone else's. "Let the wine flow free. I'm also ready for some of that *tarte au citron*. *Crème brûlée* for you, I'm guessing?"

Iz slapped his menu shut with a great beam of satisfaction.

"Why not?" he said, at which Audrey and Barbara exchanged great peals of laughter, while Billy leaned in to me confidentially and explained:

"You must not conclude from this that Mr. Diamond is unenthusiastic for *crème brûlée*. The *crème brûlée* here is the best in Los Angeles—perhaps in America. But something you will understand, if you get to know him a little bit better, is that this is his absolute peak of enthusiasm. Twenty years now we've been writing pictures together, and this is the biggest praise I ever got out of him: 'Why not?' I can throw him the best line you ever heard in a picture in your life—like the end of *The Apartment*, you know, when she says: 'Shut up and

deal'—well, you don't know it, because you only watch films
about sharks, but let me tell you, it's a pretty great line, and
when I pitched it to him, what did he say? 'Billy, you're a
genius'? 'This is going to make the picture'? No. Nothing like
this. He just looks at me with that hangdog look of his, and he
says: 'Why not?' And that's how I know that he loves the line,
even though it would kill him to say so. And that he loves
crème brûlée as well, even though he will never admit it, and the
only words you will get out of him on the subject, are these:
'Why not?'"

Audrey and Barbara had been listening to the latter half of
this speech, and watching the way Iz reacted to it, with rapture
in their eyes.

"Aren't these two just adorable?" Barbara said. "Wouldn't
it be a beautiful thing if they could be married to each other
and not to us? I don't know about you, Audrey, but sometimes
I feel so guilty, coming between them the way that I do."

Audrey laughed again. "Oh yes! I'm exactly the same. If I
hadn't snagged Billy a few years before he met Iz, I know that
I wouldn't have stood a chance."

"Look, we are not faggots," said Billy, and warned me:
"Don't start spreading that rumour around."

I nodded seriously and drank some more wine and for the
next few minutes just let the conversation wash over me.
Everyone else around the table lit up cigarettes but I have
never been a smoker so I declined. I was so happy, happier
than I'd been at any moment during my American trip, happier even than when I was lying in the sun next to Gill on
Santa Monica beach a few hours earlier. In fact, I couldn't
have cared less if I never saw Gill again, after the way she had
treated me. She was crazy to have walked out on this meal for
the sake of a few extra days with Stephen in Phoenix: because
this was paradise, right here, right now, sitting in one of the
most glamorous restaurants in Beverly Hills, surrounded by
beautiful, talented, rich, famous people, eating wonderful

food. I felt as though I'd stepped into a different universe, a different order of existence altogether. In two days' time I would be back on a Greyhound bus, making a sweaty seven-hour journey to San Francisco, with nothing to eat in my back-pack apart from processed-cheese sandwiches, but I couldn't think about that now. All I could think about was how elegant and gracious these people were, and how welcoming they had been towards me, and how that made me feel elegant and gracious in turn.

Audrey was laughing at something. Something she herself had said. It was a wicked, transgressive laugh, and Barbara was joining in. They were talking about this restaurant. It seemed that it had recently been used as the location for a film and a particularly scandalous scene had been shot in a private room upstairs.

"I mean, you are just illustrating my point," Mr. Wilder said, in that half-joking, half-serious tone that I was becoming familiar with. "This is the problem Iz and I are facing. Here we are, trying to write subtle pictures, romantic pictures, and this is what the audience expects. Ten minutes into the story and the girl is already on her knees giving the guy a blow job. Well, this is not exactly the way Garbo would behave, is it, or Ingrid Bergman, or Audrey Hepburn?"

"You've got to move with the times, Billy," his wife said.

"Believe me, I'm doing my best. We've had bare boobs in the films, twice now."

"Twice?" said Iz, sceptical.

"Yeah, we had boobs in the Holmes film, remember? The naked honeymoon story."

"The boobs were cut out."

"I know they were cut out. The whole story was cut out. But they were there to start with."

"Boobs are old news," said Audrey.

"God forbid that I should ever think boobs are old news," said Billy.

"Do you have boobs in *Fedora?*" Barbara asked.

Iz shook his head, but Billy reminded him: "Yes, we have boobs. We have boobs in the old studio scene, when they are making the *Leda and the Swan* picture."

"Oh yeah—I forgot that."

I put a hand to my forehead, and leaned my weight against it. I could feel a yawn coming on, and not just that, the whole room was beginning to feel a little unstable. My head was starting to swim.

"In fact, we still haven't solved the problem of that scene," Billy reminded him.

"Refresh my memory, what was the problem again?"

"The problem of how he's going to react. We have this young guy, the young Detweiler, and he's just a junior guy in the studio, and they're shooting the scene, and his job is to cover them up, you know—Fedora's tits. He has to cover them up for the censors. So the first time he sees her, she's naked. But how does he react?"

"How would any guy react? He'd go out of his mind."

"Yeah, but that's boring. That's the way you expect him to react."

The yawn started now. It started on either side of my mouth, I could feel it spreading to my jaw, and I tried to stop it, but the impulse was way too strong.

Iz pondered. "Well, I don't know . . . I suppose the interesting thing, in that case, would be for him to react in the opposite way most guys would react."

"And how would that be?" said Billy.

There was a long pause, and then Audrey pointed at me.

"Like her," she said.

At that moment, I was in the middle of the most enormous, most protracted yawn. I had my hand over my mouth, trying to cover it up, but then I noticed that they were all staring at me, and so for some reason I took my hand away, perhaps intending to close my mouth, but it wouldn't close. The yawn went on and on, while the room around me continued to swirl and the faces of Mr. and Mrs. Wilder and Mr. and Mrs. Diamond drifted in and out of focus.

"That's it!" I heard Mr. Wilder cry in triumph.

"That's what?" said Mr. Diamond.

"He yawns. He sees the most beautiful woman in the world lying naked in front of him, and he yawns. Because he hasn't slept all night. And *that's* what intrigues her. This has never happened to her before. That's what makes her want to sleep with him."

He looked over at his writing partner, waiting for his response. Mr. Diamond sat back in his chair, and gazed ahead for a while, thinking it over.

Finally he nodded, very slowly, and said—also very slowly: "Yeah. That could work. That could definitely work."

Billy took out one of his little cigars and began lighting it. He didn't say anything, but I think we all knew that he was disappointed. He had been expecting Mr. Diamond to say, "Why not?"

*

So I didn't pass out, exactly. I didn't lose consciousness. But I have no memory of getting back to the Wilders' apartment. They must have taken pity on me, realized that I was in no state to find my way to the hostel by myself. I suppose there must have been a cab ride, and then a ride up in the elevator, but I don't remember any of that. The next thing I knew it was morning. California sunshine was pouring into their sitting room, muted and filtered by a half-open Venetian blind, and I was lying scrunched up on a couch that wasn't really big enough to accommodate a horizontal human body, and my back was killing me and my head was throbbing and my eyelids were not at all in the mood to open.

There were noises coming from another room and at first I thought it must be Audrey so with a tremendous effort I got up to talk to her. But it wasn't Audrey. It was a middle-aged woman in a maid's uniform who was wiping down the kitchen surfaces.

"Good morning," she said. "You must be the Greek lady."

I nodded and said: "Is Audrey here? Or Billy?"

"Mr. Wilder has gone to his office to work with Mr. Diamond. Mrs. Wilder had an appointment with her ophthalmologist this morning. She told me to fix you some breakfast, so if you'd just like to go next door, I'll bring you something shortly."

I mumbled my thanks and went back into the sitting room, which had a dining table in dark oak at one end. The apartment seemed rather small but this was because it was so cluttered. Almost every inch of every wall was covered with paintings: modern paintings, mostly, lots of abstracts and lots of nudes. It was not until many years later that I realized Mr. Wilder was a serious art collector—one of the most respected in the United States—and that many of the paintings on the walls were original Schieles, Klimts and Picassos. There was also a large number of books (in several languages) and gramophone records (classical music and jazz), and several Oscar statuettes.

The maid came in with a silver tray on which was arranged coffee, pastries, jams and orange juice. She poured me some strong black coffee and I thanked her before drinking it eagerly. As I sat down at the dining table, she handed me a book. It was called *Crowned Heads*, and was written by an author I hadn't heard of, Thomas Tryon.

"Mr. Wilder put a note for you inside," she said, and left me to read it.

The note was written on thick, cream-coloured paper, headed with the name *BILLY WILDER* in discreet capitals. At the bottom of the paper was a printed address, but no telephone number. I assumed this was the address of the apartment I was in, although it wasn't.

The note said:

You probably don't remember, but last night you solved a story problem for us. This is the property Mr. Diamond and I are trying to adapt. I'm lending you my copy, in case you find time to read it and have any more strokes of genius.

Warm regards, Billy.

PS Drink lots of coffee and take lots of aspirin.

The book appeared to consist of four novellas, and on the contents page Mr. Wilder had circled the title of the first one: "Fedora." I could see that the pages which followed were covered with his handwritten notes. I drank some more coffee and shoved half a *croissant* in my mouth and began to read.

I read for about half an hour and then it became clear, from the way the maid was looking at me, that I was expected to leave. I took the book with me.

*

I thought that I would never forgive Gill for walking out on me like that, but I kind of did. A few months later she wrote to me in Athens, saying that she and Stephen were engaged, and a few years after that she wrote to tell me they were married, so I suppose it must have been the real thing, after all. After that we just swapped Christmas cards and although I came to live in London in the 1980s and we swore that we would meet up and have dinner, we never did, and eventually the Christmas cards petered out and we lost touch. A shame, really. Writing all this down has made me want to find her again, and it would be easy enough to do, nowadays. I wonder if she and Stephen are still together? They had two daughters, I believe.

I spent two more days in Los Angeles by myself. Dutifully,

I visited the Grand Central Market and trooped around some museums, but my heart wasn't in it. The thing I enjoyed most was taking the bus down to Malibu and sitting on the beach and reading the copy of *Crowned Heads* that Mr. Wilder had lent me. At least, I assumed it was a loan.

I didn't think "Fedora" was such a great story, really. The prose seemed a bit flowery to me and I never really believed in the central character, the character of the mysterious old film star. I always have this problem: it never works when writers make up a character who is supposed to be really famous, because the definition of a famous person is someone you've heard of, and if you've never heard of this supposedly famous person then they can't really be famous, so the whole thing falls apart before it's even started. But I didn't think it would be very helpful of me to tell Mr. Wilder that. In fact, after finishing the story, I couldn't think of anything helpful to tell him at all. In any case, I had no idea how you would go about turning a book into a film.

Nonetheless, I wanted to return the book, so I took a bus to Beverly Hills at about three o'clock that afternoon, a few hours before my next Greyhound was due to leave. (Gill and I had been meaning to visit San Francisco next, and then head further north, and that was the plan I intended to stick to.) I made my way to the address on the piece of paper Mr. Wilder had given me, and this was when I realized it wasn't the address of his apartment. Instead it turned out to be a plain, modern suite of offices near the corner of Santa Monica Boulevard and Rodeo Drive, a place that looked quite unremarkable from the outside and which I didn't know, at the time, was actually the famous Writers and Artists Building. There were two rows of buttons on the entryphone box but neither Mr. Wilder's name nor Mr. Diamond's was on there, so I didn't know what to do. After a few minutes two men came out. They were both in their fifties, wearing checked jackets and casual trousers.

"Can we help you?" one of them asked, noticing the way I

was loitering outside the door. I told them I was looking for Mr. Wilder and Mr. Diamond. "They went out about half an hour ago," he informed me. "I don't know where."

"Iz told me they had a meeting," the other man said (to his friend, not to me).

"D'you know when they'll be back?" I asked.

They shook their heads, and walked on. I went into a coffee shop on the other side of the street and sat down at a table by the window which gave me a good view of the entrance to the building opposite. I stayed there for as long as I could—almost an hour—until it came to the time when I knew I was going to have to leave, or I would miss my bus to San Francisco. It was desperately sad and frustrating. I tore a sheet of paper from the notebook in my backpack and wrote:

Dear Mr. Wilder,

Thank you so much for lending me this book, and for being so kind to me at dinner the other evening. It was one of the most beautiful evenings I have ever spent. I'm sorry I got drunk and had to sleep on your couch. I enjoyed the book very much and am sure you and Mr. Diamond will adapt it into a very successful film. I'm afraid I have no more story ideas for you, however. The one I gave you in the restaurant was just a fluke.

I signed my name and then, although it seemed a lame and embarrassing thing to do even as I did it, I wrote my parents' address and telephone number in Athens beneath it. Then I went into a stationery shop a few doors down the street, purchased an envelope, slid the book and the note inside and posted it through the letterbox of the Writers and Artists Building, all very quickly so I didn't have time to reconsider. And that was that. Beneath the blazing Beverly Hills sun I heaved my backpack onto my shoulders and began the long journey to the Greyhound station.

The rest of my time in America passed very slowly. I went to some interesting places but I didn't meet any more people or strike up any friendships. I was lonely and miserable, not because I was missing Gill but because as I sat eating my quarter pounder and fries at McDonald's in Seattle, I wished I was back in Beverly Hills, dining at the Bistro, listening to Mr. Wilder's jokes and drinking amazingly expensive red wine while Al Pacino and his beautiful Swiss girlfriend sat on the other side of the room. There was no pleasure in this trip any more. I would have flown back to Athens early if I could have afforded to change my ticket.

Perhaps it's to be expected that I should carry on treating my daughters as children long after they had grown up: because if the story of my meeting with Mr. Wilder in Los Angeles reminds me of anything, it reminds me that at the age of twenty-one I was still a child myself. Looking back I can see that my own parents, too, were over-protective. I was an only child and we lived in a big apartment on Acharnon Street. It was a busy, noisy, polluted thoroughfare, and we never seemed to have much money, but we were happy there—solidly, uninterruptedly happy for more than twenty years. People who only know Greece from the outside, and know that we lived through a military junta during that time, might ask, "How could you be happy?" To which I would simply reply: life goes on. Circumstances have to be very, very bad for life not to go on. There was the outside world, the world of politics and history, and there was my inside world, the world of music and family, and the two worlds never met. In the outside world there was economic stagnation and military rule and political censorship and people being tortured and sent away to concentration camps; in my inside world there was music and laughter, there were home comforts and good food and the warm glow of the unconditional love my parents felt for each other and for me. I lived in a little bubble of happiness and paid hardly any attention to what was going on around me. When the students at Athens Polytechnic rioted in 1973, I took no part in it. When my father lost his job the same year, I was simply pleased to find that he was spending more time at home and had no idea that a colleague had overheard him referring to Dimitrios Ioannidis as a fool and he'd been sacked the next day.

My father was a sweet and generous and slightly overweight man whose two passions were classical literature (in which he lectured) and Greek pastries (in which he over-indulged). My mother gave English classes to Greek students and it was kind of assumed that that's what I'd end up doing myself. Music at first was simply my hobby, but it was a very consuming one. I had no formal training. Our apartment was on the ground floor and it contained an upright piano which my father had inherited from his parents. He didn't play, but my mother could falter her way through a few simple classical pieces, while I never learned to read music or master any theory but had a talent for improvisation and playing by ear even from when I was very young. There wasn't much good music on Greek radio back then: the Colonels had a well-remembered fondness for military bands and *ersatz* folk music, and that was mainly what filled the airwaves, to the general annoyance of everybody. But twice a year my mother would visit London and come back home with classical records she had bought from the big record shops on Oxford Street, and that was how I developed my love of certain composers: composers like Ravel and Debussy whose music I listened to for hours on end, slowly learning how to play simplified versions on the piano, often just picking out the melody with my right hand and adding crudely voiced chords with my left. What I liked about these composers, above all, was that they did not indulge in big, triumphal statements, that their music was hedged around with diffidence and irony, that it implied a world in which *joie de vivre* invariably coexisted with a lingering, implacable melancholy.

Gradually I started to write pieces of my own which would attempt to show these same characteristics. I wrote for the piano at first, and then for the piano and violin. I had a friend called Chrysoula who played the violin and sometimes she would come round and play the tunes I had written for her and we would record little duets using the cassette deck on my parents' music centre. After I got back from America I wrote a piece like this which I called "Malibu." It was about four minutes long and I wrote it to remind myself what it had felt like to sit on the beach in Malibu reading "Fedora," filled with a sense of both exhilaration and loss, knowing that for a few hours I had passed through the gates of paradise but I would probably never be able to go there again. The piece was based on a very simple melody played over a pedal of alternating minor seventh and major seventh chords. There was nothing to it but people told me it was charming and memorable and I was very proud. But I had no idea what to do with this music once it was written. The thought of performing it in public or recording it professionally never occurred to me. I simply had a private cassette of me and Chrysoula playing it which, I admit, I listened to again and again.

Coming back to Greece had been hard. I had graduated from university and I had no real prospects or aim in life. I began to give a few English lessons but I was too shy and nervous to do it to a whole classroom so instead I gave private tutorials in my parents' front room. That, and my music, were the only things I had to occupy me. Life quickly began to seem grey and monotonous.

I wanted to find out as much as I could about Billy Wilder, of course, but it wasn't easy. Sometimes, when my daughters were much younger and I really wanted to scare the living daylights out of them, I used to tell them about life in the 1970s: the tiny number of TV channels and radio stations, most of them only broadcasting for a few hours every day; no internet, no social media; no mobiles, no tablets, no way of watching a film if it wasn't showing at the cinema or on television; no portable music, no downloads, no streaming. Their little eyes would widen and their respect and admiration for me and Geoffrey would increase tenfold, knowing that we had lived through those years of deprivation, survived the absence of what they considered to be the most basic human rights. For my own part, looking back on those days, it's the lack of easy access to information that amazes me most. I think, at this time, three books about Billy Wilder had been published. No bookshop or library in Athens had copies of any of them, and I know, because I scoured them all. There were a few general film reference books that made mention of him, but they didn't tell me much: just enough to make me realize that, by chance, by a ridiculous stroke of luck, I had wandered into dinner that night with a film director who was not just famous but *extremely* famous. Legendary, in fact. And, at the time, I had not even known his name! I went hot with shame when I remembered the stupid things I had said and the stupid questions I had asked him, thinking that he looked like a college professor or a plastic surgeon.

All the same, his films were not being shown on Greek television, which had imposed a ban on Hollywood studio productions that would not be lifted until the mid-1980s. That Christmas, the Christmas of 1976, we all travelled to London to visit my mother's family (who lived in unfashionable Balham) and I went to Foyle's on the Charing Cross Road hunting for film books. I bought two, one called *Halliwell's Film Guide* and one called *Halliwell's Filmgoers' Companion*, and for the next few months, back in Greece, I pored over them night and day, memorizing not just the facts they contained but also the opinions. These opinions turned out to be very old-fashioned, not to say reactionary: the author of these two massive tomes did not seem to care for any film made after about 1950, but in that respect I wondered if he was so very different from Mr. Wilder himself. In any case, by the summer of 1977, my knowledge of film had gone from being non-existent to being literally encyclopaedic. I could give you the names of hundreds and hundreds of Hollywood films, and tell you the years in which they were made, even if I'd never seen any of them myself.

And so life went on. Life went on in a blur of just-about-tolerable boredom until the last week of May 1977, and that was when everything changed, once again. That was when my father took a call from a woman who said she was from the Greek production office of the film *Fedora*, and that Mr. Billy Wilder had instructed her to contact me. Three days later I was on a plane to Corfu.

*

Four of us rendezvoused at Athens airport to take that plane. There was the assistant director—a bearded, long-haired young guy called Stavros—a blonde French lady whose role on the film I never quite understood, and then the production manager, a tall, commanding, imperious woman in her fifties who frankly terrified me.

Four seemed a small number.

"The others will be joining us from Munich," she told me.

"What have they been doing in Munich?" I asked.

"They've been in pre-production there for a month."

I did not know what pre-production was, of course.

My own job was described as "Interpretation Services." Apparently Mr. Wilder had requested me personally for this job. I was flabbergasted. As for the length of my engagement, it was undecided, although I was told that the crew were unlikely to be in Greece for more than two or three weeks. To be on the safe side I'd cancelled all my teaching appointments for the next twenty-one days.

That afternoon, as we travelled from Corfu airport towards the centre of town, I had no idea what to expect. It was early summer, the sun was dazzling and the streets were full of holidaymakers. Was Mr. Wilder really planning to shoot part of his film here? We were a silent foursome. The production manager had a folder full of papers on her knee and she was reading through them and trying to make notes as the taxi swung around corners and stopped suddenly at crossings. The other two stared out of the windows, inscrutable. There were a thousand things I could have asked them both, but the questions died on my lips.

The taxi pulled up outside a hotel called the Cavalieri, which was opposite the Leonida Vlachou square on the outskirts of the old town, a few seconds' walk from the sea. It was a handsome old building on the corner of the street, each of its five storeys punctuated by elegant balconies with wrought-iron railings. I could not help picturing myself staying on one of the hotel's uppermost floors for the next few days, in a little attic room perhaps, stepping out onto the balcony first thing in the morning and looking over the rooftops of the old town as the church bells rang and the streets came to life. At a pinch, I didn't even need to have a balcony. It would be enough to fling open the shutters in the morning and be greeted by the rich, unspoiled blueness of the sky, the salty freshness of the sea breeze. This was a long way from the Bistro in Beverly Hills, but compared to the grey smog of Athens, the shimmering filth of the air on Acharnon Street, it felt as though I had arrived in a different kind of paradise.

When we disembarked from the taxi and were standing on the street outside the entrance to the hotel, the production manager handed me a sheet of paper with an address printed on it.

"What's this?" I asked.

"This is the name of the place where you will be staying," she told me.

"Ah," I said. "Not here?"

"No. There isn't room for everybody here."

There was room for my fellow passengers, apparently, as they all disappeared inside, lugging their suitcases. Meanwhile I had no idea where the street mentioned on my piece of paper was, and had to ask for directions. A fifteen-minute walk brought me to a modern apartment building in a quiet residential area on the outskirts of Corfu Town. It seemed I was to be staying with Mr. and Mrs. Ploumidi, a retired couple whose apartment boasted a small spare bedroom overlooking the building's courtyard garden. They were very friendly and very excited to have me staying with them and wanted to know everything about the film. Unfortunately, at this stage, I couldn't tell them much.

Before unpacking, I sat down on my single bed and examined the sheet of instructions I'd been given. It was very quiet in the bedroom, and very dark. I had to turn on the bedside lamp. My duties were to start at eleven thirty the next morning, apparently. Mr. Wilder was going to give two short interviews to the local press and I was to interpret for him. More immediately, there was to be a dinner at the hotel for cast and crew at eight thirty this evening. I had asked the production manager whether I was invited or not, and she had told me, "The budget for the film does not include your food, but you are welcome to sit with us." It wasn't exactly the answer I'd been hoping for, but I supposed it was better than nothing.

Remembering my humiliation at turning up to the Bistro in my T-shirt and denim shorts, I had made sure to pack some smart clothes. I was going to be dining with famous film-makers and movie stars and I was not going to make that mistake again. I'd brought a small black cocktail dress with me, and at eight o'clock, having done battle with the Ploumidis' shower which had splattered me with tepid water while crashing and banging away like the percussion section of the Athens State Orchestra in full rehearsal, I slipped it on and added the flourish of a small fake pearl necklace. "Beautiful, beautiful!" Mrs. Ploumidi declared, and insisted on taking a Polaroid photo of me standing next to her husband before waving me off down the street, with the instruction that I was not to return without the autographs of two or three Oscar-winners at the very least.

I was overdressed for the streets of Corfu Town and drew many surprised glances as I made my way to the hotel, and by the time I had climbed the three steps to the main entrance, my heart was thumping with a mixture of self-consciousness and nervousness. I told the man behind the desk that I was with the *Fedora* crew and he too looked me up and down before pointing in the direction of the elevator and telling me to go up to the restaurant on the roof terrace.

I checked my reflection in the elevator mirror as I rode upwards—my outfit looked pretty good, I thought; all it needed was a Martini in my hand to complete the ensemble—but when the doors slid open and I saw the scene that awaited me in the glare of the late-evening sunlight, I almost turned on my heels and fled. A crowd of about thirty people was sitting at the dining tables, and every single one of them looked scruffier than the scruffiest tourist. Jeans, T-shirts, sneakers, shorts . . . Waiters were scurrying between the tables, pouring from carafes of the local wine and bearing aloft great steaming plates of *moussaka* and *souvlaki* and *kleftiko*. Everybody seemed to know everybody else. Everybody seemed thoroughly at home, even slightly bored. And there I was, in my black cocktail dress and matching clutch bag, hovering on the edge of the terrace, terrified to take another step forward and realizing once again that I had misjudged things horribly.

One of the waiters rescued me by ushering me to a seat at a bench table, where I was obliged to squeeze in between two strangers. They were so busy eating that they didn't seem to notice either me or my ridiculous clothes. The food smelled delicious. I was ravenous, but if I understood the situation correctly I was not allowed to order anything. Nonetheless, since nobody seemed to be paying any attention, I helped myself to some bread from a basket and when a waiter poured me a glass of white wine I didn't complain.

I looked around to see if Mr. Wilder was there. He was sitting at a table right over in the corner, with a bunch of other men. One of them, I could see, was Mr. Diamond. I was just wondering if I dared to go and say hello to them when the man sitting diagonally opposite to me said something.

"Not allowed to eat? Me neither."

I say "man." He wasn't really a man at all. He looked younger than me, with longish, blondish hair, and a thin attempt at a beard which only added to the impression of extreme youthfulness. But he had a nice smile and his eyes glinted at me as he took a sip of wine from his glass.

"Matthew," he said, holding out his hand.

"Calista," I said, shaking it.

"Does this mean you're another ligger, like me?" he asked.

"Ligger?"

I thought I knew most English words, but not this one.

"Freeloader. Not really supposed to be here."

"No, I'm here to do some . . . interpreting," I said, wishing that I didn't always sound so hesitant and apologetic about myself.

"Then you should absolutely order whatever you want," he said. "No question about it. Anyway, nobody ever checks these things."

Something about the way he said this made me think that he was much more experienced in these situations than I was.

"You've done this before?"

"Been on a shoot? One or two. My mother—" he nodded across at a woman sitting towards the end of the table—"is in make-up. Sometimes I come with her."

He had an English accent, but not one that I recognized, so I asked him where he was from. His family were from Cornwall, he said. After that we made small talk. He was nice: funny and self-confident and eager to ask questions about me in a way which somehow didn't make me nervous. The interest he took in me, frank and undisguised, was not something I had experienced before. The last few years in Greece had not exactly been a time of sexual or emotional liberation. Both national and family circumstances had conspired to make sure that I'd had little experience with the opposite sex, so I didn't really understand what was normal behaviour and what wasn't.

Was it normal, for instance, that this friendly young man kept stealing surreptitious glances at me between questions and even between words, clearly taking in the details of my bare arms, my hair, the line of my jaw, my bust? I had no idea, but I was acutely conscious of it, and the consciousness brought me a delightful mixture of pleasure and embarrassment. I knew that the technical term for what Matthew was doing was "flirting," but I had no idea how to reciprocate. All I could manage was to burble on with the story of how I'd met Mr. Wilder and Mr. Diamond in Beverly Hills, and when he heard this, and realized that I'd still not gone over and reintroduced myself even though they were sitting only a few tables away, he was amazed.

"Go on," he said. "Say hello to them. Don't be shy."

"Do you think I should?"

After he had practically pushed me in their direction, I walked over to the corner table. Mr. Wilder was sitting there with Mr. Diamond and four other men I didn't know. I coughed gently and said:

"Mr. Wilder?"

He turned, mid-conversation, and looked up at me. He was dressed just as he had been at the Bistro that evening, except that he was also wearing a straw hat, like a miniature trilby. I was to learn that he rarely went anywhere without one of these hats.

"Hello," he said. Clearly he didn't recognize me. "Who are you? And why, if you don't mind me asking, are you dressed like Audrey Hepburn?"

"It's me," I said. "Calista. Do you remember? The strange Greek woman who spent the night in your apartment."

"Ahh . . ." A delighted smile appeared on his face. "The Greek interpreter! Just like in Sherlock Holmes!" Turning to Mr. Diamond, he said: "Iz, you remember this lady?"

"Of course I do." He rested his cigarette against the rim of an ashtray, stood up and shook my hand. "So glad you could make it. It's great to have you on board. Please, sit down and join us."

Everybody squeezed up and a chair was placed between

Mr. Diamond and another man, who was introduced to me as "Mr. Holden, the star of our picture."

"Oh," I said, shaking his hand and trying desperately to appear natural. I think that for some reason I was beginning to speak in a posh English accent too, and probably sounded a bit like Audrey Hepburn, as well as looking like her. "Delighted to make your acquaintance."

"Charmed," he said. "Can I pour you some wine? I might as well have the vicarious pleasure, since I'm not allowed to touch the stuff myself."

"Not allowed?" I said, as he filled a new glass for me.

"Doctor's orders." He raised a glass of Perrier, and clinked it against my wine glass. "Cheers. Welcome to the madhouse."

"This is the fourth time you and Mr. Wilder have made a picture together," I said.

Since this seemed to be neither a statement nor a question, he didn't know quite how to respond to it.

"True."

"The first time," I said, "was *Sunset Boulevard. 1950.*" There was no point, after all, in having committed *Halliwell's Film Guide* to memory if I wasn't going to use it some time. And what better time than now? "An incisive melodrama," I continued, "with marvellous moments but a tendency to overstay its welcome."

Mr. Holden looked at me curiously.

"Is that so?"

I took another slug of wine. "And then of course there was *Stalag 17.*"

"There was indeed."

"Made in 1953."

"I'm sure you're right."

"High jinks, violence and mystery in a sharply calculated mixture," I told him. "An atmosphere quite different from the understated British films on the subject."

"Impressive," said Mr. Holden. "Do you have an opinion

on all of my pictures? Hey, Billy," he called across the table, "we have a walking film encyclopaedia over here."

Instead of replying, Mr. Wilder said to me: "What is your second name, please?"

"Frangopoulou," I said.

"Right. Miss Frangopoulou, please go easy on the *retsina*. I don't want you passing out on me like you did last time. You and I have work to do in the morning. As for *you*—" he pointed a warning finger at Mr. Holden—"early to bed tonight, please. Because you are looking pretty unfit to me, and tomorrow I am going to make you *run*."

*

The unit publicist had arranged for Mr. Wilder to give two interviews to local newspapers late in the morning. It was a quarter past eleven when I arrived in the hotel lobby. By then, he had already been on set for more than two hours, and he was looking very pleased with himself.

"So, now we have shot our first scene," he told me. "Now we have started, and there is no going back. Mr. Holden, like the professional he is, played his part to perfection. He walked out of the doorway of the hotel, he crossed the street, he sat down at one of the tables in the square over there, and he shouted: 'Waiter!' He did it all on the first take, and unlike some of the actors I have worked with, he did not have to have his drama teacher on the set with him, holding his hand and telling him how to dig deeper and deeper into the meaning of the scene. So it was all done very quickly, and now, while they are doing the next set-up, we have a moment to give to the journalists. I hope it's not going to take too long."

I was amazed by how happy and animated he seemed. He looked about ten years younger than he had looked in Beverly Hills the previous year. His eyes sparkled and he was lighter on his feet.

"Mr. Wilder," the publicist said. "The first journalist is here."

He was a worried-looking, bearded, dark-haired man of about twenty-five. He sat perched on the edge of an armchair while Mr. Wilder sat back on a sofa, relaxed and at ease, puffing on one of his little cigars. I was placed on the sofa next to him, sitting up straight, my body taut and alert. This was my first attempt at interpretation and I was determined to make a success of it.

"First question," the journalist said. "In your film *The Spirit of St. Louis*, James Stewart plays the great aviator, Charles Lindbergh. Was your intention to make a radical analysis of the fascist tendencies of the American state?"

I translated as faithfully as I could. Mr. Wilder gave me a brief, questioning glance, as if to confirm that this genuinely was the question, and then said:

"Well, not really, you know, I don't consider it that much of a political picture. I was more concerned with showing how he made the journey, the flight across the Atlantic."

After I had translated into Greek, the young man nodded and wrote a few words down on his notepad.

"Lindbergh himself is an archetype of the American male whose display of heroism is in reality just a thinly constructed mask for his deep psychosexual insecurities. Would you agree?"

Once again, I did my best to translate. This time, Mr. Wilder's glance towards me was not so brief, and even more questioning.

"Well," he answered, puffing on the cigar more energetically than ever, "all I can say is that Mr. Stewart must have given an incredible performance, if this is what you took away from the film. It certainly wasn't there in my direction."

After I had translated this reply, the young man scribbled on his notepad at even greater length. Then he said:

"The phallic symbolism of his plane, *The Spirit of St. Louis*, is obvious. Lindbergh, in effect, is trapped inside an enormous penis which carries him onwards to an inevitable destination which cannot be changed. Is this how you feel as a director, trapped inside your own masculinity?"

I translated the question.

Mr. Wilder leaned in towards me. "Is this guy for real?" he asked.

I answered, "I'm just translating as best I can."

He drew on the cigar a few more times, exhaled a long plume of smoke, and said:

"Look. You have asked me three questions. Not only do I not understand them—in spite of this lady's excellent translation—but they are all about a film which I made twenty years ago, which was not a success, which I should never have made, which I never think about, which I never want to talk about, and all I can say about it, frankly, is that I would burn the negative if someone gave me the opportunity. Do you mind if I ask you why it is that you are so obsessed with this particular film?"

After this question had been translated for him, the young journalist replied:

"It's the only film of yours that I've seen."

"Good," said Mr. Wilder, reaching out to shake the journalist by the hand. "In that case, the interview is over, and neither of us needs to waste any more of our time. Next!"

Next was a much more confident—indeed rather intimidating—woman of middle age, wearing a tan business suit, who flipped open her notebook briskly and said:

"Mr. Wilder, you are the director of twenty-three motion pictures. You are here in Greece to make your twenty-fourth. It is a very great honour for us. From *Some Like It Hot* to *The Front Page*, from *Double Indemnity* to *Sunset Boulevard*, you have run the gamut from comedy to tragedy, from satire to melodrama, showing yourself to be the master of every style. Who can forget the superb performances you drew from Charles Laughton in *Witness for the Prosecution*, from Jack Lemmon in *The Apartment*, from Audrey Hepburn in *Love in the Afternoon*? This morning I watched as you directed a scene from your new film. It was a privilege and a pleasure to watch a true genius of cinema at work.

"In directing the scene, you were obliged to halt the shooting at certain points because of the level of traffic noise. My question to you is this. Traffic congestion in Corfu Town is a serious problem. What do you think can be done about it? Do you approve Mayor Nikos Kandunias's proposal to close Akadimias Street to cars and re-route the traffic along Napoleontos Zampeli and Moustoxidi, introducing a new one-way system?"

I translated the question. Mr. Wilder nodded thoughtfully, and tapped ash from the end of his cigar into the ashtray in front of him. I don't remember his answer. I just remember starting, for the first time, to feel a little sorry for him.

*

The scene Mr. Wilder was shooting in the afternoon was more complicated. A track for the camera had been laid all along Nikiforou Theotoki Street—a busy shopping street, very popular with tourists—and a large crowd had gathered to watch the proceedings. One of the actors, Gottfried John, was kitted out in a chauffeur's costume and had to drive a vintage Rolls-Royce into the street. The car alone was impressive enough to attract a lot of attention. While Mr. Wilder was discussing the exact angle at which it would enter the street, and where it would come to a halt, Mr. Holden, whose character was meant to be pursuing the car on foot, stood waiting against a wall, surrounded by eager fans and onlookers. I had been told to stay close to him, and to keep these people at bay. "I'm sorry, no autographs," I kept repeating. "Mr. Holden is preparing for his scene." Sometimes a fan would say something to him and he would ask me what they were talking about, and I would give him answers like: "He saw you in *The Wild Bunch*."

"Tell them no autographs," he instructed me, and I assured him: "I've told them that already," but they were very persistent.

Eventually Mr. Wilder summoned him over to the Rolls-

Royce and they started discussing how the scene would play out. I couldn't hear what they were saying, but they seemed to be joking with each other and laughing in an intimate way.

"Look at those two," a voice beside me said. "Like two sides of the same coin."

I turned to see who the speaker was. It was Mr. Diamond.

"It's like they never stopped working together," he continued. "Although actually the last time was . . . twenty years ago?"

"Twenty-three," I corrected him. "*Sabrina*, made in 1954. Also starring Audrey Hepburn and Humphrey Bogart. 'A superior comedy, rather uneasily cast.'"

"You can say that again," Mr. Diamond agreed. "Are these your own opinions you keep coming out with, by the way, or did you crib them from someone else?"

"I've been trying to find out as much about you and Mr. Wilder as I can," was all I told him.

"That figures," he said, and laughed. "Admit it, the first time you met us, when we went to the Bistro with your friend, you didn't have the faintest idea who he was, did you?"

I shook my head.

"Was it very obvious?"

"Don't worry. He thought it was funny. Billy's an odd mix— sometimes his ego can be as fragile as hell, other times he doesn't give a damn."

"He seems very happy to be making a film again," I said, looking at the way he was talking to a jostling line of spectators and getting them to move back, with the help of the assistant director.

"He's in his element. He loves all this. The chaos, the adrenaline."

"What about you?"

"Me? I prefer a quiet life. But I don't get to choose what I do. He likes to have me around."

Ninety-five per cent of being on a film set, I was later to realize, consists of standing around, waiting for something to happen. More than fifteen minutes went by and Mr. Diamond was starting to get visibly impatient. He had got through three cigarettes in that time. "Where the hell's Marthe?" he said at last. I didn't know who he was talking about, and was about to ask him to explain, when almost immediately he sighed with relief and said: "Ah, here she is."

A woman had arrived on the set. She was wearing a brilliant-white trouser suit, a big straw sun hat that shielded most of her face, and a pair of large-framed sunglasses which made her even harder to recognize. Nonetheless, I recognized her. She had a small retinue in tow: two women walking behind her (make-up and wardrobe, I guessed—in fact, one of them was Matthew's mother) and a very lowly member of the crew in front, clearing a path for her by telling the crowds to stand back and, if necessary, pushing them aside with his hand.

"Oh!" I cried out. "It's the Swiss lady!"

"That's right," said Mr. Diamond. "The Swiss lady. Did you meet her before?"

"She was at the restaurant that night," I reminded him. "Having dinner with her boyfriend. Al Pacino."

"You're right." He nodded to himself, seemingly having forgotten this detail. "Yeah, that was when Billy met her for the first time."

"And now she's starring in his film."

"Yep." I can't say that he sounded too enthusiastic about it. He added: "What Billy wants, Billy gets."

Now that Miss Keller had arrived, they were ready to start shooting the scene. I kept close to Mr. Diamond, thinking that people might want to speak to him or ask for his autograph, but nobody recognized him. He was a very tall man and the only person who spoke to him was a rude shopkeeper who asked him to get out of the way so that he could have a better view of the filming. I told him, "Be quiet. This man is one of the writers of the film. Show some respect, please," in reply to which he grunted and gave me a contemptuous look.

This started me thinking, all the same. I thought that it must be a very strange, and perhaps uncomfortable, experience to watch the filming of a scene you had written yourself. When I composed a piece of music, an ideal version of it always existed in my head, and then when I came to record it, either by myself or with Chrysoula playing the violin, something always seemed to go a little bit wrong; there was always some disjunction between the perfect version in my mind and the final version that existed on the tape. I thought that it was probably the same for Mr. Diamond with his screenplays, only even worse. And indeed, he did not seem to enjoy watching this scene being filmed at all. Many of the shops in this street had their doorways on a raised gallery, which you approached by climbing a short flight of stone steps. Miss Keller was required to run up these steps and then hurry along the crowded gallery towards one of the shops; Mr. Holden was supposed to be following her at street level, desperate not to lose sight of her as she pushed through the crowds. Meanwhile numerous extras—local people who had been hired for the day—were milling around, adding to the scene's general sense of urgency and confusion. Time after time, something went wrong: Miss Keller tripped on the steps, or Mr. Holden dropped his sunglasses, or a spectator shouted something disruptive from the sidelines.

Mr. Diamond sighed and said to me: "This is one of those scenes that feels so simple when you put it down on paper. But in fact, we were storing up trouble. There's so many things that can go wrong." On the fourth or fifth attempt, just as it all seemed to be running smoothly, an extra got in the way of Mr. Holden as he was running, they collided with each other, and I heard a loud groan—a groan of agony—from beside me. It seemed that these logistical problems were actually causing Mr. Diamond physical pain.

"Are you O.K.?" I asked him.

"No," he said.

"Is it so painful to you, watching things go wrong like this?"

"It's nothing to do with that," he said, putting his hands on his hips and stretching with a grimace. "It's my back. My back is killing me."

I didn't know what to say. "Maybe we should go and find somewhere you can sit down," I ventured, and to my surprise he agreed.

"Shall we? Do you mind? I don't really need to be here. There's no dialogue in this scene."

We pushed through the crowds and made our way to a much quieter back street where there was a café with a couple of tables outside. We sat down and I ordered a coffee for myself and a Perrier for Mr. Diamond.

"It started in Munich a few weeks ago," he told me. "I was waking up in the middle of the night with this terrible back pain. I went to see a doctor and he said it was shingles. He told me to take Vitamin B and stop drinking and stay out of sunlight—not easy, when you're going to be in Greece in the middle of the summer—but he didn't prescribe anything. So Barbara went to see our doctor in Beverly Hills and he told me to get some Demerol or Seconal."

"Did you get them?"

"I tried the drugstores here but they didn't understand a word I was saying."

"Leave it with me," I said. I got him to write down the name of the pills he needed and promised him that I would do my best to find them. An hour or two later, mission successfully accomplished, I left them for him at the hotel reception desk.

The next day, at the same time as before, Mr. Wilder had to do more interviews and I had to do more translating. Before we started, he handed me a note from Mr. Diamond: "*I had a much better night, thanks to those pills. Thank you so much. Hiring you was definitely one of Billy's better ideas.*" I was so proud and grateful that the tears sprang to my eyes.

*

Three days later, I was standing on the balcony of my room in a different apartment building, a building which fronted on to the sea in a village called Nydri, on the island of Lefkada. The reality of my situation was starting to sink in. In the space of a few days I had gone from being a part-time (very part-time) language tutor to being the valued member of a film crew, working on a film which was being made by one of the greatest directors in Hollywood. I had stepped into a world which until recently would have been beyond the reach of my imagination. It was a world which did not seem to obey the normal rules of human affairs. For instance, there is no easy way of getting from Corfu to Lefkada—for normal people. But the production team of *Fedora* had chartered a special plane and they had persuaded the authorities to open the military airport at Actium, and when we landed there we found a convoy of cars waiting to take us across to the island by ferry. The flights I had taken from Athens to London with my mother had always been full—just as the flights I had taken to and from New York had been full—so it was a strange and miraculous experience to step onto this plane with only about thirty other people, everyone having a row of seats or even two rows of seats to themselves. Even so, even on a plane as empty as this, somehow it happened that Matthew found himself sitting in the row next to me, and just before take-off he came and sat even closer to me so that we could talk.

Perhaps I was reading too much into the fact that he came and sat so close by. It helped to strengthen my belief—or at least my trembling, hitherto somewhat incredulous suspicion—that Matthew and I were starting upon that process, that subtle, instinctive dance which two people can perform around each other, over a period of days sometimes, when they are under the spell of a mutual attraction which neither of them yet dares to express. And yet if our burgeoning friendship had a destination, we were still a long way from reaching it. On this occasion we chatted about nothing in particular for

five or ten minutes, and then he started reading. He was reading the script of *Fedora*, in fact. His mother's copy, I dare say.
He was reading the last few pages and when he had finished he
flipped it shut with a sigh.

"You didn't like it?" I asked, as he tossed it onto the seat
between us.

Instead of answering my question, he said: "What did you
think?"

"I haven't read it yet," I admitted. "Nobody's given me a
copy."

"Hm," he said, in a tone which I couldn't decipher. Then,
instead of offering a critique as I was expecting him to do, he
declared: "Well, it's not the kind of film that *I* would want to
make."

These words excited me.

"You want to make films?"

"Of course. Doesn't everybody?"

At this point I was almost ashamed to admit it, but I had to:
"I don't."

"No?"

"No."

"But if you feel you have something to say to the world," he
said, "how else can you say it, nowadays? Poetry? Nobody lis-
tens. Books? Nobody reads them. Why write a novel for two
hundred people when you can reach an audience of millions?"

"But that's just it," I said. "I *don't* have anything to say to
the world. Most people don't."

"There's creativity in everyone," Matthew said. "I firmly
believe that."

"Well . . ." It felt like I was about to trust him with a huge
secret. "I do write music."

"There you go!" he said, triumphant. "You're a closet musician. I knew it. You play an instrument, right?"

"The piano," I admitted.

"What sort of music?"

"Well, I play some classical things, some jazz . . . But mostly my own music. Just little tunes that I write myself."

"Which proves my point."

"Yes, but . . . That doesn't mean I have something to *say to the world.*"

"All right," he said. "Maybe that was the wrong way of putting it. Think of art—any work of art—being more like . . . holding up a mirror, and seeing what it reflects. So a film is like a mirror, right, a mirror to the world? And the point is that the mirror should be plain, and simple, and crystal clear. *Their* mirror—" he gestured towards the script—"is so old-fashioned, and so fussy . . . It's like they've put this massive, complicated, gilded frame around it, and it's so distracting that you can't really make out the reflection at all."

I didn't know if this was fair to Mr. Wilder and Mr. Diamond or not, but I thought it was an immensely clever thing to say. I looked at Matthew in admiration, and it struck me that I knew exactly what he was.

"You're one of the kids with beards," I said.

"What?"

"It's what Mr. Diamond calls them. The new, younger generation of directors. They all have beards, but they're still kids."

He gave me an ironic, questioning smile which made my heart flutter. "Are you making fun of my beard?" he asked.

Worried that I might have offended him, I said: "No, no, no. It's nothing to do with that."

"I mean, I know it's pretty pathetic. And I've been growing it for three weeks."

"It's not about your beard," I insisted. "And anyway—" more coaxingly: I was beginning to understand how to flirt— "I really like it. It suits you."

He smiled again, a grateful smile this time, and touched his beard, stroking it gently. "You think so?"

I said nothing—merely nodded—and then he handed me the script.

"You should read this," he said. "I'd like to talk to you about it. It seems to me . . ."

He appeared to be about to say something important, even fateful.

". . . that you have an interesting mind."

It was not quite the compliment I had been hoping for. But it would do for now.

Maybe I have not remembered our conversation exactly, but this was the kind of thing we talked about. These were the early steps in our dance. I was quite sure that this dance was going to lead us somewhere, sooner or later, but at the same time I was not tempted to rush things and neither, it seemed, was Matthew. We were content, for now, to rehearse the first exploratory moves, and to wait for this strange adventure we had found ourselves sharing—for the island of Lefkada itself, perhaps—to work its peculiar, irresistible magic.

The apartment block in which we were all housed had a striking characteristic: the building of it was not yet finished. In the year 1977, mass tourism to Greece was still at an early stage, and few holidaymakers came to the village of Nydri because it was not easy to reach by car, train, plane or any other method. But that was slowly starting to change, and as tourists grew more adventurous and stories about this beautiful, unvisited corner of Greece began to spread, developers were responding by putting new buildings up as quickly as they could. In this case they had assured the producers of the film, no doubt with hand on heart and a sincere tremble in their voices, that the apartments would be complete by the time the unit arrived in Nydri early in June. But, inevitably, they had not been true to their word, and so we all arrived to find that we would be living in apartments which had no glass in the windows. I wasn't too worried, as I considered this simply to be a natural form of air conditioning, but several members of the film crew complained bitterly, not least because it meant there was nothing to keep the mosquitoes out of their apartments at night. This was especially hard on Mr. Diamond, I think, who had the apartment next door to mine and who was now being kept awake at night by the mosquitoes as well as his shingles. Sometimes I heard him in the middle of the night, swearing loudly and banging on the walls and the furniture with his shoe in an attempt to murder the troublesome insects, who seemed to have a particular appetite for him.

The producers had hired at least a dozen drivers from among the local people and very few of these drivers spoke English, so I spent a lot of my time translating for them and for their passengers. Mr. Wilder had his own driver and Mr. Diamond had his own driver and so did Mr. Holden and so did Miss Keller and so did the other female star of the film, a German lady called Hildegard Knef. (In fact, out of the two women, it was never clear to me who was supposed to be the real star, and as I was to learn as time went by, this was always a matter of fierce, simmering dispute between them.) This struck me as being a very extravagant arrangement, as the only journey anyone ever had to make was down to the jetty on the shoreline, a distance of about three hundred metres from the apartment building. From this jetty, everyone would be ferried across to the main location, a handsome nineteenth-century villa on the tiny island of Madouri, which could only be reached by a boat journey of about ten minutes from Nydri itself.

The man who ferried everyone across was a genial character called Filippos, who owned a small boat called the *Soula*, and quickly became friends with the whole crew. On our second morning in Nydri, Mr. Wilder decided to give him a part in the film. In this scene Mr. Holden's character was making his first, clandestine visit to Fedora's villa, and he had hired a boatman to take him there. Filippos was overjoyed, of course, and did not seem put out at all by the cameras trained on him, the sound equipment recording his movements, or the large crowd of onlookers from the village, many of whom were his

friends and were shouting words of encouragement or face-
tious instructions. He even allowed one of the make-up girls,
after she had finished with Mr. Holden, to put a few dabs of
powder on his forehead, prompting loud jeers and laughter
from his friends on the quayside.

Because Lefkada is rather a hilly environment, the light
would change rapidly from hour to hour and the window of
opportunity to shoot scenes was somewhat tight. Therefore
Mr. Wilder was keeping his direction to a minimum, and he
marshalled everyone into their places rapidly. It was a simple
scene, nevertheless. Mr. Holden would arrive at the jetty,
Filippos would hold out his hand to assist him into the boat,
start up the engine and then off they would go.

Just before Mr. Wilder called "Action," however, Filippos
gestured towards him from the boat, as if he had a question to
ask before he could start. The assistant director went over to
talk to him and reported back: "He wants to know something."

"Can't you deal with it?"

"He says it has to be you."

Billy exchanged a glance with Iz, who was standing by his
side and watching the proceedings, a copy of the script in his
hand, impassive as always. Iz shrugged. In point of fact he
knew the question that Filippos was going to ask, because ten
minutes earlier he had told him to ask it. And I knew it too,
because I was the one who had translated it into Greek on his
behalf.

Billy sighed and turned to me and said, "You had better
come and help me out." I followed him as he walked over to
the boat, swishing the cane he liked to carry with him while
directing. For the next couple of minutes he and Filippos had
a very lively conversation, of which I translated both sides.
When it was over, Billy walked back to his spot beside the
camera, shaking his head, sighing more loudly than ever, boil-
ing over with exasperation.

"What was all that about?" Iz asked.

"You'll never guess what this guy just asked me. He wants to know, 'Mr. Wilder, what is my motivation for this scene?'"

"No way," Iz deadpanned.

"He wants to know his motivation, for Christ's sake. I hire him for half an hour to drive a boat across the water and suddenly he is from the Actors Studio and he needs Lee Strasberg to come over here and tell him how to play the scene."

"You're shitting me."

"I tell him—you're not an actor, you're a boatman. Your motivation is to get this man across the water. Your motivation is the fifty drachma he's going to give you for it. My God, I expect this kind of bullshit from a big movie star, but . . ." And then he stopped, having seen that rarest of phenomena spreading itself across Iz's face: an involuntary smile. The truth dawned. "Oh, I get it. It was you, wasn't it? You told him to say it, right? You and the little Greek interpreter, here, you're in this together?"

Iz was almost laughing now: an incredible thing to behold.

"Well, that's very funny, I must say." He turned to me: "Didn't you think it was funny? I won't let Mr. Diamond put any funny scenes in the script, because we're making a serious picture, so he comes up with a funny scene for me instead. Cute, isn't it? Don't you think that's cute?"

I didn't say anything. Some time afterwards, Mr. Diamond would tell me that he regretted playing this joke because it had delayed production for a few minutes, in a way that was highly unprofessional. But I remembered the fact that Billy's eyes had been gleaming again as he took up his position by the camera, and I assured him it had been the right thing to do.

*

In 1951 Billy Wilder made a film called *Ace in the Hole*, which is about a journalist who cynically prolongs a man's suffering in order to get more mileage from the story he is writing about him. "An incisive, compelling drama taking a sour look at the American scene," according to *Halliwell's Film Guide*. It took aim not only at tabloid journalism but, just as importantly, at the public which likes to consume it, prompting this notoriously curmudgeonly critic to add that it was "one of its director's masterworks." It was also Billy's first real commercial failure, because for some reason people do not like paying money to go to the cinema to have their ugliness reflected back at them.

That journalist was played by Kirk Douglas and a few days later in Nydri I encountered his Greek equivalent. This guy was quite a bit younger but he had been tagging along with the crew ever since we had arrived and, like Chuck Tatum in *Ace in the Hole*, he saw this as his potential meal ticket, his chance to find a juicy story and break into the big time. His ambition was to sell a story to one of the newspapers in Athens: his ambitions extended no further than that because Greek was the only language he spoke and this is why he pestered me endlessly to help him understand what was going on with the making of the film.

A few days after the episode with Filippos, we were all standing around the terrace of the villa on the island of Madouri, quite late in the afternoon. When I say "all" standing around, I mean that there was a real crowd. This was how Mr. Wilder liked to work. He liked a busy, gregarious set with lots of people watching from the sidelines: reporters, photographers, hangers-on, passers-by. It was one of the sources of his energy. But it was also quite hard on the actors, I would have thought.

There was another thing that made life difficult for the actors, too: Mr. Wilder's belief that the script he had written with Mr. Diamond should be treated, like the Bible, as a sacred text. After working on this script for many months—after agonizing, I would imagine, over every beat in the rhythms of the dialogue, every specific choice of words—he would not allow the actors to deviate from it at all. It was for this reason that Mr.

Diamond would be present at the shooting of every scene, sitting on a canvas chair close to the director, clutching in his hand a rolled-up copy of the script which he did not need to consult because he knew it by heart. While Mr. Wilder was watching the action, making sure that the actors were moving in the right way, that the blocking worked, that the composition was good, Mr. Diamond would listen to the spoken dialogue and if one of the actors did not speak the words exactly as written, he would glance across at Mr. Wilder when the take was done, shake his head, and everyone would have to start all over again.

This afternoon they were shooting a scene on the terrace which involved all the members of Fedora's household. Four actors, in other words: Miss Keller (playing Fedora), Miss Knef (playing the Countess), Frances Sternhagen (the Countess's companion) and José Ferrer (the mysterious Dr. Vando). It was taking a long time to set things up. The director of photography was not happy. The shadows were falling in the wrong place and everybody would have to wait until they were falling in the right place. There was a lot of sitting around and fretting and making small talk.

Tasos, the local journalist, sidled up to me and said (in Greek), "You're the translator, right?"

"Yes."

"Can you come and translate for me while I have a few words with Mr. Ferrer?"

Mr. Ferrer was sitting over by the terrace wall, his back to the sea, fanning himself, his face barely visible beneath his straw hat.

"He's agreed to give you an interview?" I asked.

"It wouldn't be an interview, exactly. I just want to ask a few things."

"No way. You have to get permission from the unit publicist."

But this rebuff, delivered quite sharply, was not enough to discourage him. A few moments later he asked me:

"So the shooting isn't going well?"

"What do you mean?"

"That's what I hear. The two women don't like each other. There's a terrible rivalry between them."

"I wouldn't know."

"And neither of them likes Mr. Wilder."

I felt like swatting him away, an impatient gesture with my hand, but now at last the assistant director was calling for everyone to be quiet and the shooting was about to start.

It did not go well. Miss Keller had to recite some lines from one of Fedora's old films while performing a sort of teasing sensual dance in front of Dr. Vando. They included the words, "Let's sin some and gin some. East of Suez there are no Ten Commandments." But she could not get them right.

On the first couple of takes, she said, "Let's gin some and sin some." The second time she said it, there was laughter from some of the onlookers.

Then, after a few more takes in which the words were spoken correctly but Mr. Wilder was still not satisfied with the way she performed her shimmy, everything seemed to go perfectly. There was a general air of relief and dissolving tension, until Mr. Diamond got up from his chair and walked across to Mr. Wilder and whispered something in his ear.

Mr. Wilder nodded and then said to Miss Keller: "I'm sorry, Marthe, we'll have to do that again."

"Why? What did I do wrong?"

He explained that she had not spoken the line as written. Instead of saying, "East of Suez, there are no Ten Commandments," she had said, "East of Suez, they don't have the Ten Commandments."

She stared at him, as if she wasn't sure that he was being serious. But apparently he was. Obediently she nodded, "O.K.," and once everyone was back in position they shot the scene again, and her dance went well—perhaps not as good as the first time—but when she came to the same line, she said,

"East of Suez, there aren't any Ten Commandments," and once again Mr. Diamond got up from his chair and went over to Mr. Wilder and whispered in his ear, and once again Mr. Wilder had to go over and have a word with his actress, who seemed to be getting visibly more distressed.

Tasos, still watching by my side, jostled my arm and whispered: "This is the kind of thing I was talking about. What's going on? Why is he being so mean to her?"

"He's not being mean," I said. "You often have to do multiple takes of a scene."

I said this with great authority. In recent days I had become quite the expert on film-making.

"Look at the German woman's face," he said. (Meaning Miss Knef, who was watching the whole scene from the wheelchair in which her character was confined.) "She's furious. If I go and talk to her, will you translate for me?"

"No, I won't," I snapped.

It was getting too painful to watch the filming any longer. The spectators were sensing the tension and they were waiting for there to be some sort of eruption; waiting almost gleefully. There was a nasty atmosphere building on the set. I felt very sorry for Miss Keller, having to perform these difficult moves and speak these difficult words in front of so many people. Still, I suppose it was her job.

To get away from it all, I turned and slipped through the crowd and then started walking up the path which led away from the villa and towards the wooded hillside at the centre of this small island. Here it was cool and shady and the only sounds were the cracking of twigs beneath my feet as I walked upwards. I soon reached the summit of the island and when I got there I stood for a while beneath the dense shade of the pine trees, relishing the silence and the cool freshness of the late-afternoon air in this isolated spot, surrounded by water and so far from the humid frenzy of Acharnon Street. But in no time at all my solitude had started to oppress me. Matthew had been one of the spectators down on the terrace: our eyes had met very briefly as I walked away from the villa by myself and it would have been easy enough to say something to him, to ask if he wanted to join me on my short walk. Why had I found it impossible to do? Why was I so shy with him, so unsure of myself? These were the questions that preoccupied me as I descended the slope on the other side of the island, scrambling down towards a rocky inlet which gave you a clear view of Skorpios, another private island a few hundred yards across the water, in this case the one where Aristotle Onassis had his home. Here I sat down and closed my eyes, tilting my face towards the sun and listening to the gentle lap of the blue water against the rocks. Perhaps it was my destiny, after all, to be always alone: that was the tragic, self-dramatizing thought that came to me, and in some paradoxical way it also brought me a kind of comfort, reconciling me to what seemed, at that moment, to be my essential nature: introverted, melancholy and solitary.

*

In this respect, after all, I was not so different from Mr. Diamond himself. Of course, he had found someone to marry, and his marriage seemed to be very happy. He also had a son and a daughter that he talked about often, and to whom he was obviously devoted. But here in Greece he was thousands of miles away from those people, his great friend Mr. Wilder was preoccupied with the shooting of his film, and meanwhile Mr. Diamond seemed to be withdrawing into himself, weighed down—it appeared to me—with private anxieties and apprehensions, feelings that he found it hard to share with the other members of the crew.

And so it was that I found him, that same evening, sitting at a table on the terrace of a bar called the Alexandros, a terrace which blurred seamlessly into the beach looking towards Madouri, so that it was impossible to tell exactly where the sand ended and the terracotta floor tiles began. He had the place to himself, and was sitting at a table close to the water, smoking a cigarette and periodically blowing the smoke up into the air in an almost-vertical straight line. I was walking down towards the beach with no fixed purpose (except to see, perhaps, whether Matthew might be there), and I was surprised when he said "Hello" to me. I said "Hello" back and then added, in my usual tone of apology:

"Please—I don't want to disturb you."

"It's true," he said, "that I came here to get away from people. But you're not one of them." I looked down, maybe even blushed a little bit. "Everybody likes the little Greek interpreter, hadn't you heard? You're the hit of the crew."

I'm not making this up to make myself look good. This is really what he said. Of course I sat down at the table beside him.

"Join me in a cocktail?" he asked.

I said, "Yes, please," and so he ordered two vodka Martinis, and then said: "Don't look so disapproving."

"I didn't mean to," I said. "People tell me it's my usual expression. But I thought your German doctor told you not to drink."

"My German doctor has never been on a film set. Certainly not one like this."

The waiter brought our drinks and I took a sip. I had never tasted a Martini before and I loved the sour sharpness of it: like a gentle slap in the face to bring you round after a faint.

"Were you there for the scene on the terrace this afternoon?" he asked, lighting another cigarette.

"Some of it," I said. "I left halfway through and went for a walk."

"That painful to watch, was it?"

"I'm sure it was worth it in the end."

Mr. Diamond shook his head. "We didn't get a usable take. We lost the light and we had to pack it in. Marthe had gone to pieces by then anyway."

"Oh." I was sorry to hear this. It didn't sound good. "What will you do? Will you try again tomorrow?"

"Billy thinks we can rewrite the scene and shoot it as an interior. We can do it in Germany next month."

"Do you agree?"

Mr. Diamond shrugged and said: "Maybe it could work that way, I don't know." I wondered whether anyone could ever make a suggestion about this film that might prompt him to say "Why not?" It didn't feel like it.

"So, once you've finished here," I said, "you're going back to Germany?"

He nodded. "Beautiful Munich. The city that gives you back pain. The Shingles City—they should put that on the tourist posters."

"You don't like it there?"

"Not much."

It was still a struggle for me to understand the practicalities of film-making, and I now said a very naive thing.

"I suppose Mr. Wilder chose to make this film in Germany because it's not so far from Greece? So if he needs to bring everyone back here, it's not too difficult?"

"That's not how it works," Mr. Diamond said, almost smiling at my innocence as he leaned forward to tap ash into the ashtray on our table. "It would be much easier to shoot the rest of the picture in Hollywood. In fact, that would suit me down to the ground. I could work nine to five and go home to my wife every night, for one thing."

"So why—?"

"We can't shoot the picture in a Hollywood studio," he explained, "because none of the studios wanted it. Believe me, we tried."

This made no sense to me.

"But it's a Billy Wilder film. He's a genius . . . He's one of the greatest . . . Who wouldn't want to make a Billy Wilder film?"

He shook his head. "Times have changed. Well, I don't know if they *have* changed, yet. But they're certainly changing."

"Why didn't they want it?" I asked.

"Because they thought it would lose money."

I was surprised by this answer, and must have shown it with a frown, because Mr. Diamond said: "There's that disapproving look again. Look, in America, film-making is a business. Nothing more, nothing less. A very healthy attitude in my opinion. To be perfectly honest, I wouldn't want it any other way. Everything else is just . . . piss and vinegar, as they say. Well, actually, I don't know if anybody really says that, but I do."

"But surely—"

"Billy and I aren't exactly on a roll at the moment," he said, anticipating me. "Our last big hit was fourteen years ago. And in the last few years, a couple of the pictures lost a lot of money. A *lot*. In Hollywood, people notice that kind of thing. You don't read *Cahiers du Cinéma* first thing in the morning before you start work. You read the trades. When we first met you, last summer, we were at a kind of crisis point with this script. If I remember correctly, you came round to our office one afternoon to return Billy's copy of the book, am I right?"

"That's right. But you were in a meeting."

"Well, that was it. That was *the* meeting."

I asked him what he meant.

"That was the afternoon we went to see Universal, because in the morning they'd sent us a note saying they were passing on the script."

"Passing?"

"They turned it down. They wouldn't put up the money."

"Oh? You mean they didn't like it?"

"You still don't get it," he said patiently. "It's not a question of whether they liked it or not. They could have been the best judges of a story in the world and we could have written them *Madame Bovary* or *Moby-Dick* and they still wouldn't have given a damn. It's not about whether you like something. They took one look at *Fedora* and decided there was no way they were ever going to turn a profit with this property."

I thought about this while drinking some more of my cocktail. "But they're wrong," I said.

It was something between a statement and a question. Well, irrespective of whether it was a question or a statement, Mr. Diamond didn't answer it. He just looked out to sea and continued to draw on his cigarette.

"Anyway," he said at last. "Hence Germany."

"So a *German* film company is paying for it," I said, slow on the uptake as always.

"They're not really a film company. They're in the tax-shelter business. It's quite something, for Billy, to get into bed with people like this. It's a big step for him." He didn't actually say "step down" but I suppose that's what he meant. "He told me a funny story, actually. When he went to see these guys in Munich, the first meeting, they asked him, 'Mr. Wilder, why do you want to make this film in Germany?' and he said, 'That's like asking a bank robber why he robs banks. The answer's obvious—because that's where the money is.'" He managed to summon a smile at his friend's joke, but it didn't last long. "Of course they didn't get it. They looked very serious and said, 'You're planning to rob us?' Germans. No sense of humour, you see." I was beginning to notice—and would see even more clearly as the weeks went by—that Mr. Diamond was not the biggest fan of Germany or German culture. Meanwhile he seemed to be thinking about something. He stubbed out his cigarette and finally said, in a low, introspective tone, "Billy must *really* want to make this picture."

It seemed that he was addressing this remark more to himself than to me, but I chose to reply to it anyway.

"Naturally he does," I said. "He's a film-maker. It's not enough for him to write films. He has to make them."

"True," said Mr. Diamond. "What's purgatory for me is

pleasure for him. Besides, what you have to remember about Billy is that really, deep down, he loves being here."

"Here?"

"Here." He gestured around him. "Europe. The cradle of civilization. Billy's a European."

"So are you," I said. "I mean, you come from Romania, don't you?"

"That's different. I came to the States when I was about eight years old. I don't remember anything about the place I was born."

He paused, as if to check whether this was true by briefly, effortfully looking back into the past and trying to summon some images.

"Nothing at all?" I prompted.

"Oh, you know what it's like. You remember little, arbitrary things." He took out another cigarette and lit it with his elegant, gold-plated lighter. I'd never seen him smoke so heavily before. "There was a little wooden chair—not even a chair, it was more like a footstool with a back to it—and it was tiny, just big enough for a small child to sit on, and I used to sit on that, next to the fire. I remember a tune my dad used to whistle. I remember a boy at school—his name was Darius—who twisted my arm out in the schoolyard one day, to get some money off me. Stuff like that. But the rest is all gone. My first solid memories are all of New York and I've always felt American through and through. But Billy was almost thirty when he came to Hollywood. He'd had all that time in Vienna, first of all, then Berlin, then Paris. That sort of thing stays with you, you know?"

"You mean he's never felt at home in America?"

"He loves America. I mean, he hates it, but he also loves it. But he also loves Europe. And also hates it. He's a mass of contradictions. I suppose that's why he needs to tell stories. And tells such good ones. You know, there are parts of him that . . . come to life, in Europe, which you don't see so much when he's in Hollywood. I saw it a few years ago, when we were making a film in Italy with Lemmon. Billy would be taking him to restaurants all the time, taking him to museums, teaching him how to understand the food, how to appreciate the art . . ."

"And what about before that?" I asked. (For I knew the subjects and titles of all Mr. Wilder's films off by heart, by now, and their chronology.) "When you went to England, to make the Sherlock Holmes film?"

"That wasn't quite the same," said Mr. Diamond. "I mean, we enjoyed ourselves there, but England is not Europe. I know that technically England is part of Europe, but . . . England is its own thing, you know?"

"Yes, I understand," I said. And it was true: whenever I went to London with my mother, I always had the sense of visiting not just a different country but a different continent. One which fascinated me, as it did most of my compatriots, but where we found many of the customs and mores to be occult, eccentric and indeed incomprehensible.

"That was a difficult picture, anyway," Mr. Diamond continued. "A lot of things went wrong." He fell into a reverie again, looking out over the water. I began to suspect that a lot of what he was going through at the moment, and a lot of what he'd been through with Billy during the last few years, was causing him to reassess things, to understand his friend perhaps better than he'd understood him before. "You know, he's actually very insecure," he said. "He's very sharp, and he's a hundred times smarter than anyone else you'll meet, and he has this incredible wit, but those things . . . I mean, that's all on the surface, isn't it? What happened with *Holmes* really shocked me. We planned that picture for years. It was so important to him, probably the most important thing he's ever done. But when the producers saw it and started telling him it was too long, he lost faith in it. Completely. He believed everything they told him about it and once he started cutting it down there was no stopping him. He cut it and cut it and

cut it. In the end *I* was the one who had to try and put a stop
to it. You know, if I'd allowed him to take out all the scenes
he wanted to take out, in the end, we would have finished up
with a ten-minute picture. And this was supposed to be his
masterpiece. This was his own baby he was chopping up, his
own . . . favourite child. Just because these assholes were
telling him to. *Fuck you,* he should have told them. *Fuck you.*
Of course—" a short sip of Martini, a long exhalation of
smoke—"it's not easy to say *Fuck you* to the guys who have all
the money."

"What sort of problems did you have," I asked, "making
that film?"

"Every sort," said Mr. Diamond. "But I guess the worst was
when we had to shut the whole production down."

"Why did you have to do that?"

"Because the star of the picture tried to kill himself."

"Oh." I was genuinely shocked. Did things like this really
happen?

"It was all . . . a big mess," Mr. Diamond continued, half to
himself. "It was his marriage, mainly . . . What was going on in
his marriage. But there was also the pressure of starring in this
huge picture. The biggest thing he'd ever done. And Billy can
be tough. Tough on actors. He puts a lot of pressure on them.
Not as much as he's under himself, of course . . ."

I thought about the phrase he had used earlier, when he had
said that the filming this afternoon had made Miss Keller "go
to pieces." She was very young, I realized, and must also have
been feeling under huge pressure. I asked Mr. Diamond if he
knew where she was and how she was coping with today's
events.

"Last I heard, she'd gone back to her apartment," he said.
"And yes, she was pretty upset. She hates Billy at the moment,
but that'll pass. He can be very charming. And very kind, sometimes. The thing is, you have to get used to his humour. You
have to work out how he uses it, what it's for. He was joking

with her this afternoon, trying to keep the thing lighthearted, but she didn't get it.

"The guy who played Dr. Watson in our Holmes picture— there was a scene where he had to dance. He was in this big dance scene with a whole chorus line of ballet dancers, and he had to keep up with them, but at the same time he still had to be acting, right? There was something important happening in that scene, an emotional thing that had to be captured. So Billy tells him: 'Colin, in this scene I want you to act like Laughton, and dance like Nijinsky.' So we did a take and afterwards Colin came running up to him and saying: 'How was it? How did I do?' And Billy answered, 'Well, you were close—you acted like Nijinsky and danced like Laughton.' And that worked, you see, because he made a joke out of it, so Colin took it on board and everything was fine."

I nodded solemnly. To be honest, I didn't really get the joke. I felt as humourless as the Germans that Mr. Diamond disliked so much.

"Charles Laughton was a famous British actor," he clarified, for my benefit.

"Yes, I know," I answered.

"And Nijinsky was a famous ballet dancer."

I hadn't known that.

"You don't know the story of Nijinsky?" he said. "He was a great dancer, but he went nuts. He ended up in a mental asylum suffering from terrible delusions. There's a funny story about that, as well."

This seemed unlikely, but Mr. Diamond was determined to tell it anyway.

"Billy was in a meeting once, with a producer. And he was telling him that he wanted to make a film about Nijinsky. So he told the producer the whole story of Nijinsky's life, and this guy was looking at him in horror, and saying, 'Are you serious? You want to make a movie about a Ukrainian ballet dancer who ends up going crazy and spending thirty years in a mental hospital, thinking that he's a horse?' And Billy says, 'Ah, but in our version of the story, we give it a happy ending. He ends up winning the Kentucky Derby.'"

And this time I did laugh, partly because I thought the story was funny, and partly because I liked the way Mr. Diamond told it, the way his eyes shone as he reached the punchline, the way that for him, briefly, the telling of this joke brought an instant of strange joy and clarity to the world. And I realized that for a man like him, a man who was essentially melancholy, a man for whom the ways of the world could only ever be a source of regret and disappointment, humour was not just a beautiful thing but a necessary thing, that the telling of a good joke could bring a moment, transient but lovely, when life made a rare kind of sense, and would no longer seem random and chaotic and unknowable. It made me glad to think that in the midst of the world's many intractabilities he still had this one source of consolation.

And now, as if reading my thoughts, he said: "You know, I would feel one hundred per cent better about this picture if it was just a little bit funnier. Writing the script with Billy, I was constantly trying to puts in bits of business, the odd line, the occasional crack. But he wouldn't have it. This is going to be a serious picture, he kept saying. A serious picture. Well, I'm a comedy writer. A comedy guy. That's why he got in touch with me in the first place, all those years ago, because he saw a couple of my sketches and they made him laugh. And not much makes Billy laugh. And since then, everything we've written together, even if it's had something serious to say, well, we've always tried to put in plenty of laughs. But this time, he wasn't interested. And I thought we were supposed to be making a satirical picture, right? That's what we always talked about. A film about the New Hollywood. The kids with beards—'They don't need a script, just give 'em a hand-held camera and a zoom lens.' But instead he decided to saddle himself with this lousy book with this crazy story about an old lady who never seems to look her age and somehow seems to have found the secret of eternal youth and I'm thinking: 'Why, Billy? Why do you want to make a picture out of this story? What's in it for you?'"

He tried to drink from his glass, but there was nothing left in it. He gazed at the empty glass quizzically but didn't seem to be in the mood to order another one.

"Well, there must be something," he said. "There must be *something* about this story that means a lot to him. There must be something here that he wants to get out of his system. But I'm damned if I know what it is." He stared out towards the old villa on the island of Madouri, glowing golden now in the setting sun, as if that might hold the solution to the enigma. "And if *I* can't work it out," he said finally, "who the hell can?"

*

The final day of the shoot came round so soon. Perversely (but quite typically, I'm afraid) I had been dreading this moment so much that I had not been able to enjoy the last few days' work at all. The thought of returning to Athens, to tutoring, to Acharnon Street, to the routine contentments of life with my parents, seemed quite unbearable. The rest of the crew would be proceeding to Munich to shoot the bulk of the film's interior scenes. The gods would be moving on, in other words; and I, a mere mortal, would be left behind, forgotten.

The Greek exteriors for *Fedora* were completed, but even so, even though these constituted only a small part of the film, it would not be right for a Hollywood crew to leave anywhere without throwing a party. And so on the last evening, from nine o'clock onwards, they booked out the whole of the Alexandros bar. The tables were piled with food. The supply of *retsina* and *demestica* seemed to be inexhaustible.

People were in high spirits. The afternoon before, Mr. Wilder and his team had shot a beautiful scene. It was a scene in which the president of the Academy of Motion Picture Arts and Sciences flies all the way to Greece to present Fedora with a lifetime achievement award. The president was played by Henry Fonda. He had arrived from Athens in a convoy of cars, led by the most important of the German producers in charge of the film. He had played his scene perfectly, with only the minimum of rehearsal. Mr. Diamond had never once had to look across at Mr. Wilder and shake his head at the misreading of a line or the misplacement of a word in the script. When he wasn't rehearsing or performing, Mr. Fonda sat quietly beneath the shade of a pine tree, an artist's pad spread open on his knees, making wonderful pencil sketches of the landscape around him. In the evening he had dined on the terrace of the Alexandros with Mr. Wilder, Mr. Diamond and Mr. Holden; and to me, sitting at an adjacent table, the three of them had never looked so happy, and so satisfied with their day's work. The presence of this quiet, gracious, distinguished man in Nydri had cast everything in a lambent glow, and even though he had left for Athens that morning, something of that glow lingered and continued to warm us.

It was a long party. The music at first was provided by a local musician. From somewhere or other a Fender Rhodes electric piano had been produced and set up on the terrace. This plucky old man was banging out what sounded to me like very approximate renditions of famous show tunes and torch songs. Really, his performances added nothing to the gaiety of the occasion. I could have played most of these tunes much better myself, by ear or from memory, and I was itching to get up and improve on his versions. A few people were gamely attempting to dance: in fact, Matthew himself came over and asked me to dance with him, and we shuffled around uncomfortably for a minute or two while our pianist performed a brutal act of assassination on "My Funny Valentine," but his playing was so jarring and lacking in rhythm that we gave up, and I was left with just the brief memory of Matthew's hand in the small of my back, the pressure of his fingers through the thin

material of my dress. After that, somehow we became separated and did not find each other in the crowd for quite a
while.

In the meantime, someone took drastic action regarding the
musical entertainment. The pianist was politely asked to leave
(having been well paid for his atrocities, I believe), and then to
everybody's general amazement, one of the producers drove
his car, a Volkswagen Beetle, right onto the beach and parked
it next to the bar. The doors were flung open and a tape was
put into the in-car cassette deck and suddenly the Rolling
Stones were pounding out into the midnight air.

This signalled an immediate change of mood. People got up
and danced, tables were cleared to one side to make more
space, and in the process there was a good deal of traditional
Greek crockery-smashing. Everything became very raucous. I
felt out of place and stood to one side, leaning against the terrace wall and looking out towards the sea with a drink in my
hand. There were quite a few of us who did not take an active
part in the revelry, mainly the older members of the cast and
crew. I was torn between conflicting emotions: gladness at the
thought that I had shared in this incredible experience, misery
at the thought that it was almost over. These emotions were
battling it out for supremacy at the very moment that Mr.
Diamond came over to talk to me.

"I just wanted to say thank you," he said, raising his voice
above the noise of the music. "It's been great having you
around. A little oasis of sanity in all this madness."

In the overwrought, emotionally heightened atmosphere of
the party, this compliment seemed to overwhelm me and
brought tears to my eyes. I looked away, preferring that Iz
should not see them.

"Hey, what's up with you?" he said, rather dashing my
hopes on that point.

"Nothing. It's just . . . this has been such an amazing time
for me. And it's all finished so quickly."

"Don't you want to go back to Athens, and see your mom and dad?"

"Of course, but . . ."

I broke free from the conversation and walked away onto the beach, furious with myself for having lost control in front of him like this. I walked up and down the beach a few times, trying to pull myself together. I rejoined the party about fifteen minutes later, feeling a bit more composed, or at any rate determined not to make a fool of myself again.

"Miss Frangopoulou?" said a familiar, Austrian-accented voice beside me.

I turned and there was Mr. Wilder, smiling at me from beneath his little straw hat. I wondered if he even took it off in bed.

"We appreciate what you've done for us these last few days," he said, shaking me by the hand.

"It's been a pleasure," I said. "And an honour. Really."

"And you've been paid for it, don't forget," he said. "This is not an unimportant factor."

I laughed and nodded.

"My friend Mr. Diamond told me you were not feeling too well just now," he said. "Is everything O.K.? Can we get you anything?"

"I'm fine," I said. "A little too much to drink. You know what I'm like. Remember the Bistro?"

"That's true," he said. "You need to watch your consumption of the *demestica*, maybe. I think this little party still has a while to run."

"I think so too."

"Well, my days of dancing till dawn are behind me, I'm sad to say. So I think I'm heading off to bed now."

"Very wise," I said, and we shook hands again, and he kissed me politely on the cheek, and then he was gone.

*

I did not take Mr. Wilder's advice. That is to say, I did not watch my consumption of the *demestica*. I danced with people a bit and talked with people a bit, and when I'd run out of people to dance with and people to talk to, and when they had run out of Rolling Stones tapes to play on the Volkswagen stereo, I sat down behind the electric piano and started playing. I was performing to myself, really—running through some favourite tunes, some of them famous, some of them not, trying out new voicings of the chords, improvising, straying off-copy—but whenever I stopped, a gratifying number of the guests gave me a little ripple of applause. But the party was starting to thin out. Eventually there can only have been about half a dozen people who remained to listen to me, and when I came to the end of "All the Things You Are," and finished my version with a strange, unexpected A-minor sixth chord, I looked up to see that one of them was Matthew.

"Wow," he said. "You told me that you played, but you didn't tell me that you played like *that*."

I smiled and felt a warmth and a tenderness and a tingling excitement course through my body.

He pulled up a chair and sat down next to me.

"Play me something you've written," he said.

"What?"

"You told me that you write music. Play some of it."

I looked him in the eyes for a moment and a lovely, nervous shiver ran through me. Then I said "O.K.," and looked down at the keyboard and placed both my hands in position, took a deep breath and played him the little tune that I called "Malibu."

I don't quite know what I expected him to say when it was finished. The last chord hung in the air for quite a few seconds before he said anything at all. Then he told me: "That's really nice. It sounds a bit like film music."

People often say this, I've noticed, about any modern music which is tonal and tries to express an emotion in direct, uncomplicated language. I never know whether they mean it as a compliment or an insult. I felt the same uncertainty when Matthew said it.

"That would make a great theme tune for this film," he added.

"*Fedora*? Oh, sure," I said. "I'll just play it to Mr. Wilder and I expect he'll hire me on the spot."

"Perhaps you should. Nothing ventured, and all that."

I smiled. "I think he might already have a composer in mind."

There was a long silence between us and then we both stood up at the same time. This exchange, and my disappointment at his response, had created a little moment of awkwardness but it was soon gone. We walked onto the beach and then down to the sea. Our hands found each other and clasped each other softly.

"It's so beautiful here," he said.

The sun was beginning to rise and the water was turning from black to magenta and soon the outline of the villa on Madouri would be visible. But I was looking at Matthew, not the view.

"What?" he asked.

"What do you mean, 'What?'?" I said.

"Why are you staring at me?"

"I was looking at your beard. It's really come along, these last few days."

I reached my hand up to touch his beard. Of course, it was just an excuse to touch his face. Soon my finger was stroking his cheek, and that was when he took my hand and moved it away and then leaned in to kiss me: a brief, gentle kiss on the lips. The first time I had ever been kissed like that. I was immediately hungry for a second kiss so I put my hand behind his neck and pulled him towards me and this time the kiss was longer and deeper, but still tentative, somehow.

We stood for a while with our arms around each other, looking out towards the island. I loved the way the curve of his body seemed to fit with mine. I rested my head against his shoulder and felt his hand starting to stroke my hair. I felt very, very happy but there was a cloud on the horizon. I said:

"I suppose . . . I suppose you're going with them to Munich tomorrow?"

Matthew shook his head. "Back to London. Which means that first of all I have to get to Athens, somehow."

I looked up at him. "Me too."

"How were you going to get there?"

"I don't know." It was true, I hadn't given it any thought.

"I was thinking it might be fun to hitch." He kissed me again. "Why don't you come with me?"

"Could I?"

"We could take a couple of days over it. Stop in some hotels on the way."

I realized what he was suggesting. The thought of it excited me, very much, but alarmed me at the same time. Also, Matthew's hands were beginning to move over my body, more freely than I had been expecting. A sudden apprehension came over me, and I tensed.

"Let me think about it," I said, pulling back.

He withdrew his hand, and looked at me: an enquiring look, with an enquiring smile. It felt as if he was amused by me as much as he was attracted to me.

"All right," he said. "Think about it. Whatever you want."

Back in my apartment, not many minutes later, I lay alone on my bed in the summer heat and I knew that I did want to go with him. All traces of doubt had vanished from my mind. I was frustrated with myself, now, for not inviting him back to the apartment, but at the same time it didn't really matter because I knew that what I wanted to happen between us was definitely going to happen in the next day or two, and perhaps it would be even sweeter this way, the pleasure intensified by the wait and the anticipation. Thinking these mixed-up, sleepy thoughts I rolled over and put my hand between my legs and soon I was dreaming about him, hot, delirious, disturbing dreams which I can still remember to this day.

*

A few hours later I was awoken from a deep sleep by a loud knocking on my door. I looked at the watch on my bedside table and it was later than I thought. Bright sunlight flooded my bedroom through the glassless window.

I went to open the door. To my surprise, it was the production manager standing there.

"Yes?" I said.

"These are for you," she said.

She handed me a folder full of sheets of paper, and a lanyard to hang around my neck.

"What's this?" I asked, stupidly.

"It appears that you have a new job," she answered.

I looked at the lanyard and saw that my name was written on it, and underneath were the words "ASSISTANT TO MR. DIAMOND" in block capitals.

I looked at her.

"What does this mean?" I asked.

"It means that Mr. Wilder and Mr. Diamond wish you to travel to Munich with them and continue working on the film."

I was lost for words. Fortunately, she wasn't.

"You'd better get dressed," she instructed. "The cars are waiting and they'll be leaving in ten minutes."

"Where are we going?"

"To the airport at Actium, and then straight to Munich."

Munich. Was this some sort of mistake, or some sort of joke? Was I now supposed to consider myself one of the gods?

"Well?" she said, impatient. "Are you coming? Or shall I tell them that you don't want the job?"

"No," I said hurriedly. "Of course. Of course I want it. I'm just so . . ."

I tailed off and she said: "Good. Ten minutes, as I told you. Don't be late or they'll just have to go without you."

I dressed and packed in a frenzy. On my way down the stairs I stopped outside Matthew's mother's apartment and knocked but there was no reply. I knocked again but nothing happened and I couldn't risk being late. He must have been in a very deep sleep. His mother was part of the crowd getting into the cars outside the building and when I asked her where her son was she just said, "Still in bed, of course." I got into the back of one of the cars, sitting beside her, and when the convoy set off a few minutes later, the only thing that stopped my sudden, bewildered happiness from being complete was the thought that I had no idea when I would see him again.

The morning after Ariane left for Sydney, I made myself some toast and some coffee and was just about to sink my teeth into the toast when, in a moment of weakness, I went to the fridge and took out the supermarket Brie I'd been keeping there. Brie and toast is not an especially good combination, in my view, but I was not in the mood to be picky. I consumed this satisfying breakfast in solitude, then climbed the stairs with a heavy heart and went into the spare room: my work room, as we called it. Geoffrey was teaching in Beaconsfield again and Fran was somewhere in the house, I didn't know where, keeping her distance, steering well clear of me. It was very quiet. I flopped down into my seat at the desk by the window and mechanically booted the computer up and turned on the Midi control keyboard even though I already knew for a fact that I would not be making any music today.

I navigated to the "Music" folder which contained two sub-folders, one called "Film Music" and one called "Other." "Film Music" contained a sub-folder called "Work in Progress" but this was currently empty. "Other" contained a sub-folder called "Billy" and this was the folder that I opened. I clicked on a file called "Press Conference" and it opened in Pro Tools.

On the screen an old piece of film footage flickered into life. I had found it on the internet a few weeks earlier. It was colour footage of a press conference given at Bavaria Studios just as pre-production on *Fedora* was about to start, about a month before I joined the crew in Greece. I found the late-1970s styles and fashions—epitomized by the dull orange of the backs of the plastic chairs on which the journalists were sitting, and the dowdy floral dresses worn by a couple of the female reporters—intensely evocative of that era, and of my early twenties generally. Billy himself, as always, was dressed casually but very elegantly: a V-necked sweater in navy blue over a white polo shirt buttoned up to the top. His silver hair was impeccably combed back and his black-rimmed spectacles gave him the look of a distinguished public intellectual.

I had asked Geoffrey to do some work on the clip for me. It began with a shot of Billy entering the room and walking towards the stage. This shot lasted for about twenty seconds but Geoffrey had slowed it right down so that it was now almost three and a half minutes long. This way, it gave the viewer the chance to understand Billy a bit more deeply, by closely observing his walk, the way he carried himself, the thought process accompanying his measured, unhurried step, his expression of amused, somewhat arrogant anticipation based (no doubt) on the fact that he already had a number of good answers up his sleeve. This was a German audience and he would be addressing them in German and he would be talking, among other things, about how it felt to be back in Germany. He knew that he was going to ruffle some feathers and he was looking forward to it.

Slowing the footage down also meant that Billy's walk towards the stage acquired a balletic quality: it made him look like a moonwalker or a deep-sea diver making his infinitely gradual progress across the floor of the ocean. Taking my cue from the slow, stately fall of his footsteps, I was in the process of composing a sombre musical accompaniment, a little piece for chamber orchestra in a minor key, with the cellos and basses steadily playing the root notes of descending chords and the subtle colourings of strings and woodwinds being punctuated, every second bar, by a female soprano voice singing the same, repeated, *vibrato*-less note. The effect was to transform the archive footage, to freeze it as a moment in time, a moment of history, even. It gave this banal walk to the front of a stage the gravity of an imperial procession, and it gave Billy himself the air of both jester and martyr: because this occasion, after all, marked his return to a country which thirty years earlier had torn his family apart, and now here he was, granting it the supreme favour of his presence and at the same time throwing himself upon its mercy: both triumphant and humiliated.

My intention was to compose four more movements in the *Billy* suite but this was the only one that was nearly finished. I hadn't even begun to think what I could do with these pieces when they were all written. For sure, nobody would ever want to perform or record them. Like everything else in my life at the moment, the writing of music now seemed Quixotic and futile, and even this "Press Conference" section, of which I had, until a moment ago, been quite proud, suddenly irritated me. So I clicked the Mute button on Pro Tools and in the ensuing silence became aware of a voice coming from the garden.

It was Fran's voice, and she was talking to someone on her mobile. The urgency of her tone made it clear that it was not a routine conversation. My guess was that she was talking to one of her close friends, but the words were indistinct. Well, that was soon remedied: I opened the window a few inches so that I could hear what was going on.

All I heard, of course, was Fran's side of the conversation:

"No. Nothing. Doesn't want to know."

...

"Fuck knows."

...

"How am I supposed to do that?"

...

"I know it is. I know that. Completely my decision."

. . .

"No! No, I just *can't*. It's driving me insane."

. . .

"Nobody. Nobody at all. And anyway, it's not the sort of thing you can decide like that."

. . .

"But that's just it. I can't. I *don't know*, Julie, I really don't know."

And on these words, she burst into tears. As soon as this happened, my maternal instinct kicked in and I was off down the stairs at a gallop. We almost collided entering the kitchen—me from the staircase, Fran from the garden. Her phone call was over and her face was red.

"What's up, sweetie?" I said.

She didn't answer but stared at me for some time, her eyes brimful of hatred.

"What's up?" she said eventually. "What do you think's up? Everything's fucking up."

She slammed the phone down on the kitchen table so hard that I was worried she might have cracked the screen.

"Whatever it is," I began, "I'm sure we can—"

"Don't talk to me," she said. "And don't come near me." (I was reaching out to her.) "I don't want words and I don't want hugs. Just leave me alone for once."

A few seconds later she had left the house and was off down the street, the forgotten phone still lying on the kitchen table.

I stood for a moment or two in the empty kitchen of my empty house, listening to what would have been silence if the drills hadn't just started up from the noisy refurbishment which had been going on for months three doors down the road. I was in a state of shock: the shock of seeing Fran in tears, and then the shock of hearing her speak to me like that. I sat down at the table, shaking. I could have run after her with the phone but instead I did nothing, just put my head in my hands and sat there, waiting for the numbness to abate and for my composure to return. Intervals of absolute silence were interrupted by bone-shaking episodes of drilling from our neighbours' house. A loose item of cutlery was rattling on one of the work surfaces.

Minutes ticked by. I believe I might have been there for almost half an hour, turning over Fran's words and trying to come to terms with what they implied: namely, that she was rejecting my attempts to support her.

After that, my thoughts led nowhere. There seemed to be nothing I could do.

I sighed, finally rose to my feet with a tremendous effort, and then slowly trudged back up the staircase.

I sat down at my desk again. Waiting for me on the computer screen was an image: the image of Billy's face. The clip of him walking to the front of the stage at the press conference had come to an end and the frame had frozen: frozen on his face at an unguarded moment. He was looking straight ahead, but not at the camera, not at the audience of journalists, not at anything, really. He was lost in thought, but I don't believe he would have been silently rehearsing his answers at this point. This was the press conference, after all, where he gave *that* response to a question from a reporter. The response that reduced an entire room to silence. But the image I was looking at did not show the face of a man privately honing a lethal one-liner. It showed the face of a man who might, temporarily, have been in command of the room, but underneath was nursing a deep, private, unassuageable disappointment. And in a strange way, it was the same disappointment that I was nursing. Billy might have known it for several months by now, and I might only just have begun to grasp it, but we had both come to the same realization: the realization that what we had to give, nobody really wanted any more.

*

A couple of months after that press conference, there were twelve of us sitting around the dinner table. Our surroundings were very grand, and very formal. We were in a private dining room at the Bayerischer Hof hotel in the centre of Munich. There was dark oak panelling, a massive dark oak table, and waiters sweltering in full penguin suits even though this was July and Munich was enjoying—or enduring—a hot, clammy summer.

I can't remember the names of everyone who was there, but I can remember most of them.

There was Billy, obviously, and sitting next to him on the right was Dr. Rózsa, the guest of honour. I was sitting between Dr. Rózsa and Iz, and on the other side of Billy, the left-hand side, was Mr. Holden. Miss Keller was there, sitting diagonally opposite Billy, and next to her was her boyfriend, Al Pacino, who was visiting from America. I can't remember exactly who the other six people were but several of them were German, and represented Geria, the tax-shelter company that was helping to finance the film. They wore business suits and didn't join in with a lot of the conversation around the table, mainly I suppose because some of them didn't speak English too well.

Dr. Rózsa—who was Hungarian, and whose first name was Miklós—was going to compose the music for the film. Although he lived mainly in Los Angeles, apparently he had a villa somewhere in Italy, where he spent most of the summer, and he had travelled up to Munich especially to see some rushes and start thinking about the score. His arrival was considered quite a major event and this dinner had been organized to celebrate it.

He was an old friend of Billy's, having worked with him several times before, most notably on *Double Indemnity*. He was also well known for composing the music for all of those Biblical epics like *Ben-Hur* and *Quo Vadis*. He had shelves full of Oscars and was without doubt one of the most famous composers in Hollywood. Needless to say, I had never heard of him.

How, then, did I find myself invited to this dinner at all, let alone sitting next to the guest of honour?

*

Iz and I had become close during the last few weeks. Obviously we were bound to become close if I was his personal assistant but in reality this was just an honorary title and he didn't need much personal assisting, least of all from me. For one thing he already spoke German, not perfectly, but well enough to get by in the city's shops and restaurants. My role, I would say, was more that of counsellor and therapist than personal assistant.

Most of the *Fedora* crew were staying in a building called the Hotel Residence on Artur-Kutscher-Platz in Schwabing, a fashionable district to the north of the city centre. From there it was a short walk to the very pleasant Englischer Garten, and rather a long drive to the film studios, which were located some ten miles to the south, in Geiselgasteig. The principal exception was Billy himself: he had a furnished penthouse apartment not far away on Leopoldstrasse. Audrey had come over from America and every day she would devotedly prepare a lavish home-cooked dinner, which would be waiting for him when he got back from the day's shooting. After that, Iz himself might come round to do some more writing on the next day's scenes, because the script, I could not help noticing, never seemed to be quite finished.

I went to the studios with Iz in his car most days, only staying behind if he had some special job for me in Schwabing. Every so often, for instance, he liked me to go to the shops and buy him some basic provisions. The Hotel Residence was a concrete brutalist building made up of self-catering apartments, and before his mid-evening trip round to Billy's apartment for writing duties, and with no wife on hand to cook for him, he would do his best to rustle up a little meal for himself—or, more likely, get me to do it. I was not a very expert

cook but this didn't seem to matter because although I suppose he was used to eating in luxury restaurants, Iz's tastes
actually seemed to be quite simple. I think one of the happiest
evenings we spent was when we threw together some tinned
sardines and tinned tomatoes and rice: I can remember him
now, standing over the saucepan and stirring the mixture
together—not with a smile on his face, of course (that would
be too much, for him), but with a rapt, satisfied expression.
And when I found a jar of black olives in his cupboard and
said, "Why don't we put these in as well?" I was rewarded
with that most precious of responses: his eyes lit up and he
rubbed his hands together and said, "Sure, why *not?*" The
result was delicious—to us, at any rate.

Through sharing these meals, we got to know each other
pretty well. His shingles had come back with a vengeance, and
I think he was often in a lot of pain. And so more to distract
than entertain him, I got into the habit of talking about myself:
my quiet life with my mother and father back in busy, polluted
Acharnon Street, my first steps into language tuition, my love
of playing the piano and listening to records. That was how he
found out that I liked to write music and had dreams of
becoming a real composer; and more specific dreams, taking
shape over the last few weeks, of becoming a composer for the
cinema.

"Dr. Rózsa's coming up tomorrow," he told me one
evening. "Billy's throwing a dinner for him tomorrow night."

"Who?" I asked, inevitably.

"Miklós Rózsa," he said. "Famous composer. Old friend of
Billy's. Don't you know *anything* about films, Cal?"

"I'm trying to learn," I said, blushing.

"Good. Well, this is an excellent opportunity. If you want to
start writing music for the movies, this is the guy you need to
speak to. You'll be going straight to the top. I'll get you invited
to the dinner, and you can sit right next to him."

*

I didn't believe him, of course. I was so far down the hierarchy of people working on this film that the key grip or best boy had a better chance of being invited. But I had reckoned without Iz's influence over Billy. Even in normal circumstances, Billy would do his best to keep him happy; but now, when he knew that the making of this film was turning into such an ordeal for him, anything he could do to make his friend and colleague feel better, he would do. So, sure: he wanted the strange little Greek girl to come to the fancy dinner party? Of course. No problem. And have her sit in the prime position at the table, right next to the guest of honour? Consider it done.

So there I was. There we were. But I'm not sure that Dr. Rózsa was happy about it.

I think that, these days, I must have a recording of every one of Miklós Rózsa's film scores—all ninety-something of them—not to mention most of his concert works. And so I know, all too well, the gentleness and lyricism of which he was capable. The beautiful love themes he wrote for *That Hamilton Woman* and *The Thief of Bagdad*. The gorgeous melancholy of the *adagio* from his violin concerto, which inspired Billy to make *The Private Life of Sherlock Holmes*. But sitting next to him at dinner that evening was not a comfortable experience, I must say. I think, looking back, that he must have been a reserved man, perhaps even rather shy, but at the time I mistook this shyness for rudeness. And in any case, that night in Munich, he would have been seventy years old. A long, distinguished career lay behind him. There were four or five more film scores to come. He had nothing to prove, least of all to a twenty-something wannabe musician from Athens.

"Is this your first time in Munich, Dr. Rózsa?" was, I believe, my opening gambit.

"I have been here many times," he answered, solemnly.

"The most recent was last year. On that occasion the Münchner Philharmoniker were giving a series of concerts in my honour."

"Nice," I said. "Did they perform your film music, or your serious music?"

Pretty good question, I thought. But I was thrown by his response.

"You don't regard film music as being serious?"

"Well, of course . . . Of course it is," I mumbled, or stumbled, or both. "I just meant . . ."

"When I came to Paris in 1934," said Dr. Rózsa, "I got to know the Swiss composer Arthur Honegger. I don't suppose you're familiar with his work?"

"As a matter of fact I am," I answered. And this was true, because I had actually heard a couple of pieces by Honegger, which were included on some of the records my mother had brought back with her from London.

He seemed pleasantly surprised. "Really? Not many people listen to his music these days. He was very famous, at the time that I knew him. One evening we were having dinner and I asked him how he made his living as a 'serious' composer, as you would call it. He told me that he supported himself by writing film music. I was astonished! I thought he meant foxtrots and two-steps, of the kind you would hear being played by the house band in a cheap café. The next day I went to the cinema to see Raymond Bernard's film of *Les Misérables*, and listened in amazement to Honegger's score. It was music of the highest quality. A revelation to me. I realized there was no shame in writing for films. Of course, that doesn't mean you don't have to make compromises. In Hollywood, one frequently finds oneself working for imbeciles. That goes with the territory."

"But Mr. Wilder is not an imbecile."

"Of course not. I regard him with the utmost respect and affection. That's why I'm here tonight. That's why I've agreed to work on this film, although I am not convinced—" he glanced around as he said this—"that it's going to be one of his big successes. No, I was thinking of other directors. Film-makers of considerable standing whose personal qualities sometimes fall short of their public reputations."

"I see."

"Mr. Hitchcock, for instance."

"Alfred Hitchcock?" Even I had heard of *him*.

"Of course. Are there any other Mr. Hitchcocks? In 1945 I composed a score for his film *Spellbound*. It is a mediocre film, as it happens—"

"Well," I said, drawing as usual on my word-perfect recollections of Halliwell's judgements, "the stars do shine magically, but the plot could have stood a little more attention."

"Indeed," said Dr. Rózsa. He looked at me closely, with a slight frown, then continued: "Nonetheless I wrote a good score. One should always give of one's best. It was for that music that I won my first Oscar. And do you know what? Mr. Hitchcock never said a thing about it. No card of thanks, no letter of congratulation, not a word. We never worked together again after that."

"That sucks," I said.

He sipped his water, before repeating: "Sucks?"

"I mean it stinks. Like the time I handed in one of my big essays two days ahead of time at the end of one semester and my tutor never said well done or anything and he still only gave me a C."

"Yes, well that . . . . 'sucks' too," he admitted, sounding somewhat friendlier than before. He looked at me even more closely over his spectacles. "Mr. Diamond tells me that you're a composer too. A musician of some merit, he assured me."

"He was just being nice," I said, glancing in Iz's direction, bashful and inexpressibly proud.

"I suppose you studied at the Athens Conservatoire?" Dr. Rózsa asked.

I shook my head. "No, I'm self-taught. I don't really compose, I just . . . make things up and record them."

He sighed. "Well, this is the fashion these days. There are no real musicians any more. Just enthusiastic amateurs, totally lacking in formal training, convinced that all you need for success is spontaneous genius. We have 'rock and roll' to thank for that."

He pronounced the three words as if he had just found a hair in his soup and was obliged to lift it clear between his fingers. After which, with a polite "Excuse me," he turned to address a remark to Billy.

While Dr. Rózsa had his back towards me, I thought about what he had just said. Frankly, for someone who had enjoyed such a distinguished career, and had received so many awards and accolades, it seemed rather petty that he should still be talking about the time that Alfred Hitchcock had behaved ungraciously towards him more than thirty years ago. But I was starting to notice that many people involved in the film business, for all the power, privilege and glamour it brought into their lives, were quick to take offence and quick to complain when things turned out to be not quite how they wanted them to be. Even Iz was susceptible. Even he maintained a constant attitude of low-level grumpiness about the hotels he was put up in, the transport arrangements made for him, the restaurants he was taken to. The only person, in fact, who didn't seem to do it was Billy himself. I genuinely believe that the only thing that really mattered to him was making films. Everything else—the conditions in which he made them, the comfort (or lack of it) in his surroundings, the tiny discourtesies of drivers or waiters or hotel bellboys—had no impact on him whatsoever. He rose above it all, preserving his good humour in the face of every minor adversity. But then, I suppose when life has thrown at you the greatest misfortune it is possible to imagine, not having your eggs cooked the way you like them for breakfast doesn't seem such a big deal.

This is not to say that he couldn't be rude or aggressive when he wanted to be. As happened, for instance, when everybody ordered their food that night. For once I didn't feel particularly out of my depth because most of the guests seemed to know as little about Bavarian cuisine as I did, and we all took our cue from Billy who asked for *Schweinshaxe* and *Leberknödel* and gave the waiter very precise instructions as to how they should be prepared. "Same for me," Iz said, and Mr. Holden slapped his menu shut and said: "What's good enough for the chief is good enough for me," and Dr. Rózsa said: "Sounds like an excellent choice." The only two dissenters were Miss Keller and Mr. Pacino. Miss Keller said, in a slightly acid voice: "Well, since Billy and Iz's script requires that I expose my naked body to the camera in a few days' time, I had probably best have a salad," and Mr. Pacino said: "I'll have a cheeseburger, please. Medium rare, fries and coleslaw on the side."

Billy looked across the table at him.

"A cheeseburger, really? What do you think this is, McDonald's?"

"No, I know this isn't McDonald's," Pacino answered. "But I'd just like to have a cheeseburger. What's the big deal? Any restaurant in the world can make you a cheeseburger, can't they?"

"Sure, but this is not *any* restaurant in the world. We are in the dining room of the Bayerischer Hof. The chef here is the best in Germany. And his speciality is *Schweinshaxe*."

"Well, that's good to know. But *my* speciality is cheeseburgers. And I'm expecting him to make me a damn good one."

"Maybe you'd like to order a chocolate milkshake as well. Or a strawberry soda. It might go better with the food than a vintage Riesling."

"Billy," Miss Keller pleaded. "Don't be mean to Al."

"I'm not being mean. In fact, I sympathize with the situation he finds himself in. Coming to Germany and being expected to eat German food—it's every American's worst nightmare."

"I have no problems with German food," said Mr. Pacino. "It's just that I prefer American food."

"Which doesn't happen to be on the menu."

"True. So I'm ordering off-menu."

"Just like you did at the Bistro, I remember."

"Exactly. So it's not a problem, right?"

The table had fallen strangely silent. Our waiter was the first to speak.

"Of course it's not a problem, sir. We can supply whatever you want."

"In that case," said Billy, "you could also bring some ketchup and some mayo, and take Mr. Pacino's cutlery away so he can eat with his hands, and maybe reset your clocks to Pacific Daylight Time so that he still feels he's back at home in Los Angeles."

"Oh, Billy," said Miss Keller. "Now come on . . ."

"Ignore him, Al," said Mr. Holden. "He's just being a mean goddamn bastard son of a bitch. Which happens to be *his* speciality."

"Bring Mr. Pacino his cheeseburger," said Billy, sending the waiter on his way. "And leave everything else as it is." He held up his hands. "*Mein Gott*—everybody is treating me as if I were the Devil himself. I'm actually the kindest, most polite person . . . Ask anybody. Ask Dr. Rózsa here. Miklós, have I ever been mean to you?"

"Frequently," said Dr. Rózsa.

"Give me an example."

"There are too many to mention."

"There you are. He has no examples."

Billy spread some butter on his bread. He didn't smile, but he seemed quite satisfied with the way the last few minutes of conversation had turned out.

"All right," Dr. Rózsa said. "I can think of one."

Billy said nothing. He took a bite out of his bread.

"It wasn't *me* you were being unkind to. But I was in the room. You did it in front of me."

"All right," said Billy, chewing his bread. "I'm waiting."

"We were working on *The Lost Weekend*," Dr. Rózsa said. "Remember?"

"This is thirty years ago. How am I supposed to remember?"

"I was in your office. I had come to tell you my ideas for the score. You remember?"

"Well, I remember many such meetings. This is nothing unusual."

"Your secretary had just brought in your mail and you were in the process of opening it. One of the letters was from a girl. One of your many conquests at the time. Remember?"

"No, I don't remember this. Not at all."

"The colour of the notepaper was pale grey."

"And this is relevant somehow? The colour of the notepaper?"

"She was heartbroken. She was writing to say you had treated her cruelly. Taken advantage of her. You remember what you did with her letter?"

"No."

"You tore it into pieces and threw them into the waste basket."

"Maybe I did. I don't remember."

"And *then*—then you had a second thought, and you reached into the basket and fished out one of the scraps of paper, and put it in your wallet. And I asked you why you had done this. Can you remember what you told me?"

"Go on," said Billy. I think he had actually forgotten, and was genuinely curious to hear the end of the story.

"You told me that your wife was currently re-decorating the family home, and you were going to show her this scrap of paper, because it was exactly the shade of grey you wanted for the wallpaper in the sitting room."

There was a ripple of laughter around the table—laughter in which a note of outrage was mingled with shocked, reluctant admiration—while Billy continued to chew his bread and stare in front of him. A glimmer of pride was discernible in his eyes and around the edges of his mouth.

"Yes, I do remember that, as a matter of fact," he said. "But she ignored my request and the wallpaper she chose was pink." He shook his head and added: "It's no wonder we got divorced soon after."

He drank some wine and gave a challenging look around the table. Nobody spoke except for Mr. Holden, who said:

"Billy, I've said it many times before, and I'll say it many times again. You are one mean goddamn bastard son of a bitch."

*

I do not think for one moment that Billy disliked Mr. Pacino. He had seen several of his films and was an admirer of his work. He did not stop needling him about his preference for American food, of course. All evening, he never let up talking about it. He was ironically solicitous about the quality and cooking of the cheeseburger when it arrived, and insisted on asking the waiter for a long list of American desserts—New York cheesecake, ice cream sundae, blueberry pie—on the hapless actor's behalf even though Mr. Pacino was quite adamant that he would like to try *Apfelstrudel*. The mockery was relentless but there was, at heart, something affectionate or even respectful about it. That was Billy's way. But very rarely—in other circumstances, and with other people—he did not pay the compliment of mockery. In fact, that was when you really had to be careful: when he stopped joking with you, when he took what you said with deadly seriousness and spoke the same way in return.

It is easy to give an example because something like this happened at this very dinner.

Sitting next to Mr. Pacino was a young German guy. I would guess that he was in his late twenties or early thirties. I assume he was something to do with the company that was financing the film, although afterwards nobody seemed especially sure what his role was. He did not contribute much to the conversation at first: not until we had all finished our desserts and some of the guests were looking at the list of *digestifs* and waiting for Billy to give them guidance.

Dr. Rózsa had been talking about the transformation of Munich that seemed to have taken place in the last few years. Apparently, since the city had staged the Olympic Games in 1972, money had been flooding in. Besides the ultra-modern, state-of-the-art Olympic Stadium, an entire new metro system had been constructed. Around the stadium itself, a new Olympic Village had sprung up, attracting millions of Deutschmarks from investors.

"One can only speculate," Dr. Rózsa said, "where all of this money is coming from."

"Well," said Iz, with a dark, mirthless chuckle, "let's not go too closely into *that*."

"What do you mean?" said the young German man.

Iz didn't answer at first. When he did, he spoke in a way which was somehow both diffident and emphatic: "I suspect that a lot of it is being funnelled secretly back from Switzerland," he said. "It's Nazi money, originally."

One of the older of the German financiers sighed and said, "Oh, please . . ."

The awkward silence that followed was broken by Billy.

"Mr. Diamond is of a much more cynical disposition than myself. In fact, I think he is the most cynical person I have ever met. Whereas I have a totally benevolent view of human nature. I believe wholeheartedly in the kindness and the goodness of the human race." Everybody waited for the punchline, which was clearly on its way. "However," he continued, "on a related note it always amazes me, whenever I come back to Germany, how at the end of the war all the Nazis simply disappeared in a puff of smoke."

"Of course they didn't," someone answered. "There were trials, there were prosecutions for war crimes, prison sentences . . ."

"Oh, I'm not talking about the big figures, the ringleaders. Of course they got what was coming to them. I mean the others, you know. The ordinary people. The ones who allowed all this to happen. Maybe you don't see it so much because you live here but when you come to a city like Munich from the outside you look at the older people, you know, and you think, O.K., what were you doing in 1942, '43, when all this stuff was happening, the really bad stuff?"

"Usually they say they were in the Resistance," said Iz.

"Like the man in your film," said the older financier.

Billy glanced across at him.

"My film?"

"James Cagney's assistant. The film in Berlin."

"Ah, yes." His eyes lit up. *One, Two, Three.* It was a good memory for him. A successful film.

The older German continued: "You know, this guy who is always clicking his heels, and Cagney asks him, 'What did you do in the war?' and he says he was in the underground, and Cagney says, 'You mean the Resistance,' and he says, 'No, no, I was working in the metro, I was underground the whole time, I knew nothing about what was going on,' so Cagney says, 'And I suppose you never heard of Adolf Hitler?' and he says, 'Adolf who?'"

There was laughter around the table. Billy nodded with satisfaction. It was a good scene. People remembered it. But the younger man, I noticed, did not seem to join in with the laughter.

"Maybe it takes an outsider," said the older financier, in a slightly sycophantic tone, "to show us as we really are. This is why we need art, after all. This is why we need films."

"Yes, maybe it's true," said Billy. "The secretary who's working for me while I'm here, I asked her where she lived—because I knew she came from out of town—and she told me 'Dachau.' You know, very matter-of-fact. To her, it's where she lives, it's just another name, another German town. To me—or to anyone from outside, you know—this is a name that sends a shiver down your spine. Thousands of people died in that place. To her, it's home. That's all it is."

Everyone around the table reflected silently upon the truth of this observation. Everyone except the young man who, after a few moments' pause, said: "Actually, there has been some interesting research lately . . ."

All eyes were suddenly upon him; none more keenly or glitteringly than Billy's.

". . . a lot of it coming from America, in fact—which argues that these numbers have been exaggerated. Taken out of all proportion."

"Research?" said Dr. Rózsa, the first to break the silence. "What kind of research is this?"

"Academic research, in the main. These people are not neo-Nazis. They are respected American scholars, from places like Northwestern University."

"Yes, I'm familiar," said Billy, pouring himself some brandy from a bottle which had arrived at the table, "with this movement which is aiming to deny historical reality. But I'm afraid that it doesn't fit in with my own observations. Or my own experience, for that matter."

"I read one of the books on this subject last year," said the young man. "I read it in America, of course—you cannot buy it over here. I found it rather persuasive."

Billy was now lighting a cigar.

"Can I tell you a story," he said, between puffs, "which you might also find *persuasive*?" When the young guy didn't respond, he continued: "And then, when I've told you the story, can I ask you a question? One which I would like you to answer."

Cautiously the young man nodded, and then, as more drinks were poured and more cigars and cigarettes were lit up around the table, we all settled back to hear what Billy had to say.

*

I'll remember what I can. And what he didn't tell us, or what I can't remember, I shall try to imagine.

It begins, I would think, something like this:

INT. CAFÉ. DAY.

A CAPTION reads: "BERLIN, 1933."

The camera takes in the whole interior of the café—waiters in tuxedos weaving their way between busy tables, old guys playing chess, businessmen reading newspapers, friends exchanging gossip and young couples lost in each other's company—before zooming in on one table near the window, where a boisterous group of young men are engaged in a loud discussion. The air is clouded with cigarette smoke and the steam from innumerable coffee cups.

BILLIE (V.O.)

So, here we are, in the nerve centre of the German film business between the wars. Which also means that it's the nerve centre of the whole European film business. The Romanisches Café in the Charlottenburg district of Berlin. Just look at the talent around that table. There you have Robert Siodmak, Edgar Ulmer, Fred Zinnemann—all before they went to Hollywood. Some of the best American movies you ever saw were made by these German guys. Oh, and look—there's me . . .

The young BILLIE WILDER is also sitting at this table, but he is detached from the conversation and is mainly looking out of the window. On the table in front of him is a bunch of flowers. He is thin, nervous, athletic, not so good-looking, but with a wit and energy about him that makes him attractive.

BILLIE (V.O.) (CONT'D)
Normally I'd be joining in the fun with everybody but today is different. You see, I'm looking out for someone and I'm not sure that she's going to show up, and—ah, but hold on a minute, here she comes!

A beautiful young woman, her dark hair cut into a bob beneath her cloche hat, taps on the window and waves at Billie. He waves back, gets up, grabs the flowers and is embarrassed by the joshing of his friends as he leaves the table.

FRIEND 1
Hey, Billie, don't you love us any more?

FRIEND 2
What's the matter, am I not as pretty as her?

FRIEND 3
Does this mean the whores on Kurfürstenstrasse are going out of business soon?

BILLIE
Very funny, guys. See you deadbeats later. Enjoy playing with yourselves when you get back to your shitty hotel rooms.

EXT. STREET. DAY.

Out in the street, he kisses his girlfriend (HELLA) politely on the cheek, gives her the flowers, and they head off down the street arm in arm.

EXT. PARK. DAY.

Montage of BILLIE and HELLA as they enjoy an idyllic morning in the Tiergarten, walking through the gardens, boating on the lake, and finally just lying side by side on the grass.

BILLIE (V.O.)

This was how it started with Hella. All very innocent. She was the daughter of a wealthy family, which didn't put me off her one bit, but what attracted me to her first of all was her beauty, of course, and her amazing love of life. And there was a kind of naivety about her which I also loved, which was such a relief after hanging out with all those know-it-alls in the café. Sure, they were my friends, but they were such loudmouths and braggarts. And I was the worst one of all, most of the time. The only guy I knew in the film business who wasn't like that was Emeric.

INT. OFFICE. DAY.

The Dramaturgie *office of Ufa Studios. A small but busy, thriving workspace. Secretaries hurrying back and forth with sheaves of man-uscript and, at a desk in the corner, a slightly harassed-looking young man with thinning hair. This is EMERIC PRESSBURGER, whose job is to act as an intermediary between the writers and the produc-tion office.*

BILLIE (V.O.)

We all liked Emeric, and we all had respect for the guy. He was very quiet—one of those unusual people who only spoke when he had something interesting to say. Maybe it was the Hungarian in him. He worked in the script department at Ufa, which meant that he was the go-to guy if you wanted to know if your idea had any chance of making it to the screen.

BILLIE *enters the office and* EMERIC *looks up and smiles, genuinely pleased to see him.*

EMERIC
Hey, Billie, what's going on?

BILLIE
Not so much. Look, is there any news on my script about the alcoholic? What does Hugenberg think of it?

EMERIC
It's still on his desk.

BILLIE
Can't you speed things along a bit?

EMERIC
I keep moving it to the top of the pile. That's all I can do. He's all tied up at the moment, making that comedy with Krauss.

BILLIE
With Krauss? That Nazi son of a bitch? How does someone like that even get work?

EMERIC
Soon people like that will be the *only* people who get work.

BILLIE
I'm keeping an eye on that bastard, anyway. If what's

happening at the moment gets out of control, I'm not going to forget the people like him who helped it along.

EMERIC
Well, anyway, I hear things are playing out very nicely with you and Hella.

BILLIE
Oh, you hear that, do you?

EMERIC
All the guys are talking about it.

BILLIE
We're going to Davos in a couple of weeks. Our first trip together. Skiing.

EMERIC
Just the two of you? Very nice.

BILLIE
Listen, I'm hungry. Do you want to come out for some lunch? I was going to pick up a sandwich at Steingold's.

EMERIC
Steingold's? It's closed. They went for it yesterday. The windows were smashed in and they wrote *Judengeschäft* all over the walls.

BILLIE (*horrified*)
Those bastards.

He broods over this, truly upset.

EMERIC

I know. It's not good, Billie. I don't like the way any of this is going. But look, don't let it put you off your stride with Hella. You've found a good one there. Enjoy your trip. Make the most of it.

BILLIE nods and smiles and pats him on the shoulder.

EXT. MOUNTAIN. DAY.

A ski run in Davos, Switzerland. BILLIE and HELLA are skiing down the mountain. The scene is shot in the artificial style of the time, with obvious back-projection. We see them exchange loving smiles as the ski run unfolds behind them.

They arrive at a ski lodge, come to an expert halt outside the door, unclip their skis and walk inside.

INT. SKI LODGE. DAY.

The chalet is full of skiers stopping off for hot drinks and food. BIL-LIE and HELLA sit at a wooden table eating sausages and hot potato salad and drinking mulled wine. There is a superb view of the mountains through the window behind them.

Next to their table is a wireless set which is broadcasting the latest news from Germany. BILLIE is listening closely while HELLA admires the view.

RADIO VOICE

It has been announced today that Reichspräsident von Hindenburg has appointed Herrn Adolf Hitler as the new Reichskanzler.

BILLIE shakes his head in sorrow and amazement.

BILLIE

Hella, darling, I think we are going to have to get out as soon as possible.

HELLA

Really? But the view from here is so lovely.

BILLIE

I'm not talking about this chalet. I mean we have to get out of Germany.

Dissolve to:

EXT. STREET. DAY.

BILLIE (V.O.)

A few days later, when we were back in Berlin . . .

Walking arm in arm, BILLIE and HELLA turn a corner and see a man being viciously beaten.

BILLIE (V.O.) (CONT'D)

. . . we watched them beating up an old Jew on Tauentzienstrasse in broad daylight. Nearly thirty SS men. Strong guys. Butchers. They'd spotted this old man with his hat, long whiskers and coat. They battered him mercilessly. And I was just standing there, completely helpless, with tears in my eyes and my fists clenched in my pockets.

BILLIE glances at HELLA. She is watching the assault, aghast, also tearful. They put their heads down and hurry on.

BILLIE (V.O.) (CONT'D)

The next day was the Reichstag fire. After that I knew

I had to get us both out. We packed two cases and bought two tickets to Paris. When we took the night train from Berlin Hauptbahnhof later that week, I had no idea when I'd see the city again. In fact, it would be more than ten years.

INT. TRAIN. NIGHT.

The train is crowded. BILLIE and HELLA are in a second-class compartment, trying to sleep, leaning up against each other. BILLIE is wearing one of his trademark little hats. It's uncomfortable so he takes it off, but keeps a tight grip on it.

BILLIE (V.O.)
We couldn't afford a sleeper so we sat up all night in a compartment with four other people. I was too afraid to let go of my hat. There were 1,000 marks sown into the lining.

He turns the hat over and runs his finger nervously around the inside of the rim.

EXT. RAILWAY STATION. DAY.

Paris, the Gare de l'Est. The train has just pulled into the platform. Amidst clouds of steam, the passengers disembark—among them BILLIE and HELLA. It is rather windy, and at one point BILLIE's hat blows off. In a panic he chases after it and just about manages to retrieve it.

Once through the ticket barrier, they look around, bewildered and tired from their long journey. BILLIE fishes a piece of paper from his pocket and looks at it.

EXT. STREET. DAY.

BILLIE (V.O.)
I'd been given the address of a hotel on the Rue de Saïgon, close to the Arc de Triomphe. It was where all the German refugees used to stay.

They walk towards the hotel down a bland, characterless residential street. The hotel itself is shabby and uninviting. Above the entrance we can read its name: "HOTEL ANSONIA." They go inside.

INT. HOTEL ROOM. DAY.

A third-floor room, sparsely furnished. It looks out over the narrow street directly into the building opposite. BILLIE and HELLA enter the room, look around without enthusiasm and put down their cases. HELLA throws herself onto the bed, then gets up again with a cry of pain. She pulls back the sheets and sees that one of the springs in the mattress is sticking out.

BILLIE
Well, it will do for now. We'll find something better in a day or two.

Fade out. Then fade in:

INT. HOTEL ROOM. DAY.

CAPTION: "One year later."

HELLA is lying on the same bed in the same room, smoking, playing patience and looking bored out of her mind. BILLIE is sitting at the little table by the window, typing a script. After a few moments he swears, tears the paper out of the roller, scrunches it up and throws it over his shoulder without looking. He is aiming for the waste basket, but actually the ball of paper hits HELLA on the head. She hurls it back.

HELLA

Do you mind?

BILLIE

I'm sorry. I hate to interrupt you when you're doing something so important.

HELLA

Just as important as writing one of your lousy scripts.

BILLIE

This "lousy script," as you call it, is going to make us—

The door opens and a young man puts his head around. (It is the composer FRANZ WAXMAN, in fact. One day, far in the future, he will write the score for Sunset Boulevard.*)*

FRANZ

Hey, Billie, are you coming out to the Strasbourg?

BILLIE

Who's going?

FRANZ

The usual guys—Peter, Friedrich . . .

HELLA (*getting up*)

Sure, why not?

FRANZ (*after a beat*)

You can come too if you want.

INT. CAFÉ. DAY.

The Strasbourg is a classic Parisian brasserie. BILLIE and his fellow German exiles are crowded around a table playing dominoes—except that they can barely see the pieces through the haze of cigarette smoke.

BILLIE (V.O.)

Now, if you recognize some of these faces, it's because they are basically the same guys I used to hang out with at the Romanisches, back in Berlin. Here we all are, having the same arguments, pursuing the same line of work—we just happen to have changed cities. See that little dark-haired guy there? Peter Lorre. You saw him in *The Maltese Falcon*, probably. See the other guy, with the sensitive mouth, and the nose like a pickle? You won't recognize him, but you've all heard his songs—"Falling in Love Again," "Isn't it Romantic." *(He sings a snatch.)* That one's my favourite, actually. Maybe I might even use it in a picture one day.

The game of dominoes is heating up. It is now essentially a duel between BILLIE and PETER LORRE, sitting opposite each other. HELLA is rather pointedly sitting beside LORRE, with her arm through his, looking at his pieces and advising him.

At the next table, a young, serious-looking COMPOSER is trying to work on his score, with some sheets of manuscript paper laid out on the table in front of him. The loudness of the Germans is putting him off, and he keeps giving them angry glances.

BILLIE (V.O.) (CONT'D)

Now *him* I don't recognize. Obviously some highly strung composer trying to write his second symphony and looking down his nose at these vulgar Germans who all want to work in the movies and never stop shouting at the tops of their voices.

RÓZSA (V.O.)
What do you mean, you don't recognize him? Billy,
that was me.

BILLIE (V.O.)
It was? You were in Paris then?

RÓZSA (V.O.)
Of course. Where else would a composer want to be?
For a while I used to go to the Strasbourg most days to
work. In fact, the only reason I stopped was because you
people were so damn *loud.*

*The noise of the dominoes game reaches a crescendo. Furious,
RÓZSA sweeps up his manuscript paper and pencils and storms out.
On his way, he glares at BILLIE one more time. BILLIE returns the
glare and, as soon as RÓZSA's back is safely turned, thumbs his nose
at him.*

*Then he turns his attention to the game again, just as HELLA col-
lects up some of PETER LORRE's pieces and places them on the
table in a final, winning move. The spectators cheer wildly. BILLIE
gazes at the table in disbelief. HELLA gives him a triumphant look.
BILLIE tips over his remaining pieces and rises from the table, putting his coat on.*

BILLIE
All right, I'm out of here.

EXT. STREET. DAY.

*BILLIE is walking through the streets of Paris, each street taking him
into sleazier and sleazier districts. As he passes one particularly cheap
hotel, a familiar figure comes out of the doorway and they almost
bump into each other.*

BILLIE

Emeric!

EMERIC

Hello, Billie. How are you keeping?

BILLIE

Not so bad.

EMERIC

Going for a little walk? Nice to get out of your hotel room once in a while, isn't it?

BILLIE

It's good to see you. Why don't you ever come down to the Strasbourg now and again, to see the old gang?

EMERIC

Oh, you know—I prefer quieter places. Hey, I heard your news—you sold a script to Hollywood! That's fantastic.

BILLIE

You heard that already?

EMERIC

Sure, it's all over town. Does this mean you'll be going to the States?

BILLIE

Yes. They sent me a ticket. I'm sailing on the *Aquitania.* First class.

EMERIC

When will you leave?

BILLIE

She sails in ten days, from Southampton. I'm leaving Paris next week. A few days in London first.

EMERIC

Well, it couldn't happen to a . . . more talented guy.

BILLIE

You almost said "nicer."

EMERIC (*laughing*)

Almost. Where are you heading, by the way? Maybe we can walk together.

BILLIE

I was going to the Avenue Wagram.

EMERIC

Really? Are you sure you want to go there? (*Lowers voice.*) It's where all the prostitutes hang out.

BILLIE says nothing. Realization dawns.

EMERIC (CONT'D)

Oh, I see.

They begin walking together.

EMERIC (CONT'D)

But look, I have to ask you—why do you bother with . . . those women, when you've got someone like Hella? She's such a catch, Billie. Every guy I know is crazy about her.

BILLIE

What can I say? Home cooking is fine, but every once in a while a man likes to eat out.

EMERIC absorbs this remark, then suddenly stops and looks at BILLIE earnestly.

EMERIC

You are taking her to Hollywood with you, aren't you?

BILLIE

They only sent me one ticket.

EMERIC

How long will you be gone?

BILLIE (*walking on*)

It's a one-way ticket.

EMERIC

But she does *know*, doesn't she? Billie, you have told her that you're leaving?

BILLIE

You have to find the right moment for these things. It has to be the right time, and the right place.

EMERIC

Well, I don't think that place is going to be the Avenue Wagram.

Disappointed in his friend, he turns and walks away. BILLIE watches as he leaves.

EXT. AVENUE WAGRAM. DAY.

BILLIE *swaggers along the street, each doorway occupied by a different prostitute. They all seem to know him. Finally he links arms with one and they disappear into the entrance of a seedy hotel. It's a scene straight out of his film* Irma La Douce.

> BILLIE (V.O.)
> I know, I know. I was a jerk back in those days. Young and full of appetite and too stupid to see the value of what I already had, right under my nose. As for finding the right time and place, I found it, sure enough—five minutes before I left for England.

INT. HOTEL ROOM. DAY.

BILLIE *is standing in the doorway with his suitcase.* HELLA *is lying on the bed, with her back towards him. He approaches her and tries to kiss her goodbye. But she doesn't turn. He kisses her tenderly on the back of the neck, but she merely stares out of the window, her eyes full of tears, which* BILLIE *doesn't see.*

Getting no response, he turns and leaves, closing the door behind him. A few seconds later it opens, and HELLA *comes after him down the corridor.*

> HELLA
> You forgot this.

She hands him his little hat. He takes it from her, they look into each other's eyes and then for a few moments they kiss passionately. Then they break apart.

INT. BOARDING HOUSE, LONDON. DAY.

It is an attic room, small but comfortable, with a tiny window looking out towards Hyde Park and the Royal Albert Hall. BILLIE stands at the window, gazing out at the view.

BILLIE (V.O.)

I did not stay in London for long, on that occasion. Three days, four days, something like that. When I came back, at the end of the war, I stayed a few weeks. And when I came again in the 1960s, to make *The Private Life of Sherlock Holmes*, I stayed almost a year. But those three or four days, my last days in Europe before leaving for Hollywood, made a strong impression.

He puts on his shoes, puts on his coat, picks up his hat.

BILLIE (V.O.) (CONT'D)

London was nothing like Berlin, nothing like Paris. I felt an unexpected kind of security there. Perhaps it was because of that island mentality, you know? These strange people, with their strange way of pronouncing words and their strange codes of behaviour and their strange class system . . . I felt you could rely on them. That they would not do anything stupid. That they would stand by you in a crisis. I never had that feeling in Paris.

He leaves the room and descends the stairs to street level. There are many, many flights of stairs. The boarding house gets less and less shabby the further down he comes.

BILLIE (V.O.) (CONT'D)

I didn't know a word of the language, and barely spoke to anyone while I was there. I bought a few novels to read on the crossing, thinking I could maybe start learning that way. In many ways, I felt less at home in

London than I ever felt in America. But still, I had the sense that, if Britain stayed strong, then there was still a chance that Europe might be saved, and . . .

EXT. STREET, KENSINGTON, LONDON. DAY.

BILLIE *steps out of the boarding house onto Queen's Gate. Standing on the steps, he puts his hat on. It feels a bit strange. He takes it off again, turns it upside down and looks inside. There is something folded into the lining. He slides a finger inside and pulls out a sheaf of franc notes—hundreds of them. There is also a note, which reads:*

"Billie, take care of yourself—H x."

BILLIE (V.O.)
. . . and all would be right with the world.

He puts the money into his coat pocket, puts his hat back on and wipes his eyes.

Then, in long shot, we see him walking away from the boarding-house entrance, north towards Hyde Park. Finally his figure exits the frame. The camera rests a while on the outline of the boarding house, this fine old Georgian building, six storeys high, rising up into the blue sky, timeless and imperturbable.

EXT. STREET, KENSINGTON, LONDON. DAY.

CAPTION: *"Eleven Years Later."*

BILLY *(his name now Americanized) is standing in the same street, opposite the boarding house. Or rather, opposite where the boarding house used to be. Now, there is just a huge pile of rubble. All around it, the buildings are shattered, half-destroyed. A gang of boys roam around this impromptu playground, climbing over the piles of bricks, the roof beams and girders sticking out grotesquely like broken bones.*

BILLY (*to himself*)
My God . . . What happened here?

BILLY looks different now. He has lost his youthful jauntiness, to be replaced by a more discreet kind of swagger. He has the look of a man who has achieved—or is on the verge of achieving—some eminence in his chosen field. His clothes are expensive (except for his hat, which looks more or less identical to the one he was wearing all those years ago). The cigarette box from which he now extracts a cigarette looks expensive, too—solid silver, perhaps?

After spending a few more astonished moments looking at the bomb site that used to be his boarding house, he walks on.

INT. CONNAUGHT HOTEL, MAYFAIR, LONDON. NIGHT.

A weary-looking BILLY trudges in, an hour or two later. The CONCIERGE nods at him.

CONCIERGE
Good evening, Colonel Wilder.

BILLY

Good evening.

INT. HOTEL ROOM. NIGHT.

BILLY is lying on the bed, staring up at the ceiling and smoking.

BILLY (V.O.)

Yes, that's right—you did hear correctly. "Colonel

Wilder," of the United States Army, or to give myself my full title, Colonel Billy Wilder, Production Chief for the Film, Theater and Music Control Section of the Psychological Warfare Division of the Supreme Headquarters Allied Expeditionary Force. Quite a mouthful. So let me explain how *that* happened.

I'd been in Hollywood more than a decade. Writing scripts, at first, and then, when I got sick of directors lousing up my ideas, directing them myself. So far, I had directed four pictures. The third, *Double Indemnity*, was pretty good, and did pretty well. Then, Brackett and I— that was the name of the guy I was writing the scripts with, Charles Brackett, a nice man, even if he was a Republican—we decided to make a film out of this book, *The Lost Weekend*. It was a tough story, a story about a man with a serious drinking problem. Not really what you might call a crowd-pleaser. Now, the picture was finished, and we had just held a few previews, and they'd been a disaster. The audience couldn't handle it. They'd never seen anything like it, and some of them even seemed to think it was a comedy and they'd been laughing at it. The studio was threatening not to release the picture at all. So my career, brief as it was, was prob-ably over. Right now, making that picture looked like being one of the worst decisions of my life.

In Hollywood, the war had seemed a long way away. Of course, I'd been following the news, and I knew what had been going on. Enough to know that I'd made the right decision to get out of Europe when I did. Some people called me pessimistic at the time. Well, as I said to them afterwards, it was the pessimists who ended up in Beverly Hills with swimming pools in their back gar-dens, and the optimists who ended up in the concentra-tion camps. So, yes, I had saved my own skin. But what about the rest of my family? This was the thing that had

been stopping me from sleeping for the last few years—
or if I did manage to sleep, giving me nightmares. And I
mean real nightmares. The kind that make you sit up in
bed covered in sweat. My father had died some time ago,
when I was living in Berlin. My mother, though—why
had I not heard anything from my mother? Was she still
in Vienna? Supposedly. But I hadn't heard from her in
years. Nothing. I'd been writing to her, but the letters
were never answered. I'd been phoning her, but the
phone was never picked up.

I suppose the truth is that, deep down, I already knew
what must have happened to her.

One day towards the end of the war I got a call from
someone I'd never heard of, a radio commentator called
Davis, Elmer Davis, who now worked for the Office of
War Information. He'd been reading a story about
Brackett and me in the newspaper, and from this he'd
picked up that not only was I a film guy, but also I spoke
German and I'd lived in Berlin for a few years and I
knew pretty much everything there was to know about
the German film business. Especially the people who
had been part of it before the war. And he said that he
had a plan for me. He said that they needed someone on
the ground out there in Germany. They needed someone
to help the Germans put their film business back on its
feet and most of all to make sure they weren't giving any
work to Nazis. And maybe also to make a little picture,
a short picture, about the camps. So that the ordinary
Germans knew what had been going on, what they'd
been part of.

Well, I jumped at the idea. Actually, it could not have
come at a better moment for me. Because of this lousy
picture about the alcoholic guy the studio bosses weren't
talking to me. It felt like I had screwed up all my chances
in Hollywood and it was time to get out for a while.

Maybe Brackett and I needed a break from each other as well. We had been a little bit getting on each other's nerves. But more than that, it was a way of going back to Europe again. I needed to do that now. I needed to know what had happened to my family. I needed to find out the truth about my mother. And maybe this was the way to do it.

First of all, anyway, they wanted me in London. I was going to stay in London for a couple of weeks and do whatever the Brits asked me to do. It was all a little bit clandestine, a little bit hush-hush. I wasn't sure what came next. I figured that I'd find out in the morning.

And that just about brings you up to date. Sorry for the long explanation. The critics always did say there was too much voiceover in my pictures.

EXT. HOTEL, MAYFAIR, LONDON. DAY.

The next morning. BILLY walks down the hotel steps, smartly dressed. A car is waiting for him. A CHAUFFEUR opens the rear door and helps him inside.

INT. CAR. DAY.

They are driving along the Embankment. Outside, through the window, we can see half-destroyed buildings, rubble and bomb sites everywhere.

CHAUFFEUR (*cockney accent*)
So you've come from America, have you, sir?

BILLY
That's right. I haven't seen London for more than ten years.

CHAUFFEUR

You'll notice one or two changes, I dare say.

BILLY

The destruction . . . It's incredible.

CHAUFFEUR

Oh yes. Jerry hit us pretty hard, some nights.

BILLY

We knew it was bad. But seeing it like this . . . It brings it home to you.

CHAUFFEUR

Well, we got through it in the end. You have to fight back, don't you? Otherwise we'd all be speaking German by now. No offence.

BILLY

None taken.

CHAUFFEUR

You make films, is that right, sir?

BILLY

Correct.

CHAUFFEUR

Anything I would have seen?

BILLY

The last one was called *Double Indemnity*.

CHAUFFEUR

Passed me by, I'm afraid. I like a good Will Hay or

George Formby myself. Something that gives you a laugh on a Saturday night. Takes your mind off things. You should ask them to be in one of your films.

                    BILLY
I'll bear it in mind.

The car pulls up outside an imposing office in Bloomsbury. A sign on the wall reads: "MINISTRY OF INFORMATION."

                 CHAUFFEUR
Here we are, sir.

INT. WAITING ROOM. DAY.

Billy sits on a bench in an impersonal antechamber, part of a somewhat decaying Victorian building. He taps his fingers nervously. This is not his usual milieu.

A door opens and a SECRETARY puts her head round.

                 SECRETARY
Colonel Wilder? Mr. Woodcock will see you now.

INT. OFFICE. DAY.

MR. WOODCOCK is about Billy's age, but there the resemblance ends. He is not the brightest of men. His accent suggests he might be the product of several generations' worth of inbreeding among the upper classes.

                 WOODCOCK
   I'm awfully sorry about this, but the fact is that Mr. Trubshaw, who was meant to be seeing you this morning, is stuck at home with the most shocking cold. They

haven't told me much about the purpose of your visit, I'm afraid.

BILLY
They haven't told me much, either. In fact, they haven't told me anything at all.

WOODCOCK
What, nothing?

BILLY
I was told it was top secret.

WOODCOCK
Yes, that's what *I* was told.

BILLY
Somebody must know the secret.

WOODCOCK
Hmm . . .

He thinks for a moment, then goes next door into the SECRETARY's office.

WOODCOCK (CONT'D)
Janet, do *you* know why Colonel Wilder has been requested to come to London?

SECRETARY
I only know what Mr. Trubshaw was told by Mr. Webster, sir.

WOODCOCK
Ah! Now we're getting somewhere.

SECRETARY

He was told that Colonel Wilder was here to advise on the kind of films to be produced in Britain for consumption in Germany after the war, sir.

WOODCOCK

Capital. Thank you, Janet.

He returns to his own office.

WOODCOCK (*sotto voce, confidentially*)

Apparently, you're here to advise on the kind of films to be produced in Britain for consumption in Germany after the war.

BILLY

I see.

WOODCOCK

Does that sound the sort of thing that's . . . up your alley, as it were?

BILLY

Well, to be honest with you, I don't think there's very much to say on the subject. My advice would be pretty simple. Make good films. Make the very best you can.

WOODCOCK (*writing this down*)

I see. Jolly good.

BILLY

Well, that didn't take very long, did it?

He sees that MR. WOODCOCK looks crestfallen, and takes pity on him.

BILLY (CONT'D)
Something that could be helpful . . .

WOODCOCK
Yes?

BILLY
. . . might be if you gave me a list.

WOODCOCK
A list? Oh yes, we have lots of lists. I can get you any
number of lists. What sort of list?

BILLY
With the names of all the most important British film-
makers.

WOODCOCK (*writing furiously*)
Righty-ho. That sounds an excellent way to proceed.

BILLY
Then perhaps I could . . . expand on my ideas, you
know . . .

WOODCOCK
Expand on them, yes, certainly . . .

BILLY
And perhaps write something a little bit longer.
Something in the form of a . . . memo?

WOODCOCK
(*almost speechless with admiration*)
A *memo*! Gosh, that would be terrific. What a simply

corking idea! A memo would . . . Well, it could be the answer to all our problems, don't you think?

BILLY

I think we should see how it goes.

There is a knock on the door, and a nervous young man—very young, about nineteen or twenty—enters the office. A trainee of some sort. His name is THOMAS FOLEY.

WOODCOCK

Yes, Foley?

FOLEY

The films have arrived, sir. The footage from the camps. They're outside on a trolley.

WOODCOCK

Oh yes. They did say those would be coming today. Well, I suppose you'd better . . . put them somewhere.

FOLEY

There are about twenty reels, sir.

WOODCOCK

Twenty? Gosh. What's on them, exactly? Did Mr. Trubshaw say what he wanted us to do with them?

FOLEY

They show scenes from the concentration camps as they were being liberated by the Allies, sir. Very disturbing, I understand. I think the idea was to have them viewed, and then used as the basis for a documentary film, to be assembled by some . . . competent person.

A short silence. WOODCOCK is clearly flummoxed.

> **BILLY**
> Perhaps I could help with that.

> **WOODCOCK**
> Well, that's awfully kind of you, Colonel, but I think this might be a task that calls for a professional film director of some sort.

> **BILLY** (*to FOLEY*)
> If you have any kind of projection room, would you take me to it, please. I would like to get started on this.

INT. PROJECTION ROOM. DAY.

BILLY is sitting in the centre of a row of seats, watching the screen intently. The camera is on his face, while in the background, in the projection booth, we can make out the figure of FOLEY.

There is silence, except for the whirring of the projector. BILLY watches. The horror of what he sees has numbed his face, turned it into an expressionless mask.

INT. PUB. NIGHT.

The end of a long, terrible day. BILLY and FOLEY are sitting at a small table, pints of beer in front of them. All around them is chatter and laughter—the routine sounds of people enjoying themselves in a British pub.

They want to talk about anything other than what they have just seen.

> **BILLY**
> I just can't get used to British beer.

FOLEY
It's an acquired taste, definitely.

BILLY
Well, I'm trying to acquire it.

FOLEY
Cheers. "Drink it while it's hot," as they say.

BILLY
That's good. I'll remember that.

They drink.

BILLY (CONT'D)
And why do they call this place the Sherlock Holmes?

FOLEY
Just cashing in, I think.

BILLY
Because I don't remember Holmes or Watson going
to a pub in any of the stories. And I read them all.

FOLEY
Me too.

BILLY
You are a Holmes fan?

FOLEY
Absolutely.

BILLY
The first Holmes story I ever read was *The Sign of*

Four. And in the very first paragraph he is injecting himself with cocaine! Amazing. I was hooked.

FOLEY

Followed by one of his best pieces of deduction—when he looks at Dr. Watson's pocket watch and works out that he had a brother who drank himself to death.

BILLY

That's very good, yes. Another moment I like very much, in the *Cardboard Box* story, is when Watson has been staring into space for a few minutes and suddenly Holmes interrupts and tells him exactly what he has been thinking. You know, he can tell that he has been thinking about the stupidity of war, what is the phrase, "the sadness and horror and stupid waste of life," something like that.

FOLEY

Yes. A remarkable passage. You think Holmes was a pacifist?

WILDER

That I don't know. But I'm pretty sure that what we saw today proves he was right. (*A beat.*) How many of those reels did we get through?

FOLEY

Nine.

WILDER

So tomorrow we might finish.

FOLEY

Another batch arrived this afternoon. And there will be more.

BILLY takes this in, and sips his drink. FOLEY searches for something in his pocket.

FOLEY (CONT'D)
By the way, I've got your list.

BILLY
What list?

FOLEY
They told me you wanted a list of the most important film-makers.

BILLY
Ah, yes. Thank you.

He takes the piece of paper and looks through the names. One catches his eye.

BILLY (CONT'D)
Emeric—of course. You know this guy, Mr. Pressburger?

FOLEY
Can't say I do. But I'm sure we can put you in touch with him, if you like. (*He finishes his drink.*) I suppose I'd better be on my way.

BILLY
Oh—I was hoping we might have some dinner together.

Foley reacts, pleased and flattered.

FOLEY
Of course. Can I get you another one of these first?

BILLY looks at his beer glass, still two thirds full, and shakes his head.

> BILLY
> Double Scotch, please.

INT. CONNAUGHT HOTEL, MAYFAIR, LONDON. NIGHT.

A slightly drunk-looking BILLY trudges in, two or three hours later. The CONCIERGE nods at him.

> CONCIERGE
> Evening, Colonel Wilder.

> BILLY
> Good evening.

> CONCIERGE
> There was a letter for you.

He reaches into a pigeonhole and hands him a large, official-looking envelope.

> BILLY (*reads*)
> "Attorney at Law." (*He puts it in his pocket.*) Probably my wife, asking for a divorce.

EXT. REGENT'S PARK. DAY.

BILLY and EMERIC are walking together.

> BILLY
> It was my wife. Asking for a divorce.

EMERIC

Oh, Billy, I'm sorry.

BILLY

I guess I had it coming.

EMERIC

Do you have children?

BILLY

A daughter. There was a son, as well. A twin brother.
But he died.

EMERIC

Will you fight for custody?

BILLY

No.

*They walk on and find a bench by the edge of a lake, where they sit
down.*

EMERIC

It was a wonderful surprise to hear from you. How
long are you staying?

BILLY

Another week, maybe two. The strange thing is, now
that I've signed up for this thing, nobody seems to know
what to do with me. The guy I met on the first day was
so vague it was incredible. If that was the Ministry of
Information they didn't seem to have much of it.

EMERIC

The British are like that. They muddle through. I

don't know how they manage it, but somehow it always seems to work out for them.

BILLY

They built this amazing empire by muddling through?

EMERIC

I suspect that if you dig deep enough into the national character you find that underneath it all there is a core of steel. But they do their best to hide it.

BILLY

Well, I can't figure them out. I've been working with this young guy, his name is Foley, and he seems O.K. Reliable. But with the rest of them, I just don't get it.

EMERIC

They are a strange and contradictory people. Sometimes I think the whole reason I'm making these films with Mickey is to try and crack the puzzle. The puzzle of the British.

BILLY

I don't know if you'll ever succeed with that, but you've got some good pictures out of it at least. *Colonel Blimp* was . . . Well, you don't need me to tell you.

EMERIC

And you! You've taken America by storm! What an achievement!

BILLY

Ten years it took me, and it hasn't been easy, I can promise you. And now I've probably thrown it all away.

EMERIC
Nonsense. You always were a pessimist.

BILLY
I'm a realist, not a pessimist. Anyway, if you could see
what I've been watching these last few days, in that little
screening room, you wouldn't call me that. I'm telling
you, these last few years in Germany, humanity has sunk
to such depths . . . You could never have imagined it.
Unbelievable.

EMERIC
Have you been officially commissioned to make a film
yet? About the camps?

BILLY
Not yet.

EMERIC
Then why put yourself through that? Why sit in that
room all day watching these scenes of . . . horror?

BILLY
I have to.

EMERIC
No, you don't. There's no need to punish yourself
that way.

BILLY
I'm looking for my mother.

Emeric is shocked into silence for a moment.

EMERIC

What?

BILLY

My mother. I haven't heard from her in three years.
My mother, my grandmother and my stepfather, to be
absolutely precise.

EMERIC

But—you're looking at these images every day, these
images of corpses, of emaciated bodies, and that's who
you're hoping to see?

BILLY

"Hoping" is not really the word I would use. (*A pause.
Then, passionately:*) I have to find out what happened to
her. I can't live the rest of my life without knowing. You
can understand that?

EMERIC

Of course I can understand. (*A pause.*) I can understand because I don't know where my mother is either.

Slowly EMERIC rises to his feet.

EMERIC (CONT'D)

There are a lot of us in the same situation.

He looks at his watch.

EMERIC (CONT'D)

I have to go.

They begin to walk together by the side of the lake.

BILLY

Look, when I have to write this memo about the films
Brits should be making after the war, I'm just going to
tell them they should all be written by Emeric
Pressburger.

EMERIC

That's very kind, thank you. Where are you going
next?

BILLY

Germany. Bad Homburg. Maybe I'll stop off in Paris
for a few days on the way.

EMERIC

A sentimental journey?

BILLY

Not really.

EMERIC

Oh. I thought you might be paying a call on Hella.

BILLY

Hella? She's still in Paris?

EMERIC

Oh yes. I had a letter from her a few weeks ago. She
married a Portuguese. Wealthy gentleman, by the sound
of it.

BILLY

My poverty was always a source of disappointment to
her. If only she could have waited a few years . . .

EMERIC

She wrote a very evocative description of their house. Out in one of the most opulent suburbs, I believe. There is a long white wall along the street, apparently, forming the border of their garden, topped by terracotta tiles, and with a door in the wall, surrounded by ivy and painted pale blue . . .

BILLY

Can you send me her address?

EMERIC

I'm not sure that's a good idea. (*Then, after a beat:*) Of course.

EXT. VICTORIA STATION. DAY.

Billy is about to board the boat train for Paris. He is drinking coffee at the station café with Foley. The air is thick with steam from the trains.

BILLY

Nice of you to see me off.

FOLEY

Not at all, Colonel Wilder. I only hope your time in Germany is productive.

BILLY

I'm sure it will be. Finally, as Holmes would say to Watson, "The game is afoot."

FOLEY

It's been a privilege working with you, I must say.

BILLY

I accept the compliment. Modesty never was my strong point.

FOLEY

"My dear Watson, I cannot agree with those who rank modesty among the virtues. To the logician all things should be seen exactly as they are, and to underestimate one's self is as much a departure from truth as to exaggerate one's own powers."

BILLY (*laughs*)

"The Adventure of the Greek Interpreter." One of the very best.

FOLEY

When all this . . . hideousness is behind us, you should make a Sherlock Holmes film of your own.

BILLY

You know, that's not a bad suggestion. I have an idea for an original story. It concerns the Loch Ness monster, and a tiny submarine which is operated by a crew of midgets.

FOLEY

Sounds fascinating. I shall be the first in the queue to see it.

BILLY (*drinking up*)

I'd better go.

FOLEY

Good luck, Colonel. And *Auf Wiedersehen*.

They shake hands.

EXT. STREET, PARIS. DAY.

A quiet suburban street. A still, sunny afternoon. Billy walks down the street, a scrap of paper in his hand, and his old hat on his head—the one he wore when leaving Paris.

> EMERIC (V.O.)
> There is a long white wall along the street, forming the border of their garden, with a door in the wall, surrounded by ivy and painted pale blue . . .

Billy has reached just such a wall, and just such a door. There is a small golden bell by the side of the door, and after taking a deep breath, he rings it.

EXT. GARDEN. DAY.

BILLY and HELLA sit drinking mint tea at a small table in a shaded corner of her lovely, well-kept garden. A fountain plays in the background.

HELLA, still beautiful, nonetheless seems to have aged more drastically than BILLY since they last saw each other.

> BILLY
> You're in love with this guy?

> HELLA
> Under the circumstances, Billy, I don't think that question is very appropriate. (*A beat.*) Our marriage is . . . very satisfactory. It was not a love marriage, at first, maybe it isn't now, but it could become one.

BILLY

So you married him to protect yourself. Well, I can't
say I blame you.

HELLA

Even on that basis, it was only a limited success. They
sent me to a camp.

BILLY reacts: shocked, distressed.

HELLA (CONT'D)

Luckily it was not one of the worst. I survived, as you
can see. (*A beat.*) It's all very well you looking so horrified. *You* were my protector, I thought, when we first
came here. But you abandoned that role. (*A beat.*) And
it's no use you looking jealous, either. What were you
expecting when I agreed to see you, a quick fuck in the
afternoon? Not my style, I'm afraid. And you are a married man, I believe.

BILLY

Judith and I are getting divorced.

HELLA

On what grounds?

BILLY

"Extreme cruelty."

HELLA

That figures. (*A beat.*) You did me a favour, in fact. I
don't think I was ever cut out to be a Hollywood wife.
What I have now suits me very well. And you were
always going to be a hotshot somewhere or other, so . . .

BILLY

I couldn't have done it without you, Hella.

HELLA

Oh, come on. No sentimentality, please.

BILLY

I mean it. (*He takes off his hat.*) Don't you remember what you put inside here? In the lining?

HELLA

Don't tell me you're going to offer a repayment. With ten per cent interest.

BILLY

I can afford it now, you know.

HELLA

Once you're in Germany, get the army to give you a couple of days' leave, and spend that money on a trip to Vienna. Don't give up on your mother, Billy. Do everything you can to find her.

INT. OFFICE, US ARMY COMPOUND, BAD HOMBURG. DAY.

BILLY (V.O.)

A few days later I arrived in Bad Homburg, and was introduced to my commanding officer. Unlike the people I had met in London, he actually seemed to know what he wanted from me.

BILLY is sitting in a very different office to the one where he met Mr. Woodcock at the Ministry of Information: this one is improvised, rough and ready, and forms part of a large compound of

wooden bungalows. An imposing, confident-looking officer—
COLONEL PALEY—paces the room as he gives instructions.

PALEY

The reels of film you requested to be sent on from
England have already arrived. And we have plenty more
for you to view here. I appreciate that you want to have
this information film completed as soon as possible. But
before you do that, there are some people we want you
to interview. Actors, directors, producers. We need to
know what they got up to in the years before the war,
and where their . . . sympathies lie these days. If there's
anyone you recognize from your own time in Berlin, just
let us know.

EXT. FARMHOUSE. DAY.

An isolated farmhouse, deep in the heart of the German countryside.
BILLY emerges from the house and shakes hands with the owner,
who gives him a basket of milk, butter and eggs. BILLY gets into a
jeep and drives off.

BILLY (V.O.)

There were other important matters to deal with, however, such as making sure that we had adequate supplies
of acceptable food. Army rations I did not regard as
acceptable. However, there were always deals which could
be done. I came into contact with a lot of ordinary
Germans in this way. But funnily enough, in all these
encounters, I never met a single Nazi. Most of these people seemed to barely recognize the name of Adolf Hitler,
and if they did, they insisted that they had opposed him or
even fought against him from the very beginning. When I
started interviewing some of my old colleagues from the
film business, however, it was a different matter . . .

INT. BILLY'S ARMY OFFICE. DAY.

BILLY (V.O.)

One of the first people I found myself face to face with, for instance, was my old friend Werner Krauss, who had made such a good living for himself with all those terrible portrayals of evil Jews in the propaganda films of the 1930s.

KRAUSS is sitting in BILLY's office, squirming in his seat as he tries to justify himself. BILLY has a form in duplicate open on the desk in front of him.

KRAUSS

The thing is, Billy, of course everything got out of hand as the war progressed, but at the beginning, the Führer had some good ideas.

BILLY

Go on.

KRAUSS

He understood the German people, and he understood that many of them had . . . legitimate concerns about the influence of the Jews. Of course, that doesn't excuse—

BILLY

I don't think we need to proceed with this interview any further, Krauss. (*He looks at the form on his desk.*) You are applying, according to this, to make a performance of the Passion Play in Oberammergau later this year. You intend to take the role of Jesus Christ—is that right?

KRAUSS
Yes.

BILLY
Well, I don't see that there will be any problem with
that.

KRAUSS is visibly relieved. He is about to say thank you.

BILLY (CONT'D)
On one condition, that is. When you come to the crucifixion scene, I want you to use real nails.

KRAUSS reacts. He can hardly believe what he's just heard.

BILLY (CONT'D)
Now get the hell out of my office. I will do everything in
my power to make sure you never work in Germany again.

INT. CINEMA. DAY.

*A film is showing. The camera is on the audience, who are watching
in silent horror, flinching occasionally. The narration comes to an end
and the grim music swells to its climax.*

BILLY (V.O.)
After a few weeks we had a rough assembly of the film
about the camps. We called it *Death Mills*. We screened
it for a test audience in Würzburg.

PALEY (V.O.)
And what did they make of it?

INT. OFFICE, US ARMY COMPOUND, BAD HOM-
BURG. DAY.

BILLY is reporting to COLONEL PALEY on the reception of the film.

BILLY

I don't know. They said nothing. We gave them all preview cards and pencils, but not one of them filled in the card.

PALEY

Not one?

BILLY

Not one. But they all stole the pencils.

PALEY thinks about this for a moment.

PALEY

You know, Billy, it's too soon. These people are in shock. Their country has been under attack for six years. Bombs have been raining down on them. And then to confront them with this horror, something which they had no knowledge of but which implicates them all. We should wait some months before screening it again. Perhaps even a year or more.

BILLY

Respectfully, sir, I disagree. It should be screened in every cinema in Germany, and they should be made to watch it.

PALEY

Made? How do you do that?

BILLY

No film, no ration card. No ration card, no bread. We give them no choice.

PALEY stares at him. He has never heard such passion in BILLY's voice before.

EXT. BERLIN. DAY.

From above, we see the shadow of a plane as it flies over the shattered city. It's the same image as the opening shot of Wilder's film A Foreign Affair.

> BILLY (V.O.)
> Well, I never got my way about that. But I did get permission to spend a few weeks in Berlin. As we flew into the city that used to be my home, I couldn't believe my eyes. It was in ruins.

EXT. STREET, BERLIN. DAY.
Billy is being driven along in an army jeep. He looks left and right, searching for landmarks he might recognize. Nothing.

> BILLY (V.O.)
> The Romanisches Café? Gone. The Ufa Writers' Building on Friedrichstrasse? Gone. Ruins everywhere, and people still scattered amongst them, trying to scratch a living like animals. It was one of the hottest summers in years, and the city stank. Stank of people dying. Stank of corpses.

EXT. STREET, VIENNA. DAY.

BILLY is standing outside number 7 Fleischmarkt, the apartment building where he used to live with his mother. A woman emerges from the doorway and he begins to talk to her, questioning her urgently.

BILLY (V.O.)
Some time that summer I visited Vienna, too. I spoke
to my mother's friends, her neighbours . . .

Their conversation quickly over, the woman shakes her head and hur-
ries on.

INT. OFFICE. DAY.

Billy is questioning a bureaucrat, who is looking through a ledger of
names.

BILLY (V.O.)
. . . I questioned all the relevant authorities, got them
to search through the records . . .

The man closes the ledger and shakes his head.

BILLY (V.O.) (CONT'D)
. . . But my mother and my grandmother and my stepfather had vanished. Nobody could say what had
become of them. Someone had spirited them into thin
air, and there was nothing left. I never saw my mother
again. Never found a single trace of her.

INT. PROJECTION ROOM, US ARMY COMPOUND,
BAD HOMBURG. DAY.

The camera is on BILLY's face as he stares intently at the flickering
screen.

BILLY (V.O.)
I only had a few more days left in Germany, and my
picture was finished, but still the reels of film kept coming
in. And still I couldn't stop myself from watching them.

On one of those final reels, there was an image I've never been able to get out of my head. There was an entire field, a whole landscape of corpses. And next to one of the corpses sat a dying man. He is the only one still moving in this totality of death and he glances apathetically into the camera. Then he turns, tries to stand up, and falls over, dead. Hundreds of bodies, and the look of this dying man. Shattering.

There is a long pause. Then:

BILLY (V.O.) (CONT'D)
And even then, I wasn't really looking at him. You know? I was looking at the bodies. The bodies behind him. All around him. And all the time, the only thing I was thinking . . .
Was it her? Could one of them be her?

FADE OUT.

*

Billy fell into silence. Nobody spoke. Finally he became aware of the waiter hovering by his side.

"Another brandy, sir?" the waiter said.

Billy looked at his glass. It was almost empty. He swirled the remaining liquid around a bit and drank it down.

"Sure," he said. "Fill it up." He looked around the table: "Anybody joining me?"

A few people did, including Iz and Mr. Pacino. Iz had been smoking almost non-stop while his friend was talking, and was still smoking now, swathed in fumes from the cigarette. In the silence that followed Billy's story—a silence which must have lasted two or three minutes—the sound of people swirling their drinks around in their glasses, and swallowing them down, seemed very loud. It was late and the main restaurant next door was empty. There was almost nothing to disturb the contemplative stillness in our private room. The young German man whose comments had prompted the reminiscence was looking down at the space where his plate had been, too scared to meet anybody's eye. He only looked up when Billy spoke again, and it was obvious that he was being addressed.

"So . . . yes," Billy said, with a steely coldness in his voice that I had never heard before. "Yes, I am familiar with these theories that have been circulating—not just recently, but ever since the end of the war, in fact. That the numbers are wildly exaggerated. That those pesky Jews, once again, are telling lies for their own benefit. That there was never really a Holocaust." He took another sip of brandy. "Which brings me to the question I was going to ask you. And it is a very simple question, I must say. The question is this. If there was no Holocaust, where is my mother?"

As he looked directly across the table at the man to whom this question was addressed, there was a tiny, militant smile on Billy's face. When no answer was forthcoming, the smile remained: steadfast, immutable.

After ten seconds or more, he repeated: "Where is she?"

The young man tried to hold Billy's gaze, but it was impossible. It was not a battle of equals. Their eyes met briefly, but then he looked down again, down at the tablecloth. There was another long silence. Mr. Pacino coughed into his napkin, but nobody spoke.

"You may leave now," Billy said to the young man.

The young man got up, scraped back his chair, and left without saying a word. Billy watched him leave, then took off his glasses, rubbed something from his eyes, and put them back on again.

"I'm glad my wife was not here to witness that," he said. "She is very sensitive on this particular subject. She would have found it very upsetting. *This*, gentlemen—" he looked to his right, towards Iz and Dr. Rózsa, and then to his left, towards Mr. Holden—"this is why you should never invite your wives out to dinner with you."

"For once, Billy, something that we can agree upon," said Dr. Rózsa, as he drained the last droplets of water from his glass.

*

One more time, I played back the press conference clip, and listened to the music I had written for it. And when the clip had run its course, I looked again at the frozen image of Billy's face on the screen: the face of a man nursing a deep, private, unassuageable disappointment. What he had to give, nobody really wanted any more.

Then I found the original footage of the press conference, and started playing it back with the original sound, at the normal speed. I'd seen it many times before, so I fast-forwarded through most of it, until I reached the moment that I wanted to revisit.

It's a female journalist, a young German reporter with reddish hair, who stands up to ask the question. A bland enough question, one which could have been answered in any number of equally bland ways.

In German, she asks: "Mr. Wilder, you lived for several years in Berlin between the wars. How does it feel to be back in Germany, for the making of your new film?"

And Billy thinks for a few moments, and then says, without smiling—so deadpan that nobody on earth could tell whether he was making a joke or not: "Well, you know, it was difficult to raise the money for this picture in America. So I was very glad when my German friends and colleagues stepped in. And now, I think it puts me in a kind of win–win situation."

"What do you mean by that?" the woman asks.

"I mean," Billy says, "that with this picture I really cannot lose. If it's a huge success, it's my revenge on Hollywood. If it's a flop, it's my revenge for Auschwitz."

The silence in the room is hard to describe. It is sudden and fathomless. It lasts for maybe eight or nine seconds—until a couple of the journalists start to laugh nervously—but it seems much, much longer. It has a resonance, a harmony, a texture that is more rich and complex than any music I have ever heard.

I wish I could somehow record this silence. It would render all the music in the world obsolete: especially my own.

After a while, I turned off my computer and went downstairs to see if Fran had come home yet.

I n fact Fran did not come home until later that afternoon. I was in the living room, sitting on the sofa working through the contents of a couple of cardboard boxes. I heard the front door open, and then I heard her walking into the kitchen and putting something down on the table. But I didn't rush in to talk to her this time. I'd been doing some thinking, and I realized now that I'd been coming on too strong. I couldn't force her to talk to me. The last thing she needed was me breathing down her neck. If she wanted to chat about things, fine. But it would have to be at her pace, and on her terms.

I dipped into the cardboard box again, and took out a small Manila envelope filled with photos. The pictures inside were quite old. Italy, late 1980s. Geoffrey and I had been married a couple of years and we had spent a fortnight in Puglia and my mother (because he was such a sweet man) had joined us for the second week. There we were, the three of us, on the steps of the cathedral in Lecce. She was starting to look happy again, for the first time in about seven or eight years . . .

"Hi," said Fran.

I gave a little start, not having heard her come into the room.

"Oh. Hello," I said, smiling up at her.

"What are you doing?"

"Just going through some of Mum's old stuff."

She sat down beside me and picked up one of the photographs.

"Looking for anything special?"

"A letter that I wrote her once, from France. I know it's in here somewhere."

Fran inspected the photograph in her hand and laughed. "Your hair!" she said.

"Very fashionable at the time," I informed her, primly. I took the photograph gently from her hand and replaced it with a different one, taken about fifteen years later. "Nice one of you and your sister," I said.

It was true, it was a good picture of them both (aged nine or ten) but it was an even better photograph of my mother. She was sitting on a bench in a London park—Hyde Park, probably—with her arms around both of her granddaughters. The striking thing was that she looked so much younger than in the other photograph. The shadow of widowhood had long since left her and had been replaced by the thrill of finding herself a grandparent. The energy of these two little girls, their freshness, their enthusiasm for life, had seeped into her as if by osmosis.

"I miss her," Fran said. "So much."

She told me she was sorry she had been angry with me that morning, then she gave me a hug and went upstairs. I carried on looking for the letter I had written to my mother from France all those years ago. While I was looking for it, my mind was working and it occurred to me that actually the person Fran would have found it easiest to talk to about her current predicament was my mother. That was why she had just said: "I miss her," in such a heartfelt way. Randomly, a few more thoughts popped into my head. It's strange how sometimes the most important, most truthful ideas come to you when you're doing something routine and part of your mind is focused on something else entirely. I thought about what I'd overheard of Fran's telephone conversation this morning, and the anguished tone in which she had kept saying to her friend Julie, "I don't know." And that was when it dawned on me: if you are discussing whether or not you want to keep a baby, and you say, "I don't know," then what you are really saying is that you do know.

This realization stole over me slowly, becoming more and more solid, more and more dazzling in its clarity, as I allowed myself one final look at that joyous picture of my daughters and their grandma on the park bench, before putting it back in its envelope.

A few minutes later I found what I had been looking for: the letter I had written to my mother (one of very few that I ever wrote to her, strangely) from France in that extraordinary summer of 1977. And as soon as I started reading it I felt myself carried back to that relentlessly sunny August, to the shooting of *Fedora*'s final scenes, and the closing phase of my encounter with Mr. Wilder.

*

9th August 1977
Hôtel Ambassadeur
Cherbourg

Dear Mum,

Thanks so much for your letter, which reached me in Munich a few days ago, just before we left for France. It's lovely to hear from you and to get all your news. I'm glad Dad's tests from the doctor are all looking o.k.

Thanks also for sending me the article from Το Βήμα. However, as I'm sure you do not need me to tell you, you should be wary of believing everything that you read in the newspapers. I actually met this journalist while we were filming in Nydri. He struck me then as a troublemaker: someone out to make a name for himself, who was asking all sorts of people (including me) questions about the film, looking for a story. It is not true that the two leading actresses dislike each other. It is not true that Mr. Wilder himself is unpopular with the cast. I have been there every day, watching the filming, for the last six weeks or more, and I can tell you that every-thing is going smoothly. What this man has written makes me so angry! But I can console myself that nobody on the crew here reads Greek so nobody is likely to see it.

So, now we are entering the final stage of our great adventure.

Last week we flew from Munich to Paris and were taken to our new hotel and I have to tell you that it is AMAZING! It is called the Raphael and it is in one of the most beautiful parts of Paris, only a couple of minutes' walk from the Arc de Triomphe. Honestly, I think we have nothing like this in Athens. The furniture in my room is wonderfully old-fashioned. It's the kind of furniture where the chairs have striped cushions to match the curtains and the curtains are thick and heavy and you open them by pulling on a cord with a big golden tassel on the end. My room has its own bathroom with a shower and a bath and even a bidet! which I haven't used yet because I'm not quite sure how it works. (Mr. Wilder told us a funny story about bidets over dinner last night. Apparently, the last time he was making a film in Paris, his wife asked him to purchase a bidet and have it shipped out to her in the United States. Instead he sent her a telegram saying: "Unable to obtain bidet—suggest you do handstand in shower.") The view from my room is not so great—just a view of the side street—but still, I'm not complaining, every morning I wake up and it takes me a few moments to be certain that this is all real and not part of some fantastic dream.

However, as you will see from the address at the top of this letter, we are not in Paris at the moment, because only a few days after we arrived, while the set decorators were getting everything ready to film the big funeral scene at the Studios de Boulogne, some of us came here, to the coast of Normandy where tomorrow they are going to film another important scene. The hotel here is not quite so nice—it's right opposite the big industrial port—but we are not going to be staying in it for long. The scene they are going to film takes place on a beach nearby and it has to be filmed at dawn and after that I think we will be packing up again and going back to Paris.

In fact, I only came here because Mr. Diamond has a lot of correspondence he wants me to help him with, regarding another film project he intends to pursue when he gets back to Hollywood. We had a long meeting about it this morning and now I have some letters to type. Actually, I don't think the project will come to anything. From talking to him over the last few weeks I know that he sometimes tries to write films on his own or with somebody else but in the end he always ends up working with Mr. Wilder. They are married for life and I don't think either of them will ever do anything with another collaborator again.

I told you in my last letter from Munich that Mr. Diamond was in poor spirits but he seems to have cheered up since we came to France. This could also be because his wife has come to join him for a couple of weeks: she is here with him in Cherbourg now and it seems to make him much more cheerful and at ease with himself. Mr. Wilder's wife Audrey is here too, but I think she is also flying back to the States quite soon.

A new actor has joined us today, a very handsome guy called Stephen Collins. He is meant to be playing the young Mr. Holden and I must say that the resemblance is very strong. This is for a scene where he and Fedora are having a conversation in their car on the beach after spending the night together. The beach is meant to be in Santa Monica and I must say it seems hard to imagine, because Normandy is nothing like California, but everyone seems confident they can make it work and I suppose that's the magic of the movies. One beach is much like another, I guess, although the light here seems very different. European light, not American. Anyway, I have read the scene and I do think that it's quite beautiful. There are lots of touching moments like this in the script and this is why it puzzles me that Mr. Diamond can't sound a little happier about it. But I suppose this is just his way.

Well, Mum, I had better get on with my work. I never thought that I would end up as a screenwriter's secretary but that seems to be what I am at the moment and I suppose it just proves that life is full of surprises. Only another three or four weeks of this strange, fabulous existence and then I will be coming back to Athens. I hope you won't be hurt if I say the thought frightens me a little bit, even though of course it will be great to see you and Dad. But I think it will be hard to go back to normal life.

Well, I'm not going to think about it, for the moment.

All my love to you both, always,

Cal

*

That afternoon in Cherbourg, while I was typing up the proposed treatment for Iz's film project, the telephone rang in my hotel room. I answered the call and heard a female American voice and it took me a little while to recognize it: not because I was unfamiliar with Audrey's voice, but because she was the last person I was expecting to call me.

"Calista, dear," she said, "Barbara and I are going for a drive while the boys are working. Please say that you'll join us."

I told her I would have loved to, but I was also working at the moment.

"Oh, phooey! Have you seen the weather outside? It's glorious out there. We're in France in the middle of summer and you're not going to be cooped up in some dingy hotel room typing out a silly treatment. Come on, we're waiting for you in the lobby."

It seemed that I had no choice. Ten minutes later Iz's car was taking us out of town. I sat in the back, next to Barbara, and Audrey sat in the front, next to the chauffeur.

We drove for about half an hour, uphill at first, and then, as we left the traffic behind and the houses started to fall away, along winding coastal lanes. The chauffeur seemed to know the area well and to have a specific destination in mind. Eventually he pulled up on a grass verge by the side of the road.

"You can all walk to the beach from here," he told us. "About fifteen minutes, along that path."

It was a perfect August afternoon and the sun was blazing away in the sky. There was no breeze and the sea stretched out

towards the distant horizon, languid but shimmering, silver-blue.
There were a few yachts sculling backwards and forwards, and
the outline of a ferry at the edge of our vision, either arriving
or leaving, many miles away. It was very hot and I took off my
coat, folding it over my arm, wondering why I had brought it
in the first place. The three of us set off along the path. We
didn't meet many people on the way.

"So," Audrey said, falling into step beside me, "what did
you think of Munich?"

I was surprised to find myself flanked by both women, now,
as they moved in close on either side of me and each took me
by the arm. I looked from one to the other, but neither of them
gave the impression that this was anything other than perfectly
natural.

"It was . . . O.K.," I said. "Quite a fun city, I thought."

Towards the end of my time there, in fact, I had discovered
the more bohemian end of Schwabing and had spent quite a few
enjoyable nights at a club called the Schwabinger Sieben, drinking and listening to bands with the younger members of the crew.
Unsurprisingly, however, this had not been Audrey's experience.

"Fun!" she laughed. "My God, it's the most boring city on
earth. While Billy was down at the studio all day I had nothing
to do but go shopping and the only food you could find in the
shops were cabbages, potatoes and five hundred different kinds
of sausages. Believe me, there are only so many ways you can
dress *those* up on a plate. If I'd known that making this crack-
pot film was going to involve four weeks in *Germany*, of all
places, then I promise you I would have talked him out of it."

"As if you could talk Billy out of anything," Barbara said.

"Well, I would have had a damn good try. How did Iz manage to put up with it, anyway?"

"Well, I really don't know—since I wasn't there at the time.
We shall just have to ask Calista." She squeezed my arm more
tightly than ever, and suddenly I realized what the real purpose
of this walk was: it had been set up so that Barbara could enquire

after the physical, mental and emotional well-being of her husband. And I was the one who was going to provide the information. After all, I'd spent more time with him in Munich than anybody. "You saw a lot of him while you were there, didn't you? I mean, I heard that you were practically inseparable."

"Well, I was just . . . trying to do my job," I said, a tad defensively.

"Of course you were, dear. And what was your impression?"

"My impression?"

"Well, for one thing, did he eat properly while he was there? Because it looks to me like he's lost about fifteen pounds at least."

Iz was always skinny. To my eyes, he looked no different now than he did on the first night I met him in the Bistro, more than a year earlier.

"Yes, I think he ate very well. We cooked lots of meals together."

"Well, that's a relief because on his own he can hardly boil an egg. And was his back hurting the whole time?"

"It came and went. But I think that was just stress."

"Ah—now we're coming to it," Barbara said. "Stress. Why is he so stressed? He's never been like this before when they were shooting a film. Not even on *Sherlock Holmes*—and that was a *really* stressful shoot."

I thought about this and tried to formulate a truthful answer.

"I'm not sure that he . . . believes in this film, in quite the same way that Mr. Wilder does."

"That's interesting," said Barbara. "Why, what did he say about it? Anything specific?"

"Two or three times," I said, "he's told me that he wonders why Mr. Wilder was so keen to adapt this particular book, this particular story."

"I've been wondering that myself," Audrey said, unexpectedly.

We had reached a point on the path which had been set aside for picnickers or simply for those who wanted to rest their legs. There were four or five tables with benches attached to them, overlooking the sea. We sat down at one of these tables.

"What a beautiful afternoon," Barbara said.

The beach spread out beneath us was surprisingly busy. Or perhaps this was not so surprising—it was just that I had forgotten, in the unreality of the last few weeks, that we were now at the beginning of August, the height of the holiday season. I looked down at the tiny figures on the beach, swimming, sunbathing, playing football and Frisbee, and wondered how they could tolerate it—ordinary life, mortal life—when up above them, high on the cliff, the gods were sitting, discussing the god-like concerns of their god-like world. Ignorance is bliss. I had never really understood that phrase before. I understood it now.

"It is," Audrey agreed. "Quite heavenly. Even so, there's no situation which can't be improved by a vodka Martini. Here, help yourself."

She took a silver hip flask from her handbag and passed it to Barbara.

"You're a genius, Audrey," she said. "An evil genius, but a genius all the same."

She drank from the flask and passed it to me. I only pretended to drink from it, though. I had recently developed quite a taste for vodka Martinis but still, it was a little early in the day for me, and I didn't feel the need right now. After taking my fake sip I passed the flask back to Audrey.

"You were saying, Aud?" Barbara prompted.

"What was I saying?" She took a big sip and wiped her lips on the back of her sleeve.

"You said that you'd been wondering why Billy wanted to make this film."

"Yes. Well, I have my theories, but . . . that's all they are. As you know, he *never* talks to me about the picture he's making. Not a word. I assume Iz is the same."

"Of course. *We're* the ones who have to live with the fallout, who put up with the moods and have to deal with the highs and lows, but God forbid either one of them would ever confide in *us*. Their wives. The very idea! I mean—" addressing me—"it doesn't worry me at all that you got so close to him in Munich, dear, but it seems a little hard, somehow, that you should end up with more insight into my husband's state of mind than I have."

"Honestly," I said—on the defensive again—"that's all I know. Just one or two things that he said while we were making dinner and so on. I'm sure he would have said them to anybody."

"Well, let me give you both my take on it," Audrey said. "And I'm speaking now as someone who's known Billy for more than thirty years."

The vodka flask was passed around again, and I took another of my fake sips. Then Audrey began:

"Let me say from the start, Billy and I are not exactly soulmates," she said. "Not in the traditional sense, anyway. I mean, you and Iz, Barbara, you're both writers. You're both creative types. So that gives you a certain . . . affinity. Well, I never did anything creative in my life."

"Oh, come on—no need to be so hard on yourself."

"I'm not being hard on myself. I'm a damn good cook and a damn good companion and a damn good *wife*, if it comes to that. And back in the day I was one hell of a singer."

"You were a singer?" I asked. No one had told me this before.

"There's no need to sound so surprised, dear. I was indeed. Going places, too, once upon a time. I toured with the Tommy Dorsey band, you know . . ." She looked at me, and said, with a note of despair: "Oh. You don't have the faintest idea who that is, do you? I know, it was all long, long in the past.

Anyway, I gave all that up. Not that Billy asked me to, of course. He's never made me do anything I didn't want to.

"We had such a sweet and lovely courtship. I was an extra on *The Lost Weekend*—you can just see my left arm in one of the scenes—and we dated a couple of times round about then. But Billy's love life was pretty complicated at the time. He was still married, and he was having an affair with somebody else and . . . well, you wouldn't want to think about it. And his star was already on the rise, but as soon as that picture turned out to be a hit, he became the most incredible hotshot, you know? Nothing improves your sex life more than success, and suddenly *everybody* wanted to be with him. I was well aware of that, of course, and I didn't really feel that I had a hope in hell, but for some reason . . . he liked me. Don't ask me why, but it was as simple as that. He liked me. Nothing much happened, at first, apart from those couple of dates, but then I went on tour, I went on tour for a few months with the Dorsey band, and after the shows I'd find myself alone in the middle of the night in some hotel room, in some two-bit town—in Albuquerque or Tulsa or somewhere—and I needed to talk to someone, I needed to feel just that little bit less alone, and for some reason, he was the one I would call. Can you imagine? I could have called my mom, or anyone in my family, or any one of my girlfriends, but instead I called the most successful young director in Hollywood. In the middle of the night. When he was in the middle of making a film. And you know the strangest thing? He answered. Every time. Even when it was three o'clock in the morning and I was waking him out of a deep sleep. He always answered. And he always sounded pleased to hear from me, and he would always talk for as long as I wanted him to. I suppose I just loved hearing that voice. That funny little Austrian accent. And he was always so funny, you know? He would always say the funniest things. He liked to make fun of me because I came from downtown LA. He used to say, 'Audrey, I would worship the ground you walked on, if only you came from a better neighbourhood.' Always with the jokes. The same a few years later, when he was shooting a picture in Paris and I asked him to get a bidet for our bathroom and he wired back, 'Unable to obtain bidet—suggest you do handstand in shower.' Honestly, how can you not be in love with a man who sends you a telegram like that? We had the strangest wedding. The strangest but the most perfect. It was in Nevada. A little place called Minden. Have you heard of it? No, neither had I. Neither had Billy, so far as I know. But we were on a road trip and suddenly he just stopped there and said, 'This looks like a good place for a wedding.' He'd bought me a ring in a little jewellery shop on Ventura Boulevard in Encino and paid the princely sum of seventeen dollars fifty for it. And look, I'm still wearing it today." She held out her hand for our inspection. "I hadn't brought a dress with me or anything like that. Why would I? I had no idea this was happening. I got married in a pair of old blue jeans with a bandana on my head. Who cares? It doesn't matter what you're wearing, does it? What matters is who you're marrying.

"So you see, the thing is, Billy and I may be very different people—one of us is a creative genius, while the other one . . . well, isn't—but I can tell you now there isn't another person on the planet who knows him as well as I do. And he may not be showing it the same way Iz is showing it, but he's known, deep down, for quite some time now, that the writing is on the wall for him. He's not the King of Hollywood any more, he hasn't been for quite a while, and that kind of glory is not going to come back again. You know, one morning a couple of years back he'd finished having breakfast out on the balcony, and he was sitting there with a cup of coffee, and he'd been reading one of the trades, and it was a piece about Spielberg, about *Jaws*, about how much money this goddamn film had just made for the studio. The paper was on the table next to him and he was just sitting there thinking, looking out over the city. And I asked him what he was thinking—which is a big mistake, normally, with Billy, but this time he didn't snap at me or anything, he just gave me a little smile and said, 'What I was I thinking? Nothing much. I was just thinking that I was Steven Spielberg . . . Once.'"

Audrey fell silent, and the only sound that reached us for a few moments was the sound of a little child, a toddler, wailing in some kind of distress down on the beach. Shouting "*Maman! Maman!*" over and over. The cry pierced me, for some reason. The sound always does. Even now I can never hear a child crying without wanting to run over and comfort it.

"So what you're saying," I began, as the meaning of her words started to sink in, "is that Mr. Wilder and Mr. Holden's character in the film are the same."

"Well, anyone can see *that*," said Barbara. "Even the character's name sounds like Billy Wilder. And he wears the same hat as Billy in practically every scene."

I felt very stupid for not having realized this before.

"But if that's all there was to it," Audrey said, "they would just be making a comedy and Iz would be much happier about the whole thing. Billy sees this picture as a tragedy. It's a tragedy about someone who used to be on top of the world but now it's all over for them. The picture isn't about Barry Detweiler. He's the sideshow. It's about Fedora. She's the tragic heroine. And *that*'s who Billy identifies with. *That's* why he wants to make this picture."

*

Billy and Iz and their wives remained in Cherbourg for a few more days, staying with the film's art director, Mr. Trauner, who had a house nearby. I went back to Paris by train the morning after my conversation with Audrey and Barbara.

The days began to pass quickly. The shooting of the film was coming to an end. I wish I had kept a diary because so much of that month, my long hot Parisian August, is now forgotten, lost in the haze of my unreliable memory. I know that

I revelled in the opulence of my room at the Raphael Hotel, and the glamorous ambience of the Studios de Boulogne where the final interiors were being shot. Iz, on the other hand, went round grumbling that the hotel was going to pot and the studios were a shadow of their former selves. Barbara had flown home, and he was miserable again. Audrey had gone home, too, but Billy seemed to be enjoying himself as much as ever.

Day by day, the dreaded moment was getting closer: the moment when the last scene would be filmed, the production would be wrapped, and we would all be sent home. The weekend before that was to happen, however, someone unexpected turned up at the hotel. It was Matthew.

I must be honest—I had not given him very much thought since the last time I had seen him, on the beach in Nydri. Perhaps that seems surprising, because it was certainly true that the party on the beach, and our first kiss just before dawn, had been magical experiences for me, and during the first few days in Munich, immediately after we had been separated, I had dreamed of him constantly and often thought about asking his mother how I could get in touch with him. But at heart (perhaps you have guessed this already) I'm a sensible person rather than a romantic one, and as the days went by I began to feel that perhaps I had simply been seduced by a place, an atmosphere—and a person, of course—and as those precious memories started to recede, to become more and more indistinct, and as I adjusted to the new duties and rhythms of my life in Germany, I thought about Matthew less and less. Needless to say, lodged deep inside me there was still some trace of the feelings that had been stirred in me that night, some sweet or rather bitter-sweet residue, but for the most part it did not disturb me too much. Sometimes in the early hours of the morning it would flare up, or suddenly, unexpectedly present itself to me during working hours while I was in the middle of some quotidian administrative task, distracting me with fleeting, intense visions of the sunrise over Madouri, or

Matthew's hand on my breast. But these were isolated moments. I started to tell myself that it had been nothing more than a teenage crush (I still thought of myself as a teenager) and that the wise and grown-up thing to do was to get over it: to forget all about him, and move on.

That was all well and good. But it made no difference whatsoever to how I felt the second I glimpsed him checking in to the Raphael one Friday evening towards the end of that month. You know the routine—my heart performed cartwheels, my legs turned to jelly. All clichés, and all completely true. I took some time to calm myself—luckily Matthew was busy signing the register and handing his passport over—before approaching from behind and tapping him on the shoulder.

"Matthew?" I stammered.

He turned around and broke into a smile.

"Cal! I was going to call you. I was going to call you the minute I got up to my room."

"You've just arrived?"

"Flew into Charles de Gaulle this afternoon."

"How long are you here for?"

"Three nights."

He took me in his arms, hugged me and kissed me. I think the kiss was aimed at my mouth but for some reason I turned my head and made sure it landed on my cheek instead. I suppose I wasn't sure we were ready to pick up exactly where we'd left off.

Matthew was having dinner with his mother that night, and I had work to do for Iz the next day, so we weren't able to talk much until Saturday evening, when we went out for dinner to a restaurant close to the newly opened Pompidou Centre. It was a warm evening and we were able to sit out at a table on the street. Matthew was in an expansive mood. He seemed to have changed since Greece: more confident, more worldly, a little more full of himself. He had signed up for film school in the autumn and was making grandiose plans for the movies he was going to shoot over the next few years. I too had grown in confidence during these last weeks and I'm afraid that I did not take these ideas quite as seriously as he would have liked me to (and as I might have done had he put them to me during our conversation on the plane from Corfu to Actium, for example).

"We have to start making films that reflect the world we live in," he told me. "I don't know what it's like in Greece, but in Britain our film industry is a joke. All we make are sex comedies and trashy horror movies. A film should be so much more than that. Film-makers have a moral duty to hold up a mirror to the society they live in."

He had used this mirror analogy before, of course. I remembered it, but he seemed to have forgotten. Still, even though I could now tell that these theories of his were well rehearsed, I found the *braggadocio* with which he expressed them to be even more adorable. It made me want to reach across the table and kiss him. For now, however, I resisted the temptation.

"I'm sure Billy and Iz would agree with you," I said. "I think *Fedora* has many important things to say—about age, about beauty, about how we worship youth and fame . . ."

Matthew snorted.

"I read the script," he said—again, seeming to forget that I'd been there when he finished it, sitting right next to him, in fact—"and to be honest, I wasn't impressed. Sure, it's well constructed and so on, but nobody cares about that kind of thing any more. It's so old-fashioned, so . . . *creaky*. And the stories I've been hearing, about how he makes the actors say every line just as it's written, how he won't let them improvise, he won't let them *inhabit* the characters. No wonder they all hate him."

"They don't all hate him. That's not true. Where did you read that? In one of those stupid newspapers?"

"Cinema has changed," he said. "It went through a revolution in the 1960s—just as society did. If you aren't able to take that on board, then you're finished. Dead in the water."

I didn't try to argue with him. I went back to eating my *steak tartare*.

The next afternoon, on a bright and beautiful Sunday, we sat on the grass in the Jardin des Tuileries with a copy of *Pariscope* and planned how we would spend the rest of the day. Matthew was transfixed by the listings magazine, unable to believe the number and variety of films being screened. Feeling very worldly, I explained to him that this was perfectly normal for Paris: this was a city of *cinéphiles* (the word tripped off my tongue elegantly) and there was no better place in the world to catch up on foreign films or revivals of classics. Indeed, in the last few weeks in Paris, I had finally been able to plug the yawning gaps in my knowledge of Billy's films: I had laughed my way joyously through *Certains l'aiment chaud*, I'd been transfixed by the amoral schemers of *Assurance sur la mort*, I had witnessed Billy and Iz at their peak in *La Garçonnière*, watched their collaboration sour and misfire in *Embrasse-moi, idiot*, and belatedly come to understand the mythology that surrounded *Boulevard du crépuscule*. My admiration for these films now knew no bounds, and I would have defended Billy's genius to the hilt if anybody had challenged me.

There were no Billy Wilder films showing in Paris that day, I was disappointed to find. What should we go and see instead? Matthew and I agreed on a compromise: we would watch two films, with dinner in between. He could choose one of them and I could choose the other. And so it was that we set off towards the Rue Jacob for a six o'clock screening of *Taxi Driver*. (His choice.)

"What's it about?" I asked, as we stood in the queue outside the little cinema with a lot of other, mainly young people. The tag line on the poster said: «*Dans chaque rue, il y a un inconnu qui rêve d'être quelqu'un. C'est un homme seul, oublié, qui cherche désespérément à prouver qu'il existe.»*

"It's about alienation," he replied.

Well, I could have worked out that much.

"Alienation and violence."

"Oh. I don't like violent films."

"It exposes the dark underbelly of the American dream."

"Have you seen it before?" I asked.

"Three times. It's a bloody masterpiece. Come on."

We went inside.

*

Two hours later, we were studying the menus in a nearby brasserie. I was in a state of shock.

"Didn't you like it?" Matthew asked.

"It's not really a question of *liking* it," I said. "Of course, it's . . . brilliant. But I feel like . . ."

Words failed me. Matthew supplied them instead.

"You feel emotionally drained. You feel like someone's beaten you to death. Your soul is crushed. Your faith in humanity has been shattered. You've never seen such ugliness, such horror on the screen before."

"Pretty much," I said.

"That's it! That's *exactly* how I want the viewer to feel when they've seen one of my films."

"Well, O.K., but . . . it's not really what I want from a night out at the cinema."

"Come on, Calista. Don't be such a *bourgeois*. It's not like I took you to see a porn movie, like Robert de Niro does with Cybill Shepherd."

"No, of course not . . . I think I'll have the *confit de canard*."

"I mean, when you see a film like that, can you not see how silly, how pointless it is to make something like *Fedora* in this day and age?"

"But Billy's from a different era, a different generation."

"Well, now another generation has taken over. Mine. *Ours.*"

He leaned across the table and clasped my hands in his. The thrill of his touch was sudden and electric. He was very persuasive, but I didn't want to talk about this any more. I was beginning to feel that perhaps I had been born into the wrong time.

Over dinner, we talked about Matthew's summer holidays at his grandparents' house down in Cornwall. It sounded lovely. While he was talking I allowed myself a private fantasy that he would take me down there some time. I paid for the meal, just as I had paid for last night's. Matthew didn't seem to have much money. I got my little stipend from the film company every Friday morning, and since my living expenses were almost non-existent, I had saved up quite a tidy sum. It didn't bother me that I was paying.

"So what are we going to see next?" Matthew asked, as we sipped our brandies. I hadn't been planning on a drink, but after that film, I felt I needed it.

"This," I said, pointing at a title in the magazine. "It's on at the cinema just along the street. Come on, it starts in ten minutes."

*

Ernst Lubitsch was a name that Billy and Iz mentioned all the time, but I had never seen one of his films. Their feelings for him clearly went beyond admiration, into reverence. Hero worship. Billy, I was told, even had a framed tapestry on the wall of his office, embroidered with the words, "How would Lubitsch do it?" For him, the Lubitsch approach to storytelling was the ultimate in elegance, slyness and obliqueness, underpinned by a sort of gentle, quintessentially Middle-European cynicism.

The film Matthew and I went to see was called *Rendez-Vous* in French. In English, its title is *The Shop Around the Corner*. It was strange seeing it on that hot August night in Paris because it was basically a Christmas movie. It told a beautiful, simple love story about two shopworkers in a little department store in Budapest, who fall in love with each other as pen pals but can't stand each other in real life. The thing I remember most about that screening is how quiet it was. I don't mean in the auditorium, because the cinema was full of people and there was plenty of laughter. I mean quiet on the screen: because the film had absolutely no music (except over the opening and closing credits), and nearly all the dialogue between the two lovers was spoken in murmured undertones. It was not just a film without gunshots, explosions or revving car engines, but a film in which hardly anybody raised their voice at all. But in spite of—or perhaps because of—this understatement, the warmth of the film slowly seeped into you, suffusing you with its amber glow, until you, too, wanted nothing more than to share in the hushed, tender glory of the love declared between James Stewart and Margaret Sullavan in the final scene. I think it might just be the most romantic film ever made.

As soon as we came out of the cinema and started walking along the street, my hand reached out for Matthew's and he clasped it in return.

I leaned into him and hooked my arm around his as we continued walking.

I waited for him to say something about the film. I wanted to know if it touched him in the same way that it had touched me.

Eventually he said: "That was so sweet."

I looked up at him expectantly, waiting for him to say more, but there was no more. It was not exactly what I'd been wanting to hear. But it would have to do.

We didn't talk much after that. As we approached the river and began to cross the Pont Royal, I noticed that he was humming a tune to himself.

"What are you singing?" I asked.

"It's the tune you wrote," he said. "The one you played to me at the bar in Greece."

"'Malibu'?"

He nodded. He wasn't quite singing it properly, but still.

"I love that you remember it," I said. "But that's not quite how it goes."

I hummed the tune for him, the way that I had written it.

"That's it," he said. "It's so lovely. Did you ever make a recording of it?"

"Yes," I said.

"Could you send it to me?"

"Of course."

My heart was ready to burst with happiness at this sign that he remembered our last evening in Nydri, and associated it with the romantic aura that was now enveloping us in the wake of the film. As we crossed the bridge, we stopped to lean against the balustrade and to look out over the dark, glimmering water. When we were tired of looking at the water, we looked at each other, and then we kissed. It was a long kiss, and also rather a scratchy one, because of his beard. But I didn't mind that.

When we returned to the hotel, we asked for our room keys—his was Room 313, mine was 422—but in the lift he looked at my key and said, "I don't think you'll be needing that tonight."

I laughed and we kissed again.

And then . . .

Well, Billy is reported to have once said—rather crudely, I suppose—that "Ernst Lubitsch could do more with a closed door than most directors can do with an open fly." So I shall now follow the technique of the master, and close the door of Room 313, gently but very firmly, on what happened next.

*

In the morning, we decided to call for breakfast in bed. We ordered coffee, orange juice, pastries, scrambled eggs and bacon, fresh fruit and yoghurt.

Love, I was starting to discover, gives you a terrific appetite.

While we were waiting for breakfast to arrive, Matthew took a shower. I lay stretched out diagonally across his double bed, revelling in my shameless nudity and in the tousled comfort of the sheets which were still warm from our morning lovemaking. My mind roamed idly, contentedly over the prospect of the days and weeks to come. Work on *Fedora* might almost be over, but that didn't matter any more, because I would not be returning to ordinary life after all. From now on, my life would have Matthew in it. He could come and visit me in Athens for a week or two, before the start of his first term at film school, and then perhaps I could move to London to be with him. Or find my own place, if he didn't want to feel crowded out. Perhaps it would be a bit much to live together after only a few weeks. Men could be funny about things like that, although personally, I was ready to begin tomorrow if he could be persuaded.

I stretched and yawned, listening to the splash of the shower water coming from the bathroom. My limbs were aching in the sweetest, most delicious way.

Suddenly I remembered that when the boy arrived with our breakfast trolley, he would expect a tip. Still naked, I got up and rummaged around in my handbag, but all I found in my purse was a ten-franc note (too much) and some small centime coins (too little). What I really needed was a fifty-centime piece. Matthew's jeans were strewn on the floor. I stuck my hand into one of the pockets but instead of finding any coins, I found a sheet of paper. It was a letter.

I took it out of his pocket and glanced at it—just glanced at it, that's all—and the first word I saw—the only word—was "*darling.*" My stomach lurched and I unfolded the letter but still only read one sentence—the final sentence—which was "*Can't wait to see you again—Juliet.*" There were lots of kisses and hearts after her name.

I felt nauseous now, and shoved the letter back into the

pocket of Matthew's jeans. Then I sat on the edge of the bed
for a few moments, shaking, until I became conscious of my
nudity and quickly pulled some clothes on.

There was a knock on the door. I was still getting dressed,
so I didn't answer it. Then the knock came again and a voice
called out, "*Service de chambre!*" and from the bathroom
Matthew called, "Can you get that, Cal?"

Fully dressed but for one shoe, I opened the door. The uni-
formed bellboy wheeled the trolley in and I signed for it and
in my confusion I tipped him with a ten-franc note after all. He
looked pretty satisfied as he said thank you and left.

There was no way, however, that I was going to have a cosy
breakfast in bed with Matthew after what I had just seen. I had
no idea what I was going to do but within a few seconds of the
bellboy's departure I had put on my second shoe and followed
him out into the corridor, closing the door of Room 313
behind me.

*

What happened with the rest of that day? Where did it go?

I can't say with any certainty. I wandered through the
streets of Paris, confused and mortified by the events of the
last few hours. I felt abused, betrayed, violated. And also angry
with myself: angry for having succumbed so readily to a
romantic delusion, to have been prepared to believe that
Matthew felt something for me when it was clear that all he
had wanted was to get me into bed. I had offered myself a mas-
terclass, I realized, in projecting my own feelings onto someone else. That film, which had flooded me with such fuzzy, loving thoughts, had not made any impression on him
whatsoever: that much was clear. It seemed I was just a quick
sexual interlude to be enjoyed before he returned to the real
love of his life, this woman Juliet—whoever she might be.

It was late in the afternoon when I made my way back to the
Raphael. I wanted to leave it late because I didn't want there

to be the smallest risk of running into Matthew when I was there. I knew that he had been taking a flight back to London at midday. That evening they were going to be shooting Fedora's suicide scene at Montcerf railway station—the very first scene in the script, and the very last to be shot. I had a couple of hours to spare before I was due to travel to the location with Iz in his car. All I wanted to do was lie on my bed and stare up at the ceiling and wait for this miserable feeling to pass.

I was just about to enter through the revolving door at the front of the hotel when someone came out through the same door and nearly bumped into me. It was Billy.

"I'm very sorry," he said.

"No," I countered, "it's my fault. I wasn't looking where I was going."

"Well, now you mention it," he said, glancing at me a bit more closely, "you do look slightly distracted. Is everything O.K.?"

"I'm fine," I said. "Everything is fine."

"Have you been taking advantage of this very nice Parisian sunshine?"

"Yes, I've been in the . . . Jardin du Luxembourg," I improvised.

"Good. Very good. I was just going for a little walk myself."

"That sounds nice."

"Well, it's a funny thing . . ." He leaned on his cane, seemingly in no hurry to depart. "This is our last day in Paris, and just the other night I was saying to my friend Mr. Diamond, you know, this has been the most horrible few weeks."

"Horrible?"

"Sure. Because Paris is one of my favourite cities, and for the last few weeks I've seen nothing of the city at all, I have done nothing but work, and I feel like, you know, the piano player in a brothel—everybody else is screwing and having a good time and I just have to keep the music going." At this point, it only seemed to occur to him for the first time who he was talking to. "I'm sorry, that's not a very nice comparison to make to a young lady. I'm sure you've never seen the inside of a brothel. Still, you played the piano yourself, or so I'm told, at our little party in Greece a few weeks ago, so perhaps you know what I'm talking about."

"Perhaps," I answered, not knowing what else to say.

"Anyway, as you know, I have some filming to do tonight, so if I'm going to take my walk . . ."

"Of course."

He was about to leave, when a thought appeared to detain him, and he turned round to say: "I don't suppose you'd care to join me? There's always the chance we might end up in some bar, and there might be time for a cocktail before work starts. I hate to drink alone."

Whether he was being kind, because he could see the distress I was in, or whether he really wanted my company, I couldn't tell, and I still don't know. Either way, I was grateful for the offer, and we started walking together across the street. He was surprisingly quick on his feet—but then that cane, as I knew, had always been a theatrical prop, nothing more.

Billy appeared to know exactly where he wanted to go, even though the streets we were walking through were hardly the most picturesque or interesting in Paris. First we seemed to be in a business district, then a residential one, but the houses and offices in both were equally characterless. Paris is always quiet in August, of course, but here the absence of cars and people on the streets seemed positively eerie this late afternoon, as the shadows lengthened and plunged these unfrequented byways into melancholy shade.

"We are heading for a bar, believe it or not," Billy explained to me, "but I'm taking you by a devious route. Don't worry, there is a reason. A method to my madness. And here it is."

He laid a hand on my arm and stopped walking as we found ourselves opposite a tall building, seven or eight storeys, which seemed to be nothing more nor less than a run-of-the-mill apartment block. I looked across at Billy and he was gazing with uncommon fixation at a window on the third floor.

"This building used to be a hotel," he said.

"The Ansonia?"

"That's right. And that room there—" he pointed upwards with his cane—"was where I lived for one year. I lived there with a woman, my girlfriend."

"Hella," I said.

He looked at me in surprise.

"How come you know these names? The hotel, the girl-friend."

"Because you told us all about them," I answered. "Remember? At the restaurant in Munich."

"You were there that night?" he asked.

I was disappointed—but not too surprised, frankly—to learn that my presence had made no impression on him.

"Yes," I said. "I was there."

He looked up at the window again.

"Forty-four years ago," he said. "We had a pretty tough year together. Hard for two people to have a year like that and survive. You know, to stay together I mean—as a couple."

"Does she still live in Paris?" I asked.

"I couldn't say. And I'm pleased to report that I have no curiosity any more. What's done is done."

"I guess so."

"Well, I don't suppose you'd understand. You're too young. As you get older, the hopes get smaller and the regrets get big-ger. The challenge is to fight it. To stop the regrets from taking over. Right?"

I nodded, not really sure that my opinion was much use to him.

"Come on, there are plenty of bars round the corner, on this big street here."

We set off again. I took one last look at what used to be the Hotel Ansonia, the cultural hub of Paris for German refugees in the 1930s. Billy didn't bother.

"There used to be a brasserie here," he said, "called the Strasbourg. But that disappeared a long time ago. During the war, I think. It didn't survive the occupation. Never mind, any place will do. Luckily the weather is nice enough for us to sit out on the street."

We took our seats at a touristy sort of place, on a busy thoroughfare leading up to the Arc de Triomphe which was only a few hundred yards away. Billy ordered a vodka Martini and I was happy to follow suit.

"So," he said, raising his glass. "Cheers. Chin-chin."

"Cheers," I answered, raising my glass in return.

He took a sip and let out a little sigh of satisfaction.

"So we are almost done," he said. "Can you believe it? With every picture, you know, there is the thought that we're never going to get there. And with this one, even more so . . ."

"I never doubted it," I said. "Not for a minute."

"Really? Well, there have been a few times during the last few months, I can tell you, when I would have liked to hear you say that. As I said to Mr. Diamond only the other day: 'In the time it's taken me to do this, I could have shot three lousy pictures.'"

"But it's not going to be a lousy picture," I said.

"And the problem is," he continued, taking no notice of my comment, "that we are not out of the woods yet. 'We're not out of the woods yet, Baxter'—that's one of Mr. Diamond's lines from *The Apartment*. Now we actually have to cut the thing together, and something tells me this is not going to be an easy process. Not easy at all." More Martini. "Well, you have to be optimistic, don't you? We've come this far. We've got to get it finished."

"I didn't think you were an optimist. I thought you were a realist."

"I'm a realist when it comes to life. When it comes to making pictures, I'm an optimist. You have to be, or you would never even write a single word of script, you know? I mean, the fact that any kind of picture ever gets made at all is kind of a miracle. Of course, it's harder now than it ever was. It never used to be as hard as this. Now you spend three months of the year writing the script and the other nine months making the deal. It's soul-destroying."

"I went to see two films last night," I said, and told him what they were. He smiled with almost childlike happiness when I mentioned Lubitsch's name.

"*The Shop Around the Corner* is really a very good picture. One of his best. Very hard to find anything wrong with it. A beautiful script by Mr. Raphaelson. Perfect script. You liked the picture?"

"I loved it. *Taxi Driver* . . . not so much."

"Yeah, I saw it. Mr. Scorsese is a very serious guy, a talented guy. He's one of those kids with beards we were talking about, you know? I thought it was a great picture, in many ways. Just too much. Too violent—for me. Too depressing. But this is the fashion these days. You haven't made a serious picture unless your audience comes out of the cinema feeling like they want to commit suicide. It's not just an American thing, in fact the Europeans are even worse. This German kid, Fassbinder, they told me that he is coming to the studios in Bavaria soon to shoot a picture called *Despair*. Seriously—that is the title. I think it is based on a story by Nabokov or some guy like that. Now, something tells me this is not going to be a comedy. So just imagine. This is the situation I'm thinking of, when the picture is released in a year or two. Imagine a family in Düsseldorf. The husband is despondent—he comes home and there is a letter from the income tax people. He owes 11,000 marks or he's going to jail. The wife tells the husband, 'Look, I'm in love with the dentist and I'm leaving you.' The son has been arrested because he's a member of the underground. The daughter is knocked up and has got the syphilis. And now somebody comes to see them and says, 'Look, I know you've had a very bad day, but let's cheer ourselves up. Let's go and see Fassbinder's *Despair.*'" I laughed and laughed when he gave this example, and he could not help smiling back, because it always made him happy when people liked his jokes. "You see, it's not going to happen, right? It's not what people want when they go to the movies. I know that this picture, the one I'm making now, it's one of my most serious pictures, of course— I want it to be serious, I want it to be sad—but that doesn't mean, when the audience comes out of the cinema, they feel like you've been holding their head down the toilet for the last two hours, you know? You have to give them something else, something a little bit elegant, a little bit beautiful. Life is ugly. We all know that. You don't need to go to the movies to learn that life is ugly. You go because those two hours will give your life some little spark, whether it's comedy or laughter or . . . just, I don't know, some beautiful gowns and good-looking actors or something—some spark that it didn't have before. A bit of joy, maybe."

He took the olive from his Martini and ate it off the cocktail stick, chewing it in small bites, enjoying the flavour.

"You know, my theory about these guys—the kids with beards—is that someone like Lubitsch, he lived through this huge war in Europe—the first one, I mean—and once you have experienced something like that, it's inside you, do you see what I mean? The tragedy becomes part of you. It's there, you don't have to shout about it, to splash the horror of it on the screen all the time. There is a lot of pain in all his films—even *The Shop Around the Corner*, even then the old man, the shop owner, tries to commit suicide—but it doesn't dominate. It's not the whole story. He doesn't need to shout about it. In fact, sometimes, the very thing you want to do is to shut up about it, not even mention it at all, you see? The stupidest picture I ever made was right after the war, just after I came back from Germany. You know, I had seen all these terrible things, the most terrible things I have ever seen in my life, but at that point the last thing I wanted to do was write a picture about it. So instead, Brackett and I, we wrote this stupid story with songs, about two dogs who fall in love, and we set the story in Austria but not the real Austria, this one was just a fairy tale, and for the leading man we cast Bing Crosby, of all people . . . Well, maybe it's not a good example because it turned out to be a lousy picture. What I'm trying to say is . . . look at this man, Mr. Spielberg. He is a genius, I have no doubt about it, but he was born just at the end of World War Two. He doesn't know what it means to live through something like that. And for me, I think you can feel that in the pictures he makes. The storytelling is brilliant, the technique is brilliant, but there's something else, something not there . . . Can you see what I mean?" He drained the last drops of liquid from his glass. "Well, here I am, starting to sound like one of those guys from *Cahiers du Cinéma*, with my fancy theories. I suppose I'm just old-fashioned these days. People call me a cynic and sure, I've made some cynical pictures, but actually, I think I have quite a romantic image of what a picture should be. Just don't let it get around."

"I think people will understand that," I said, "when they see *Fedora*."

He shrugged. "God knows what they are going to think of it," he said. "I don't even know what I think of it myself at this point."

"I think you've improved on the book," I said, trying to be encouraging.

"That wouldn't be hard."

Trying another tack, I said: "Speaking personally—and I don't want to speak out of turn—I think it is going to be a very . . . *compassionate* film."

His eyes flared up with an enquiring light: "Compassionate? Well, that's a good word. I like that word. Compassionate to whom?"

"To all the characters. But to the old Countess in particular."

"Well . . ." Billy signalled to the waiter to bring two more drinks. "You know, there might be a reason for that. I'm seventy-one now and I know what it's like to be old, and I can tell you that it's a big pain in the ass. Everything starts to fall apart, nothing works the way it used to do. But it's different for men and for women. For me, getting old is an inconvenience. For women it's a tragedy. And I've seen this myself. I've seen it with my own eyes.

"Back in Berlin, back in the 1920s—very soon after I arrived in the city, way before I started writing scripts and getting into the picture business—I worked at a couple of hotels. The Eden and the Adlon. Big hotels, famous hotels. I was a professional dancer. So what I would do, there were these women attending the *thés dansants* in the afternoons, sometimes with their husbands but more often by themselves, and they needed someone to dance with. Some good-looking young man who knew how to dance, either because they didn't have anyone to dance with at all or their husbands couldn't dance or couldn't even stand up or maybe just couldn't bear putting their arms around their wives' waists, you know? Which I have to say wasn't always easy, because a lot of these German women in their sixties and seventies, they were big women, you would have to admit, with all those years of eating *Spätzle* and *Knödel* and *Wurst* and *Sauerkraut* and *Apfelstrudel*. We are not talking an Audrey Hepburn kind of a figure here. But actually it wasn't the ones who were overweight who made the big impression on me. They often seemed to be quite cheerful women, quite happy with themselves. It was more the ones who had kept their figures but lost their looks, and now they were just lonely. Maybe their husbands had left them or maybe their husbands had died, and they were never going to get another man in their lives, not in a million years, because they were *old*. That was it. The only reason. And when they put their arms around you,

you know—and I was no Holden, I was no Cary Grant, I'm telling you that—still, you could feel this hunger, this need, just to be touching another human being, you know? And it was kind of a horrible feeling, from my point of view, it used to send these shivers down my spine, you could feel the neediness in the way they were touching you. But still, you had to feel sorry for them. Once a woman loses her looks, that's it. She's invisible. That's why the plastic surgeon guys are making a fortune but, you know, that's serious stuff, they're not performing some minor operation, most of these guys, what they're doing to these women is . . . Well, it's all in the film. You read the script. And I've never forgotten that—even after all these years, what is it?—fifty years—my God—even after all that time, I've never forgotten what it was like to have those women put their arms around you, and to look into their eyes, and . . . the sadness you saw there. The sadness and the need. It was . . . Well, just thinking about it makes me want to have another Martini. Do we have time?"

He looked at his watch.

"No, we don't have time. That's a pity. We have to shoot at nine o'clock, just before it gets dark, and I have to get there before that, because they are laying a track, a track for the camera along the railway platform, and I should make sure that they're doing it properly. My car will be here in five minutes."

"I'd better get back to the hotel," I said. "Iz will be expecting me."

"You don't have to go to the location with him," Billy said. "You can come with me and meet him there. I'll phone the hotel from my car and let him know what's going on."

"You have a *phone* in your car?" was all I could say.

He chuckled at the naivety of this question.

"Come on," he said, rising to his feet. "This is the final chapter in the Adventure of the Greek Interpreter. We might as well make it a good one."

*

As we drove across Paris, making our way towards the eastern suburbs, Billy kept up a running commentary on the landmarks we were passing and his personal memories of them. This was the street where Marlene Dietrich lived nowadays, that was the restaurant where he'd once had an eight-hour lunch with Maurice Chevalier . . . He remarked to me that "Paris is a city where the money falls apart in your hands but you can't tear the toilet paper," and told me again about the telegram he'd sent to Audrey, the one about doing handstands in the shower, and even though this was the third time I'd heard this story now I still laughed because he recounted it with such deadpan glee and was so happy when people thought it was funny.

The car rolled smoothly through the quiet city streets and soon we were entering the suburbs. Places with unfamiliar names like Vaires Torcy, Lagny Thorigny and Esbly. Calm, prosperous neighbourhoods. Large family houses: sometimes with couples sitting on balconies or in their gardens, having pre-dinner drinks, but mostly empty. No doubt people were still away at their holiday homes. And soon, beyond that, we were into the countryside: flat, featureless countryside, which persisted for three or four miles until a town came into view in the distance. We could see the towers of an impressive Gothic cathedral casting long summer shadows over the huddle of shops and houses clustered at its feet.

"I wonder where we are," said Billy, who had been writing some notes on a page of his script and now looked up to observe his surroundings for the first time in a while.

"We are approaching Meaux, sir," the driver said.

"Meaux," Billy repeated. The name didn't seem to mean anything to him.

"Where they make the Brie," said the driver. "The best Brie in France comes from here."

"Ah, of course!" said Billy. "*Brie de Meaux.*"

"Maybe you'd like to try some?" the driver said. "My cousin has a farm nearby. He would be very happy to welcome you."

"That," said Billy, with some emphasis and sincerity, "is very tempting, I must say. But we have to get to the location."

"My cousin's farm is very close. Just a few minutes."

Billy hesitated, and then turned to me: "What do you think? I mean, it would be ridiculous to come to this region, the very place where it's made, and not to taste it, don't you agree?"

I thought about everybody waiting for us at the location. And how Iz was always so clear on the need to be "professional."

"We mustn't be late . . ." I said.

Billy looked at his watch. "Well, first of all they have to lay the track along the platform of the railway station. We can't do anything until that's done. I think we have time." He leaned forward and said to the driver: "O.K., please, you can take us there for a few minutes."

"My cousin will be so happy," the driver said. "It will be an honour for him."

In less than a minute we had taken a right turn off the main highway and were snaking down a narrow country lane. Soon we could see a farm to our left, which could only be reached by a long, straight, unpaved road. Loose gravel churned beneath the wheels of the car and clouds of dust were thrown up on either side of us. It was very bumpy, and the driver was taking it fast. Billy and I were thrown backwards and forwards, and he clutched onto my arm for support as we bounced over a pothole.

At the time I felt that it seemed rather a lot of trouble, just to taste some cheese. But later, when I thought back to another thing that Iz had said to me in Greece, I realized that perhaps there was something about this detour that was more symbolic for Billy. At heart he was a European, after all: this year he had spent more than four months in Europe and, as he had only recently complained to me, in that time he'd barely been able to sample any of the things he loved about it. The filming of *Fedora* was almost over. He was about to return to the States. Why not grab one last chance to remind himself what Europe really meant to him—how it *tasted*, to someone who had been forced to leave it behind all those years ago? One last chance to do something that he could only do in the continent that had raised him.

Maybe that was it.

We pulled up in a farmyard surrounded by outbuildings, and as soon as the engine was switched off we were plunged into the most profound, restful silence. No birdsong, no lowing of cattle, nothing. The driver went over to the back door of the farmhouse to find his cousin, while Billy and I got out of the car to stretch our legs and arms. It was a beautiful evening, hot and cloudless. I leaned against the warm body of the car and tried to get used to what was happening. It was an unreal turn of events, but every turn of events in my life had been unreal for the last few months.

"This way, this way!"

The driver had returned with his cousin and there followed a vigorous bout of handshaking and hugging and backslapping, during which the farmer repeated over and over again that *Ben-Hur* was his favourite film and was a masterpiece of cinema. Billy was used to being mistaken for William Wyler— it had been happening to him for at least thirty years—so he cheerfully accepted these compliments on behalf of his fellow director. The farmer then led us in the direction of a large stone barn with a green door. He unlocked the door and we followed him inside, into a decidedly chilly space with three or four tables set up for guests. It was pretty gloomy and uninviting in there.

"Perhaps you want me to move one of these tables outside for you?" he said.

"If it's no trouble," said Billy. "That would be wonderful."

"For the man who put that chariot race on screen," the *cinéphile* farmer said, "nothing is too much trouble."

He and the driver set up a table in the sunshine for us and brought two plates, two knives and two wine glasses.

"With Brie," the farmer said, "I always recommend a Pinot Noir. It's not too fruity, not too heavy. It brings out the flavours perfectly."

"I will be guided by you, of course," said Billy, offering up his glass.

Two glasses of wine were poured and then the first cheese was brought to the table.

"This," said the farmer, "is a *Brie de Melun*. We sell it here but it is actually made a few miles away, on my wife's brother's farm. Still from the Seine-et-Marne region, as every genuine Brie must be. It has quite a strong flavour, rather salty. If you ripen it for too long, it becomes bitter. This cheese has been ripened for five weeks."

"Did you ever taste this before?" Billy asked me, spreading some of the cheese onto a crusty slice of *baguette*.

"I never tasted any kind of Brie before," I admitted.

"That doesn't surprise me so much, coming from Greece," he said. "There you have *feta*. A nice cheese, but not really in the same league. Like comparing *Asti spumante* with champagne." He bit into the bread and cheese, closed his eyes and chewed thoughtfully. "Ah, yes, this is good. This is one of the best I ever tasted."

I took my first bite, not knowing what to expect. At once a complex blend of flavours began invading my mouth. The cheese was smooth and milky but it also had distant overtones of walnut, and a distinctly earthy quality. To my unformed taste buds, it was a strange flavour but also immensely pleasant. Also, the creamy texture of the cheese, combined with the crustiness of the bread, was amazing.

"It's really nice," I said.

"Try it with the wine," Billy advised. "He's right, they go together well."

I held the wine glass up to the evening sunlight. Shafts of light were reflected back from its rich, ruby depths. I drank a large sip and allowed its dark, berry-flavoured notes to blend with and then overtake the lingering flavours of the cheese and bread.

"Mmmn," I said. I couldn't find the words to express my approval. I was reduced to making guttural noises. "Mmmmn-mnmnm . . ."

We ate and drank some more and then the farmer went to fetch the next cheese.

"So, if I may start getting . . . a little personal, at this stage," Billy said, dabbing at his lips with a handkerchief, "I could not help noticing, a little bit earlier, that you seemed slightly depressed in your spirits today. I wondered if there was anything wrong."

"Well . . ."

"Because, I mean, if you are sorry that the shooting of the film has come to an end, we're all sorry about that, but there's not very much we can do about it."

"It's true that I—"

"You know, I'm very glad that we found something for you to do, so that you could come with us to Germany and France, and Mr. Diamond, I know, has been very grateful for all your assistance, but you cannot come back to Los Angeles with us, unfortunately."

"Of course. I never dreamed of it."

The farmer had returned with another cheese.

"This one," he explained, "is also from my wife's brother's farm. It is another *Brie de Melun*, but it has only been matured for four weeks, so it is a little harder, and it has been finely seasoned. See if you can guess the seasoning."

Billy spread some of the cheese onto his bread and took a bite. He stared into the middle distance as he chewed. Then he said:

"Mustard. Am I right?"

"Yes, you are right. Mustard seeds. Not many. The flavouring is very delicate. I'll leave you to enjoy, and go to fetch the best of all."

While he was gone, and while I was eating more bread and cheese and drinking more wine, unable to believe that the simplest kinds of food and drink could taste as good as this, Billy resumed his line of enquiry.

"So I'm guessing that this is something more personal happening, yes?"

I nodded, and swallowed down my mouthful of mustardy cheese before saying:

"When we were on Lefkada, there was a boy. His name was Matthew. We kind of got friendly, and then there was some . . . unfinished business, I suppose you'd call it."

"Continue," Billy prompted, as I drank some more wine.

"Well, on Friday, he turned up in Paris, at the hotel—his mother is one of the make-up artists on the film, actually—and last night we went on a date and after that . . ."

"After that, I'm guessing, you finished the business," Billy said.

It was a blunt way of putting it, but I nodded again.

"And now he's gone?"

"It's worse than that," I said, and told Billy the whole story of the letter that I'd found that morning in the pocket of Matthew's trousers, and how used and betrayed it had made me feel. I couldn't believe how easy it was to confide in him. I suppose it's a truism that wine loosens the tongue and makes it easier to talk. But in this case I don't think it was the wine. I think it was the cheese.

Speaking of cheese, just then the farmer reappeared with the third and final sample for us to try. It was a bigger wheel of cheese than he had brought before, with a slightly thinner crust. Billy leaned forward eagerly to inspect it.

"And this is . . . ?"

"This, sir, is my own cheese. Made on this very farm. A genuine *Brie de Meaux*. Matured for the full eight weeks. We take the milk from our own cows. The cheese is drained in the traditional way, on straw mats, then salted, then cured for two days and then left to ripen in a refrigerated cellar. In the first week of this process, this is when the rind starts to appear, which—" he added, with a disapproving glance at my plate—"you should eat, *mademoiselle*. It is very nutritious. Also, it tastes good. During the ripening period the wheels of cheese are turned over, by hand, every few days. You will not taste a better cheese than this in the whole of France, sir. I guarantee it."

Billy looked at his watch, then asked the driver: "How long to get to the location from here?"

"About half an hour, sir."

"All right. We'd better hurry with this."

"Sir," said the farmer, protesting. "It takes *eight weeks* to make this cheese. You cannot hurry with *Brie de Meaux*. Either making it or eating it."

Billy thought about this. Then he nodded his agreement, settled into his chair and reached for another piece of bread.

"You are quite correct. Any chance of some more wine?"

"Of course, sir. Please—" he gestured at the wheel of cheese—"take some. Don't wait for me to cut it for you."

He left to fetch another bottle of Pinot Noir. Carefully, very carefully, Billy cut a sliver of cheese from the wheel and slid it onto my plate. The cheese was a buttery yellow, almost liquid, and gave off a delicate but tantalizing, somewhat fungal aroma. Then he did the same for himself. I broke off two pieces of bread. We looked at the food on our plates expectantly, our mouths watering.

"Shall we go in?" he said, raising his knife.

I raised mine too.

"But before we do," he said, abruptly, lowering his knife and pointing it at me. "Allow me to say something about the story you just told me."

I waited.

"The letter you found in this boy's pocket," he said. "I don't regard it as conclusive evidence."

"No?" I could feel a morsel of hope stirring in my heart when I heard these words.

"All you saw, if I understand things correctly, was the word 'darling.' And the phrase 'Can't wait to see you again.'"

"That's right."

"Well, why jump to hasty conclusions? 'Can't wait to see you again' is the kind of thing anybody might write."

"I suppose so . . ."

"And in England, there is a certain class of people who call each other 'darling' all the time. It's the whole Noël Coward thing. It means nothing. They even say it to their window cleaner."

This sounded plausible, I had to admit.

"So I would consider the possibility that this woman is just a casual friend. That's all."

"A casual friend," I repeated, and as I turned this phrase over in my mind, weighing its probability and feeling waves of longed-for relief course through my body, the farmer returned with our second bottle of wine and refilled both our glasses. Then Billy and I spread some of the cheese onto our bread, and delicately eased the food into our mouths.

Well. That cheese—and I am not exaggerating here—that cheese was simply the most wonderful thing I had ever tasted in my life. The flavours came at you, one after the other, each one more complex and subtle than the last. I closed my eyes so that I could savour them more intensely.

"Good, yes?" said Billy, after we had both been eating in silence for a while.

"Oh yes."

"I'm tasting a little bit of hazelnut, a little bit of mushroom. It's almost as if, you know . . . almost as if you can taste the soil in there, like a good Scotch whisky."

I nodded but, unlike Billy, I couldn't put my feelings into words. All I know is that I experienced something like an epiphany at that moment. Everything came together at once—the rush of hope that his words about Matthew had provoked in me, my pleasure, my still-astonished pleasure at being in his company, the gorgeous taste of the cheese, the warming effect of the wine, the sheer loveliness of the natural world all around us as we sat in that farmyard, the setting sun on our faces, the cloudless blue-pink-yellow sky above us, the melancholy beauty of that evening in late August—it all came together so that even now, even today, if anybody asks me what my idea of perfect happiness is, that is the moment I will always talk about, always return to. Such a moment! Such a memory!

"I'm in heaven," was all I said.

"Good," said Billy, with the professional satisfaction of someone who has set out to give pleasure, and succeeded. He ate his last morsel of cheese, then looked at his watch again. "However, heaven or not, now we have to leave."

"Yes, of course."

He disappeared into the house to give our thanks to the farmer—perhaps even to give him some money, I don't know. When he came out he was walking more quickly than usual.

"We are going to be late onto the set. This has never happened to me before. Look what you've done to me!"

Mortified, I was about to apologize: then I realized he was joking.

"Anyway, it was worth it," he said, taking one last look around the farmyard as the chauffeur opened the back door of the car for him.

"I'm glad you think so."

"Of course I think so." He was about to get into the car, but paused in order to smile at me and say: "You know, we've both been reminded of something important this evening." I wondered what he could mean—what he and I could possibly have in common. "Whatever else it throws at you," he said, "life will always have pleasures to offer. And we should take them." And then this man who had achieved so much in his time, and suffered so much as well, tilted the hat on his head so that it sat at just the right angle, and tipped it to me. "Remember that," he added. And I always have.

*

We were indeed late getting to Montcerf. But—just as Billy had hoped—the crew had anticipated his needs and already laid a dolly track along the station platform, parallel to the railway line. So that saved some time.

The shooting went smoothly. I felt decidedly light-headed after the wine, but it took more than a few glasses of Pinot Noir to make Billy tipsy. The only hitch was when Miss Keller did not speak one of her lines exactly as written. Instead of saying, "That call—it wasn't Michael on the phone. Who was it?" she said, "That call—it wasn't from Michael. Who was it?" Naturally, Iz pointed out that she had deviated from the script, and they had to do another take. Miss Keller didn't object or complain. She understood how it was with these two by now. She got it right on the third or fourth attempt, and then they were done. That was a wrap, as the saying is.

But there was no wrap party as such. Instead, when we got back to the hotel, there was a subdued gathering at the bar. Many of the cast and crew had already gone home, in any case. Mr. Holden was not there, nor were Miss Knef or Mr. Ferrer. There were about ten of us, drinking champagne and smoking a few cigarettes. Gradually people drifted away, until the only ones left were me, Billy and Iz.

The two old friends sat in silence for a while. They looked exhausted, rather than triumphant.

"Oh well," said Iz gloomily, after a few minutes. "We made it."

"Yes," said Billy. "We made it."

The silence re-established itself. Billy was puffing away on his little cigar. Iz was staring at the table. I had no idea what he was thinking, but I was happy to see that slowly, almost imperceptibly, a tentative smile began to spread on his face. It was a rueful, lopsided smile, but a smile all the same. Finally he looked up and at the very same moment, as if they were connected by some telepathic understanding, Billy glanced across at him and their eyes met. He smiled too.

"We made it," Iz repeated, raising his glass.

"We made it," Billy said, and they clinked their glasses together.

After that they fell silent again, having no further need of words or gestures to express what they were feeling, and suddenly I felt like an intruder. It was time to say goodnight and goodbye to them both.

On the way to my bedroom, I stopped by the reception desk and found that a note was waiting for me. It was from Matthew.

Dear Calista,

What happened? Why did you leave? Where are you?

I hope nothing is wrong. I have to go to the airport now. Please drop me a line at—

But the address he had given me, when I tried writing to it from Athens a few days later, turned out to be wrong. I sent him a long letter, and enclosed a cassette recording of me and Chrysoula performing "Malibu" on the piano and violin, but the letter and the recording never reached him. Maybe he had already moved out, and was now in student accommodation somewhere near his film school. I suppose I could have tried writing to him a second time, using his mother's address, but something stopped me: the suspicion that he might deliberately have given me a false address, because he didn't want to hear from me again. The more I thought about it, the more likely that seemed. That was how crushed I felt, by my first experience of love. Anyway, whatever the reason, the cassette I had sent him came back undelivered.

F*edora* had wrapped. But its difficulties were not yet over. When they returned to the States, Billy and Iz engaged a new editor and produced a rough cut of the film. But then Billy took a fateful decision. Wanting the two main actresses' voices to sound similar, for plot reasons, he decided to have *all* their lines re-recorded with a single voice, belonging to a German actress called Inga Bunsch. Hundreds and hundreds of lines—the complete vocal performances of Marthe Keller and Hildegard Knef—were junked and replaced by Ms. Bunsch's flat, monotonous loops.

In December 1977 he returned to Munich for the recording of Miklós Rózsa's score with the Symphonie-Orchester Graunke. But when the time came to add music to the picture, he used very little of it. He dropped Dr. Rózsa's opening title music, for instance, and used Edvard Greig's "The Last Spring" instead. Rózsa was furious. I was told that he did not speak to Billy for years afterwards. In his autobiography, *Double Life*, he discusses the scoring of almost every picture that he was involved with: but he does not mention *Fedora*. He was too angry.

A test screening of the film in Santa Barbara did not go well. Towards the end of the picture, the audience started laughing at lines which were supposed to be deadly serious. Next it was shown at the Cannes Festival, where the European critics liked it but the Americans hated it. Only in 1979 did it receive a limited release in America. It did well in New York but nowhere else. It turned out to be Billy's revenge for Auschwitz after all; not his revenge on Hollywood.

Billy and Iz made one more picture together in the early eighties, a comedy called *Buddy Buddy*. It was somebody else's idea, it had no personal resonance for them, their hearts were not in it, and the less that is said about that film, the better.

After that, they fell silent.

*

And what of my own life?

Tragedy struck my little family in 1981: all those years of indulging in delicious Greek pastries caught up with my father, and he suffered two heart attacks within a few weeks of each other. The second one was fatal.

Bereft and grieving, Mum and I sold the flat in Acharnon Street and moved to London. We bought a two-bedroom flat close to her relatives in unfashionable Balham.

She kept her married name and since there were not many families called Frangopoulou in Balham (in fact, there was just one, to be precise) it was easy enough for Matthew to find me in the phone book a few years later.

It was early in the spring of 1985 when he called. My romantic life in the intervening years had not been very exciting and I admit that I was irrationally happy to hear from him again. He invited me to dinner at an Italian place in Soho and I spent most of that day wondering what it would be appropriate to wear. After all, I have a track record—as you will know by now—of making epic sartorial misjudgements. In the end I decided it would be too humiliating to put on a sexy outfit for him (even if I'd possessed one) so I opted for something pretty but conservative: a 1920s-style needlecord dress from Laura Ashley, with a drop waist and sailor collar, in dark red. Even so I felt somewhat overdressed, because Matthew turned up in an old fisherman's jumper and a pair of jeans that must have dated from about ten years earlier, judging by the flares. I was disappointed when I saw him, I have to admit. In my memory he had been impossibly handsome: handsome in a boyish way, despite his beard or perhaps even because of it. Anyway, now the beard was gone and his face looked a little fatter and in fact he had put some weight on around his stomach as well. But it didn't matter that I found him less attractive than I had found him in Greece and Paris, because my assumption that this might be a date did not last much beyond the *apéritif*. Within a couple of minutes I learned that he was married and I also learned that his wife's name was Juliet. Well, I was relieved in a way. At least it meant that my instincts back in Paris in the summer of 1977 had been correct. But I had been rather hoping that he might ask if he could go to bed with me, so that I could have had the satisfaction of turning him down.

O.K., so Matthew had not summoned me in order to rekindle the flames of our youthful romance. Instead, he had a business proposition. It turned out—slightly to my amazement—that he had been given the money to make a feature film. Remember, if you will, that at this point in time, the mid-1980s, British cinema was undergoing one of its periodic moments of renaissance. Channel 4 had just come into being and was pouring money into production and development. Resistance to Thatcherism had galvanized film-makers. *Chariots of Fire* had given everybody confidence. Matthew had been marked out as a Talented Young Thing and he had been given a few hundred thousand pounds to bring his personal blend of Martin Scorsese, Nicolas Roeg and left-wing polemic to the screen. You might not remember the film—not many people do, these days—but it drew a fair amount of attention at the time. But when I met him that evening it had not yet started on post-production, and there was a key member of the creative team who had not yet been appointed: the composer.

Over our *antipasti* he hummed a melody to me.

"What's that?" I asked.

"What do you mean, 'What's that?'" he replied. "It's your tune. The one you played to me at the party in Greece."

"You never could remember how it went," I said, and sang "Malibu" to him properly, the way it was supposed to sound.

"That's it!" he said. "That's exactly it!"

"I know it is," I replied, calmly, trying not to sound too patronizing.

"We *have* to use it," he said. "Even when I was shooting I was already hearing it, over every scene. Please say you'll do it, Cal."

"Do what?"

"Write the music for my film."

And so that was how it started. Matthew had to provide me with a full team of assistants to teach me how music for films was written and orchestrated and recorded and synced and edited, because all I had—my sole contribution to the whole project—was this simple little melody with the bitter-sweet feeling which stuck in your head, but that was enough. Just recently there had been a spate of films in which the music had been almost as memorable as the story itself—sometimes even more so. *Chariots of Fire* was one, *Merry Christmas, Mr. Lawrence* was another, and I was lucky, something similar happened to me. The cinema audience took to my tune and liked it and remembered it and I won a couple of awards and soon, for a few brief years at least, job offers started coming in. In fact, my next offer was from a Hollywood studio and before I knew what was happening I was flying to LA for meetings and viewings and recording sessions.

It was on one of these visits, in the spring of 1987, that I saw Iz and Barbara for the last time.

Barbara was as glamorous and effusive as ever. Iz, I thought, looked thin and elderly.

They invited me for dinner at their house on El Camino and Iz told me that he and Billy were still meeting at the office every day, still throwing around ideas for scripts and stories.

"But it's never going to happen," he said.

"Why not?" I asked.

"A couple of reasons. The first being that there's only one more film Billy wants to make, and it's not for me."

I asked him to tell me more.

"There was this book published a few years ago, *Schindler's Ark*, did you hear about it? Australian writer. It's about a German guy who saves lots of Jews from the Holocaust. Billy's trying to buy the rights."

"He would be the perfect person to make that film."

"Maybe," said Iz, not sounding altogether convinced. "But a lot of other people are chasing the rights. A *lot*. He has some . . . pretty powerful rivals."

He didn't tell me the other reason why he and Billy would never complete another script. I only realized it the next year, when I read Iz's obituary in the newspaper. He had been seriously ill for some time, with multiple myeloma: in fact his "shingles" during the shooting of *Fedora* may have been the start of it. He had known for some time, but had never mentioned it to Billy. Billy only found out a few weeks before his friend died. "The way we had plotted this script," he told an interviewer, "the script of our lives, was that being fourteen years older I was supposed to go first. As you see, that didn't happen."

*

The film that had brought me to LA on that occasion had several British people on the creative team, including the editor, a gentle, kindly, sweet-natured man called Geoffrey. Maybe ours wasn't the most fiery or passionate courtship (I know he won't mind me saying this) but we fell for each other pretty hard, in our quiet, undemonstrative way. We were married within three months of meeting each other.

Geoffrey and I both wanted to have children as soon as possible but it didn't work out so easily. In the end I wound up having IVF and that was how Francesca and Ariane came about, in the spring of 1994. That was when I discovered that the one thing I loved more than composing music for films was being around young children and giving them the love and care that they needed. Ever since my daughters were born, my life has been devoted to the task of finding some sort of equilibrium between these two vocations—writing music, and bringing up my kids, and although it has not always been an easy process, it has always been a joyful one. Composing for films has been a wonderful adventure but I can honestly say that I never regretted turning down a job if it meant I could spend more time with the girls, taking nourishment every day from their energy, their curiosity, their youthful zest for life.

And so I continued working, just not as much as before. My jobs came mainly from the UK, sometimes from Europe, once or twice from Hollywood. The last of my American films was in 1996. That was when I went to Los Angeles again, and had my final meeting with Billy Wilder.

We went for lunch, Audrey, Billy and I, to one of their favourite restaurants, Mimosa on Beverly Boulevard. When we had finished our desserts Audrey had to leave for a doctor's appointment. I was about to stand up and leave as well, but Billy put his hand on my arm and said, no, I should stay for a coffee. So we ordered a couple of espressos and settled down for our final chat.

"Well, the little Greek interpreter," he said, "has come quite a long way in the last few years, don't you think?"

"I suppose she has," I said, and reminded him that it was almost exactly twenty years since Gill Foley and I had shown up at the Bistro in our awful T-shirts and cropped denim shorts, and I had got drunk and yawned so long and so hard at the end of our dinner that it had given Billy the idea for one of the scenes in *Fedora*.

We talked for a while about the making of that film. His memories of the shoot were quite clear; clearer, in fact, than his memories of the film itself. I mentioned some details from a couple of scenes and he didn't seem to be entirely sure what I was talking about.

"I never think about my old pictures," he said. "What's the point? All you see is the mistakes you made. You would go crazy doing that. All you can think about is the next one."

"You're going to make another film?" I asked.

He stared at me and laughed.

"My God, Calista, I am ninety years old. You think I'm going to get up at five in the morning to drive to some location in the middle of nowhere? Give me a break."

"Iz told me once," I said, "that you wanted to make a film of *Schindler's Ark*."

"Correct."

"Did you see it?" I asked. Spielberg's version—retitled *Schindler's List*—had come out three years earlier.

Billy nodded, and fell silent for a long time. Then he said:

"Yeah, I saw it. I saw it once. I couldn't bear to watch it another time. I think it is one of the . . . the *greatest* films. The very greatest. Better than anything I could have done."

I was very moved to hear him say this. My mind went back to one of our last conversations in Paris, and I said:

"I remember you telling me, once, that Spielberg, and the other people of his age, could never really make serious films because they hadn't been through what you went through. People of your generation. The two wars."

He looked up.

"I said that?"

I nodded.

"Well, that was bullshit. And what's more, I don't remember saying it. When did I say it?"

"Don't you remember? It was the final night of shooting. The evening we went to the farm, and ate Brie."

His eyes lit up. "Ah, yes. I remember that. I remember the cheese, definitely. But I don't remember saying anything like that about Mr. Spielberg. And if I did, I was wrong."

Neither of us spoke for quite a while. I was contemplating, again, my memory of that precious evening, turning it over in my mind. But Billy's thoughts were somewhere else entirely.

"You know," he said at last, and suddenly it felt as though the whole restaurant had fallen silent, that we were the only two people talking in that place or indeed in the world. "When I saw that film . . . Those scenes . . . The scenes in the camps, the death camps. They were so real. Do you know what I realized I was doing?"

I shook my head, and looked into his eyes, which had become cloudy.

"I wasn't looking at the actors any more. I was looking at all the figures in the background. It felt as if I was watching . . . the thing itself, while it was happening, and I realized I was still looking for her. I was still looking to see if she was there."

I reached across the table and clutched his ninety-year-old hand. Our eyes met for the last time. And then he finished his coffee, ordered a couple of brandies, and told me a funny story about Jack Lemmon and Shirley MacLaine.

*

I completed my musical suite inspired by Billy Wilder in the end, although it still hasn't been performed or recorded. But it took me longer than expected—three or four years, altogether—because something intervened and distracted me. It began on the day that I overheard Fran in the garden, talking on the phone to her friend, and looked through those old photographs of my mother and her grandchildren. I had an idea that day, one which would change my family's story for ever.

And what was it that gave me this idea? *Fedora*, of course.

I don't know why I ended up taking the DVD out of its case and slipping it into the machine later that night. I was bored of watching terrible screeners, I suppose, but there must have been more to it than that. Fran and Geoffrey were both upstairs, in bed. It was getting on for midnight and I was feeling restless and unhappy but I didn't want to drink alcohol or eat Brie. I felt like watching *Fedora* again.

What an odd film it had turned out to be.

After seeing it again, a strange thought occurred to me: back in 1977, when I was trying to hide the fact that I knew nothing about films, I would go around quoting lines that I'd memorized from Leslie Halliwell's film guide. But for some reason I had never looked to see what Mr. Halliwell had written about *Fedora* in the later editions. So that night I took the fat paperback volume down from my shelf and read his verdict: "*Sunset Boulevard* revisited, with a less bitter approach and less effectiveness." To which he adds: "But any civilized film is welcome in the late seventies." I rather think Billy might have appreciated that. There are a lot of assumptions packed into that word "civilized," but I think Billy would have understood them, and probably shared them. Perhaps it's a generational thing, more than anything else.

There is a lot wrong with *Fedora*. The awful dubbing of the two actresses' voices. The creaking melodrama and implausibility of some of the scenes. Even the film's eccentric final line—"The electric blanket I had sent her came back undelivered"—shows that Billy and Iz were losing their touch, were not firing on all cylinders. It's hardly "Nobody's perfect" or "Shut up and deal."

Also, it was a difficult film for me to watch. That is to say, the film itself—as assembled by Billy and his editor—was in a constant tug-of-war with my ever-vivid memories of the days we spent making it. When William Holden walks across the street in Corfu and sits down at a café table and calls out: "Waiter!" it takes me out of the story and brings to my mind, instead, the morning I started working for Billy and had to translate those two crazy interviews for him in the foyer of the hotel. When I see the old boatman taking Mr. Holden across the water to Fedora's villa, it reminds me of that funny, cheerful little man and the way that Iz used him to play a secret joke upon his friend. And at the very beginning of the film, when Fedora throws herself under the train at Montcerf station, it makes me think, of course, only of the time I spent with Billy sitting in that farmyard in the Seine-et-Marne region east of Paris, drinking wine, watching the sunset, and eating *Brie de Meaux*.

So it's a film I struggle to see clearly. But when I do see it clearly, it remains, for me, a thing of great beauty. Great beauty and determination. Billy's urge to create, to keep on giving something to the world—a fundamentally generous impulse— had been as strong as ever when he made it. And, as I had tried to convince him at the time, the film shows such compassion for its characters: for its ageing characters, in particular—be they men or women—struggling to find a role for themselves in a world which is interested only in youth and novelty.

I watched the film again that night and felt an overwhelming gladness that it existed. An inexpressible sense of gratitude towards Billy, of thankfulness that he had taken the trouble to conceive and nurture this strange, unique creature, to bring it into the world so that in manifold ways it could touch and inspire the people who saw it.

It was in the warming, clarifying light of this gladness that my great idea took its sudden shape.

*

There was still some lamplight coming from beneath the door of Fran's bedroom. I went inside and asked her a question. When the answer was yes (as I knew it would be) I went to my own bedroom to speak with Geoffrey; because everything, now, depended upon his response.

*

At first I was not even sure that he was awake. But when he knew that I had something urgent to discuss with him, he rolled over to face me as I lay beside him, and started to listen.

Fran wants to keep her baby, I said. But she also wants to go to university. So it's down to us.

"To us?" he repeated.

We can do it, I told him. We can bring up the child for her. For a few years, it can be our job, our responsibility. Almost two decades may have gone by since we last did anything like this, but we won't have forgotten. The impulse is still there. The will and the energy are still there.

Even as I said it, I had a fleeting vision of my encounter on the escalator at the Tube station a few days earlier. The little girl clasping her mother's hand. That huge, priceless instant of connectedness. I so wanted to feel something like that again. Not wanted: needed. The need was terrifying, overpowering.

"What do you think?" I whispered, as Geoffrey lay there in silence.

He didn't answer.

"We could still do it," I prompted, my voice starting to shake. "We've still got it in us."

For the first time, his eyes opened fully, and he looked at me in the half-light.

He kissed me. Then he turned away again until he was lying, once more, with his back towards me.

And then he said, "Why not?" murmurously, before falling asleep.

Cascais, 14 October 2019—
London, 22 May 2020

ACKNOWLEDGEMENTS AND SOURCES

My two main sources for this novel were the feature-length documentary *Swan Song: The Story of Billy Wilder's Fedora*, directed by Robert Fischer in 2014, and Rex McGee's lengthy article "The Life and Hard Times of *Fedora*," in *American Film*, February 1979, pp. 17–32.

Rex McGee (who was taken on, in his twenties, to be Wilder's personal assistant on *Fedora*, almost as unexpectedly as happens to Calista in my novel) also supplied me with endless valuable information via email. I can't thank him enough for his generosity and patience.

Similarly, Paul Diamond, son of Iz, answered many questions by email and on Twitter, took me on a tour of his father's and Billy's haunts in Beverly Hills in January 2019, and—most valuably of all—gave me access to his father's memoir, *A Definite Maybe* (currently unpublished—but not for much longer, I hope). My thanks to him are boundless.

In Greece, Alkistis Triberi and Marilena Astrapellou patiently answered my many queries. Chrissoula Sklaveniti shared her detailed local knowledge of Nydri and Lefkada, and told me the story of her grandfather, Filippos, who has a small part as the boatman in *Fedora*, although I don't believe he ever asked Billy Wilder what his motivation was.

Many valuable details about life in 1970s Munich were passed on to me by Tanja Graf and Patrick Süskind. Volker Schlöndorff, who knew Billy Wilder well and attended some of the shooting of *Fedora* at Bavaria Studios, gave generously of his time and knowledge.

Thanks also to Julie Gavras, to Frederic Tuten (source of the

Jaws in Venice idea) and of course to Marthe Keller, who answered my lengthy and unsolicited text messages most courteously.

*

The first half of this novel was written during a two-month residency at the Pestana Cidadela Hotel in Cascais, Portugal. This residency was funded by the Fundação D. Luís I, F. P. and the Câmara Municipal de Cascais. I was invited to take part in the residency by Filippa Melo and cannot thank her enough for the kindness, warmth and hospitality she extended to me while I was there. I must also thank her colleagues at the Fundação, Salvato Tenes de Menezes and Pedro Viagre, for making me so welcome. Among the others who helped to make the experience so productive and enjoyable were Joana Soreiro, Nareen Figueiredo, Francisca Prieto, Elisabete Pato and Manuel Alberto Valente.

*

The following books were consulted in the writing of this novel:

Cameron Crowe, *Conversations with Billy Wilder* (Faber and Faber, 1999)

Robert Horton, editor, *The Billy Wilder Interviews* (University Press of Missouri, 2001)

Kevin Lally, *Wilder Times: The Life of Billy Wilder* (Henry Holt & Co., 1996)

Ed Sikov, *On Sunset Boulevard: The Life and Times of Billy Wilder* (Hyperion, 1998)

Anthony Slide, editor, *It's the Pictures That Got Small: Charles Brackett on Billy Wilder and Hollywood's Golden Age* (Columbia University Press, 2015)

Billy Wilder and Helmuth Karasek, *Billy Wilder* (Hoffmann und Campe Verlag, 1992)

Maurice Zolotow, *Billy Wilder in Hollywood* (WH Allen, 1977)

*

Specific incidents in the narrative, and many of the direct quotations from Billy Wilder which appear in the text, were sourced as follows:

p. 56 "I can't just make pictures for six people in Bel Air . . ." Zolotow, p. 179

p. 57 Iz Diamond's highest expression of enthusiasm: "Why not?" Sikov, p. 389

p. 101 "That's like asking a bank robber why he robs banks . . ." Horton, p. 144

p. 105 "I want you to act like Laughton, and dance like Nijinsky . . ." Zolotow, p. 236

p. 105 "Billy was in a meeting once, with a producer . . ." Zolotow, p. 236

p. 131 "You told me that your wife was currently redecorating . . ." Slide, p. 251

p. 142 "We watched them beating an old Jew . . ." Sikov, p. 86

p. 181 "When you come to the crucifixion scene . . ." Zolotow, p. 137

p. 182 "But they all stole the pencils . . ." Sikov, p. 240

p. 185 "There was an entire field . . ." from Volker Schlöndorff's three-part filmed interview with Wilder, *Billy, How Did You Do It?*, BBC TV, 1988

p. 187 "If it's a huge success, it's my revenge on Hollywood . . ." Horton, p. 145

p. 192 "Unable to obtain bidet . . ." Zolotow, p. 235

p. 212 "I feel like . . . the piano player in a brothel . . ." Sikov, p. 558

p. 215 "In the time it's taken me to do this . . ." McGee, p. 32

p. 216 "Imagine a family in Düsseldorf . . ." Horton, p. 160

p. 222 "*Brie de Meaux* . . ." In the documentary *Swan Song*, *Fedora*'s production manager, Harold Nebenzal, recalls: "We shot in a railroad station in Montcerf, on the outskirts of Paris. We had to wait for dark. And I went with Billy and the chauffeur took us out to Montcerf, and on the way we went through Meaux. And the driver said to Billy, 'You know, this is where they make the good Brie.' He said, 'Brie? Wonderful cheese . . . do you think we could taste it?' 'Oh yes, monsieur' . . . So we went to one farm after another, and we went in, and we tried the cheese here, and we tried the cheese there, and we had a glass of wine here, and a piece of bread there, and—this was certainly unusual for Billy Wilder—we got to the location site late. LATE! I don't think Billy's ever done this in his life . . ."

p. 237 "The way we had plotted this script . . ." Sikov, p. 580

p. 240 "I wasn't looking at the actors any more . . ." This story about Wilder's reaction to the film *Schindler's List* was told to me during a conversation with Volker Schlöndorff at his home in Berlin, 13 March 2020.